Love is the riskiest business of all

He's the hot new guy in the small-town Wyoming office, a bachelor from L.A. with a trail of divorces behind him. But something about Blake Cobb has Sadie Felix setting her sites on him—even though he might just be her biggest competition in the race for a much-coveted promotion. Still, a little workplace rivalry will only make the tension between them more thrilling. At least, that's what Sadie hopes, until she learns Blake's already dating the boss's daughter...

She's an ambitious corporate climber with a face and a body that could stop a clock. Which is exactly why Blake steers clear of Sadie Felix—he's been there, done that, with disastrous results. Besides, his new girlfriend is a dead ringer for his first love—the one who got away. But when an office scandal throws the boss's daughter in a new—and unflattering—light, Blake's forced to see what's been right in front of him all along...

RUNNING THE NUMBERS
A Long Shot Romance

Books by Roxanne Smith

Long Shot Romance Series
Men Like This
Relapse In Paradise
Running the Numbers

Published by Kensington Publishing Corporation

Running the Numbers

A Long Shot Romance Novel

Roxanne Smith

LYRICAL PRESS
Kensington Publishing Corp.
www.kensingtonbooks.com

For my dad,
Gary Lain,
who loved the West

You are missed.

Acknowledgements

I've been waiting for this. The final book in the series, my last opportunity to put it all out there. A new author, I've been timid in my acknowledgments, but this might be the last chance I get to mention everyone who deserves it.

And so. Deep gratitude for my agent, Dawn Dowdle, and my editor at Lyrical Press, Marci Clark, who both make me look really, really good on paper. I shovel words, but they shine the light.

My husband and ultimate bestie, Matt Smith, who takes my crazy in stride and continues to wait patiently for the love story I'll dedicate to him. (Not yet, honey, but I'll get there.) My brothers, Jesse, Spencer, and Dakota for hearing me out when I need a sounding board. And, finally, a huge thank you to my friends who were there when the first book only existed in a spiral notebook and didn't laugh when I said I wanted to get published—
Ray (Louie) Barrera, Tarran Clack, Beth Kopcho. You are the elite.

"You don't need a certain number of friends, just a number of friends you can be certain of." —Anonymous

Chapter 1

Sadie Felix leaned against the solid oak filing cabinet in her office and waited for the fax to bleep-bloop its way over the wire. "The offices of Avery & Thorp are Daniel Boone meets caviar. What d'you think, Ken?"

Kennedy, Sadie's best friend and coworker, didn't glance up from attacking her nails with an emery board. Her heeled feet were propped on Sadie's desk. She shrugged.

Sadie drummed her fingers across the polished wood. "Spacious and modern, with rich dark wood, gleaming gold accents, marble fireplaces, and deer antler chandeliers. This place exudes all the grandeur and luxury of mountain wealth."

"Sure," Kennedy finally agreed. "Your point?"

"Only that using a fax machine here is a lot like standing at a state-of-the-art airport waiting for a horse-drawn wagon to roll in. I wish old people would learn to e-mail, already. I hate to say it, but you know it's the octogenarians out there keeping the fax machine alive."

From the corner of her eye, Sadie caught sight of Duncan Perry, her boss, striding past her office.

"Duncan!" She called out his name, knowing full well her knee-length pencil skirt wouldn't allow her to catch up before he hit the spiral staircase that would take him to his lofty upstairs office. At the same time, with her other hand, she swatted toward Kennedy, warning her.

Kennedy jerked in surprise, swiftly planted her feet back on the ground, and hid the nail file from view, all with the practiced ease of a veteran's habit.

Duncan walked past but returned shortly and dipped his head around the frame. He'd gone fully bald on the top of his head and wore what hair was left like a graying crown, with fierce pride. "Yes, Sadie?" He looked past her, at Kennedy sitting at Sadie's desk. "What're you doing in here?"

In her best prim tone, Kennedy supplied a believable alibi. "Sadie asked for advice handling an older client. You know how ornery octogenarians can be."

"Can I assume you're finished? You have plenty to do, getting Henry's office ready for Mr. Cobb."

Kennedy jumped up. The emery board mysteriously vanished from sight. "Yes, I'm going. Though, Sadie, you really should think about less restrictive garments." She gave Duncan a harassed look as she sashayed past. "She almost face-planted flagging you down."

Sadie smoothed her skirt, wrapped around her legs like a mummy's bindings. "It's true. I'd be more mobile on a pogo stick."

Duncan finally heaved in a sigh as Kennedy slipped out of the room. "If you called me in here to discuss your wardrobe malfunctions, I'm afraid you've mistaken my job title."

"Just a quick word," Sadie assured him with her best smile, which he usually saw right through. There were downsides to being pals with the boss.

His kind, light brown eyes were understanding but firm. "Is this about Kennedy? I've explained to her for the last time why I hired Blake Cobb, rather than promote her. She's done a great job as Henry's secretary, but Blake has experience I can't ignore."

"No, sir. My dog's not in that fight." Duncan might respect her opinion and expertise as a senior accountant, but not enough to score Kennedy a job she wasn't the best candidate for. Especially not a job like the audit director. "I did, however, want to get some information on Blake, since I'll be picking him up on my day off tomorrow." She enunciated a few choice words, letting Duncan know how she felt about being tasked with work on a requested personal day.

Secretly, Sadie couldn't wait to meet Blake. Nina Walsh, Duncan's secretary and another of Sadie's long-time friends, had let a particularly juicy tidbit slip at lunch last week—her friendly balding boss was considering ditching Jackson Hole, with its harsh nine-month winter, for Salt Lake City, his wife's hometown. Which meant the chief accountant spot might soon be at Sadie's fingertips. It was one more step toward the end of the longest con of her life—becoming partner.

And the last thing she needed was more competition. If Duncan left the firm, the promotion to chief accountant would come down to her and Wes Black, the other senior accountant. He was also her nemesis and all-around least favorite person.

But what about this Blake Cobb guy?

Nina talked about his resume like it shined with the brilliance of an Olympic torch. He'd been partner at his firm in L.A. and was taking a major step down to come to work for Avery & Thorp as the firm's internal auditor.

If Nina had her facts straight.

Sadie wanted to get them from the source.

Duncan's mouth thinned in a thoughtful way, and his shoulders relaxed, a sure sign he'd stick around for a minute to chat. "Honestly, I can't believe we got so lucky. This guy, he's top of his field. A major player in Los Angeles. His firm held accounts for top-billed actors and city officials. Given our own list of clients, he's exactly what we need."

In the auditing department? Sadie chewed the inside of her lip. "Why isn't our new golden boy coming in further up the chain? I mean, obviously, auditing is critical, but it sounds like we're replacing a Pinto with a Corvette." She abruptly shut her mouth and cleared her throat. "No offense to Henry, of course. Henry's great."

Henry Rupert was ancient, hard of hearing, and had earned his retirement five years ago.

Duncan's knowing gaze lingered on her face, and a smile flirted with his lips. A consummate professional, he didn't let it have run of his mouth. "It's a little early for nicknames. As for golden boy's reasons for taking a step back in his career, I can assure you, they're personal. They're definitely not professional, and that's all we need to concern ourselves with." He smiled then, a fatherly gesture more than a show of mirth. "If that's all, I have a handful of messages to answer from yesterday."

Indeed, he had a stack of little pink notes in his hand. They used to be plain old pale yellow ones, but since Reba Garcia had taken over as receptionist, there'd been a few colorful changes around the office.

Duncan shuffled through them before a final glance up at Sadie. "Lunch?"

Sadie did some quick calculating. She'd milked Duncan for all he was worth—at least all she'd risk. She didn't want him to guess she was on a recon mission. "Actually, I think I might've made plans with Nina. Can you ask her to give me a buzz?"

He nodded absently, back to his messages. "You got it." Then he disappeared.

Since she was already at the door of her office, Sadie peeked out into the large main room they referred to as the bookkeeping parlor. It played host to the bookkeeping team and Kennedy, whose desk was clustered among the others in the center of the room in a complicated configuration designed to give each worker some semblance of privacy. The rear of the room held a fireplace made of dark maple, humbler by far than the grand marble monstrosity in the roomy client waiting area. Next to it, a wrought iron spiral staircase led to the upstairs offices and conference room.

Sadie waved at Kennedy, who waved back with a bored frown, and thanked her lucky stars for her private office. There were four of them, one at each corner of the bookkeeping parlor, sporting panes of frosted glass etched with aspen trees. The two offices across from Sadie's belonged to the firm's only junior accountant and the audit director. Next door to her, Wes Black's.

His last name suited him. He kept his gleaming black hair long enough to sweep to one side. His black eyes were unremarkable. While Sadie appreciated a man who understood the importance of grooming, Wes had a tendency to over-pluck his eyebrows. She could tell when he'd been at it recently, because they'd look penciled in for about a week, until they had time to grow in.

Women—Kennedy and Pearl Harris, the payroll clerk, in particular— found him terribly attractive. To Sadie, he was plain terrible. Unlike them, she had the benefit of experience to form a proper opinion.

She went back to the fax machine to retrieve the sheet from the paper tray and sat in her wheeled chair at the same time her interoffice call light lit up orange.

She snatched up the receiver and double-checked the line number on the digital display. "Hi, Nina. I'm hoping you learned something new about golden boy. Duncan won't tell me anything."

At least not anything Nina hadn't already told her.

"Well," Nina drawled in her theatrical manner, "I just might. You tend to get quite an education speaking one-on-one with a man."

This was why Nina was her "long-time" friend. Not her *best* friend. Her flair for the dramatic was exhausting, but damn if she wasn't a useful ally. Sadie attempted to sit back and cross her legs before the tight fabric of her skirt reminded her of her restrictions. She settled for crossing her ankles. "What d'you got? You think he's after Duncan's job?"

"I don't know, but if he is, you can step right on down, honey. This guy has chops. You know he audited a senator last year? I can't fathom why else he'd take Henry's job unless it's to bide his time before he can snag Duncan's. Could be that's their end game. I get the sense Duncan knows more than he's saying on the matter."

Sadie pressed her lips together. Duncan probably had a good idea of how mouthy of a secretary he had. He'd be cautious of giving Nina fuel to feed the gossip mill.

Nina sighed disappointedly. "Obviously, asking would be a tricky thing."

Sadie grunted in frustration. "I wouldn't normally care. I have my five-year plan, and a promotion would put me a few years ahead of schedule. But something about Wes's face makes me want to take a mallet to it. I can't work for him." Plus, he'd adore the chance to rub it in for the rest of eternity. "If Blake's gunning for Duncan's job, I'd rather he get it than Wes."

"Oh, come on, now. Don't give up! You deserve the promotion, and not a single person in this office would say otherwise. Except Wes, but don't mind him." Nina had big, round cheeks framed by a halo of frizzy chestnut hair, and plump little lips perpetually puckered. Sadie imagined them pursed sympathetically. "I'm as unhappy as you are, you know. You think I want to take calls and run errands for Severus Snape?"

Sadie snorted. The nickname did Wes justice. "I'll do my best to make sure it doesn't happen, Nina. Now, back to Blake. Learn anything juicy during your conversation with him?"

"Did I? Who're you talking to, girl?" Nina tutted. "It may not be anything as profound as his personal reasons for moving to Jackson, but I picked up a few details it couldn't hurt to have. For starters, he had to fax over a copy of his driver's license for me to book his airline flight from Los Angeles. I'm not sure it matters, since he might be the competition, but you ought to prepare yourself. Blake Cobb is a *looker,* honey."

Sadie rubbed her forehead. Perfect. Another Wes strutting around the office.

As if reading her mind, Nina sniffed. "Not like Wes. You know how some of the girls downstairs are about *him,* though, Lord help me, I can't figure out why."

"Me, neither." Sadie had long since let Wes's personality overrule his physical appeal. Kennedy thought Wes was the hottest thing to hit Earth since the sun. It didn't say much, of course. Kennedy could develop a crush on a stock photo.

Nina rambled on. "This Blake fella has sandy blond hair cut nice and neat the way a professional man ought to wear it"—a not-so-subtle dig at Wes—"and the most striking eyes. The kind of hazel that really stands out, you know? Deep green mixed with gold. Real stunning. And that's just his DMV photo! Now him, I wouldn't mind running around for. If you take my meaning."

Sadie huffed. "Great. We haven't even met the guy, and you've turned traitor."

"Oh, come now. I'm one of your best friends." Nina slipped into grandma mode, which Sadie begrudgingly admitted she found oddly consoling. It was like a superpower women earned the minute they hit sixty. "I'm merely *saying*, he's not a bad runner-up."

If Nina thought Blake was good-looking, Kennedy would probably have fits over him and declare herself madly in love at first sight.

Sadie tapped her fingernails across her desk. "I guess we'll find out tomorrow if he's apt to sweep me off my feet."

"Not likely with your history, sweetie."

Ouch. Sadie couldn't deny she had a hell of a track record. Not necessarily her fault, though. The ski bum had managed to keep his drug problem well-hidden the three months they'd dated. And how was she supposed to know the trust-funder had faked his job as a chef, slaving over another woman instead of a hot stove? Before those two, there'd been the guy who'd lived in his van and the deli owner with the alcohol-monitoring anklet.

Yep, she had a talent for attracting real losers. They were always good-looking, smooth as a glass surface, and hiding drastic, unmanageable flaws. Despite her embarrassing relationship rap sheet, she still believed she'd meet a man one day who wouldn't be anything more or less than what he advertised. She'd at least wait to hit forty before she gave up hope entirely.

She pursed her lips. "Given my history—thanks for that, by the way—if I do like him, we can pretty much take it on faith he's got skeletons doing a jig in a closet somewhere."

"Oh, hon." More sympathy. "It's not you, you know. It's where we are. The gender ratio is all out of whack. There are a dozen men for every female. You attract them like flies with your Snow White appeal."

Sadie despised the nickname. Her short black bob ended at her jawline. She kept it perpetually tucked behind her ears so the ends flipped out like little raven wings on the side of her head. She didn't particularly care for that, but the ear-tucking habit wasn't going anywhere, and she didn't have time to wrestle with long hair.

"Besides," Nina continued, "I have to admit. Blake sounded awfully formal on the phone. He's probably a boob. Not your type. In fact, we ought to do Amanda a favor and send *her* to the airport. They'd probably hit it off."

Amanda Avery was the daughter of Iris, the Avery half of Avery & Thorp. The boss's daughter. She was the head of the bookkeeping team and the most boring, sedate, mundane, unruffled human being Sadie had ever met in her life, the woman's wacky wardrobe notwithstanding.

Sadie slumped in her chair. "Just what we need—another humdrum accountant to make us all look bad."

* * * *

Blake scanned the sidewalk for his name on a sign or someone waving from one of the three vehicles parked curbside. A topless Jeep, a red Ford pickup, and a minivan were his options so far. In his mind's eye, he was waiting for a newer model black sedan with tinted windows to pull up—a vehicle suited to a well-to-do accountant in one of the country's wealthiest counties.

The Jackson airport defied his expectations. The sidewalk out front for loading and picking up passengers was no larger than an L.A. bus stop, and the parking lot for the whole airport hardly competed with a Kmart's. Small and a little rundown, it had one major redeeming quality—the mighty, massive Tetons rising up in the distance, jagged peaks thrusting into thin wispy clouds as if they were too intimidated to hold their fluffy shape in such grand company.

Blake peered at the imposing summit of the Grand Teton—ten thousand feet in the air, a swift four thousand foot rise from the valley— and shook his head slightly in awe. Pictures hadn't prepared him for seeing the stunning, commanding mountains in real life, up close. In hollows between the razor sharp pinnacles sat white masses. Snow. In early September. Supposedly, a glacier lived up there somewhere, but he'd have to see it to believe it.

He swallowed and gave Seth his full attention. Difficult, between fumbling with his rolling suitcase, his cell phone, and the impossible view of the mountains. He turned his back on them, eyes toward the loading zone. "Look, bud, I think your mom will understand if you decide to go to Purdue in the spring."

Of course Quinn would mind, but she wouldn't tell Seth that.

Seth sighed wearily into the phone. "I know she will, but—Maddie, no! Sorry, Dad, she's trying to take the phone."

Blake grinned to himself as his eighteen-year-old son explained to his two-year-old half sister why she couldn't play with his *pone* right now.

Quinn's child with her new husband, Jack Decker, little Maddie had plowed into her terrible twos with gleeful impishness. A charming troublemaker, she'd give a winsome smile while putting JELL-O in your loafers, which made getting angry an impossibility. Annoyed, at times. Exasperated, definitely. Mostly amused.

She had her uncle Blake, and just about everyone else in the family, wrapped around her tiny, sticky fingers. "Sounds like Maddie's keeping you on your toes."

"Yeah, well, you were here two weeks ago when she learned to walk." Seth's wry tone held a hint of amusement. "Since then, she's discovered her range has expanded. She grabs *everything*. Last night, she went for Jack's glass of wine, and it spilled inside his guitar. I thought he would freak out, but he laughed and said his guitar would probably only play Irish pub songs from now on."

Against his will, Blake cracked a smile.

As much as he wanted to hate the guy for being his ex-wife's new love, Jack had a certain quality that made him impossible to dislike—women adored him, children loved him, and men envied him. The British accent thing probably didn't hurt.

Blake rubbed his forehead and refused to think too hard about Jack, Quinn, and Maddie. They defined a whole world of regret. Instead, he focused on his son, the one thing he'd gotten right. "Seth, if your heart says go to Purdue, then go. Your mom will be happy as long as you are. You know that."

Maddie's happy squawk echoed in the background.

Seth shushed her, almost politely. "That's exactly what Jack said."

A wrench to the gut. Well, why wouldn't Seth go to his stepdad for advice? A few short years ago, the kid hadn't wanted anything to do with Blake. That he'd asked Blake's advice at all was a testament to how far Blake had come as a father. Not far enough, however, when he stopped to consider the years he'd wasted being too busy for his son.

And it's not like it wasn't my own fault.

Unhappy thoughts of an unhappy time. It seemed like in the last decade, all Blake had were unhappy times. Which was exactly what had landed him in remote Jackson Hole, Wyoming. Fewer than ten thousand full-time residents, but elitist enough for him to have no trouble finding work suited to his résumé. His job was the one thing in his life he hadn't managed to completely screw up.

An arm shot out of the driver's side window of the Ford pickup. A few dents and dings, but waxed to a perfect shine, the truck gleamed in the September sunlight. The hand waved.

A second later, the door opened and a woman stepped out. She looked right at him and waved again. She had on a dirty navy blue baseball cap. Short black hair tufted out on the sides. Her eyes were wide-set and almond-shaped, like a cat's. Hard not to notice the way she gazed at him as she came around the bed of the truck, openly curious.

Attractive.

Blake's stomach curled into itself instinctively, and a bone-deep desire to run back the way he'd come struck him like a blow.

Why is this happening to me? What have I done this time? Blake stared at the woman, a ghost from his past. One he'd long considered vanquished. The resemblance made the short hairs on his neck dance.

"Dad?" Seth's inquisitive voice brought Blake back around.

Blake swallowed and gave the woman a hollow smile and perfunctory nod of greeting. "Hey, kid, I'm going to let you go. I think my ride is here."

"Wait." A pause while Seth shuffled with something in the background. "Maddie wants to say good-bye."

Blake gave the woman another half-assed smile and a what-can-you-do shrug and turned so she couldn't watch his face. "Okay, put her on the *pone*. I mean, phone."

Seth snorted. "Yeah, don't let Mom catch you encouraging the baby talk." Another scrabble that sounded like someone scratching their nails over the phone's tiny microphone.

"Uckle Bake!"

The garbled shriek made Blake jerk back from his cell phone with a wince. "*Heeey*, Maddie. Are you gonna tell me bye?"

"Bye, Uckle Bake!"

"Bye, sweetie. I love you—" A loud crack told him the phone had been dropped on Maddie's end. He waited patiently for Seth to rescue the call. He was in no hurry to confront the woman behind him.

Seth came back to the line, sounding harassed. "Sorry, Dad. I better go. She's headed for the coffee table at full speed."

A sudden sensation of loss hit Blake like a quick pellet shot to the chest. He didn't want to say good-bye. When would they see each other again if Seth went to college in Indiana? It was like a hole opening up inside him that loneliness rushed in to fill.

Blake cleared his throat to dislodge the emotion growing thick in his esophagus. "No problem, Seth. Just, uh…you know. Keep in touch. Whatever you decide to do." They signed off.

Reluctantly, Blake turned back to the woman. He wracked his brain for the right thing to say. She was a stranger, and he shouldn't let his first impression become a permanent mark against her. After all, it wasn't her fault she was a dead ringer for his old mistress, the one responsible for his split from Quinn years ago.

She saved him the trouble by speaking first. "Uckle Bake, huh? Your niece sounds cute." A wide grin split her face. Her eyes, a striking shade of pale gray, like pools of clear water, seemed to tease him from beneath the bill of her cap.

It would've been better if she hadn't said anything. Blake kept a straight face and his gaze trained on the generic symbol stitched onto her ball cap. He determined to cling to the one thing about this woman that didn't remind him of Kira, who wouldn't have worn a baseball cap if he'd paid her in solid gold bars engraved with her name. "Blake Cobb."

Her smile faltered at his stiff introduction. It didn't disappear but turned wry. "Sadie Felix." She stood up straighter and renewed Blake's attention with the subtle change a few calculated adjustments made to her demeanor. Authority flooded her sharp gaze, and Blake was once again reminded of Kira in a bad way. "Senior accountant at Avery & Thorp." Her smile changed yet again, this time into something plastic and false. "I'm here to take you to your temporary housing, Mr. Cobb. May I take your luggage?"

Ah. Emasculation. He'd missed the feelings of inadequacy and self-loathing Kira had always inspired within him. Ms. Felix apparently had the same withering touch.

Blake reevaluated his coworker. Mud-crusted, ankle-high, tawny hiking boots, rumpled khaki shorts with a tear in one pocket, a dirty ball cap, and still she wore her title like armor over it all. She'd hold her chin high in a potato sack. She was his equal, not someone he could get away with talking down to. Not that he'd meant to be a jerk.

I never mean it, do I? Quinn's dry response snapped across his brain like a horse-whip, a trained response anytime Blake thought about feeling sorry for himself or making excuses.

"I apologize if I seem short," he offered Sadie. "Long flight." Ever an excuse but an honest one, at least.

Mostly honest. Was he supposed tell his new coworker he could hardly stand to look at her because it was like a waking nightmare? At least her eyes were a different color, very unlike Kira's coffee-brown ones. Blake cleared his throat and tried again. "Not my niece, actually. More like stepdaughter." Or so he liked to think. His relation to Maddie was complicated.

Blake lifted his luggage and swung it into the bed of the truck, denying Sadie further opportunity to emasculate him. He didn't doubt she'd get his luggage for him, just to remind him to feel small for talking down to her. He made for the passenger door after another halfhearted smile for his host. It wouldn't repair the damage, but maybe he'd look inoffensive enough for her to let it go.

A different yet equally abrasive emotion gripped him now, familiar and as old as little Maddie, who had Quinn's pale blond hair and looked out at the world through Jack Decker's remarkable aquamarine eyes.

Blake had been there when she was born in L.A., been one of the first to hold her in the nursery. He'd changed diapers, scrubbed spit-up off hundred-dollar silk ties, and fed her in the small hours of the night when Quinn and Jack had both been hit with the flu. Since Quinn worked from home, they didn't have a nanny to call on in an emergency, but Blake hadn't minded. He'd been Uncle Blake since the moment she was born.

But he should've been Daddy.

Sadie Felix was no litterbug.

Blake could tell by the crumpled sandwich baggies, drained soda cans, empty water bottles, wadded napkins, discarded gum wrappers, and other assorted garbage scattered across the floor and dashboard of her pickup.

He climbed into the truck with what he hoped was less than a grimace as his feet made loud, crunchy work of the trash. A four-foot long hiking pole was wedged into the cab at an angle so it made a barrier between him and Sadie. It appeared to be sanded down to perfect smoothness and glazed with some sort of sealant.

Sadie noticed his gaze, smiled, and patted it as she got in behind the wheel. "Pine. I carved it myself."

She *carved* it herself? Blake resisted giving her a once-over, but an unmistakable zing of curiosity made it a test of will. Not because she sported a Snow White black bob he historically found attractive, but because any man might look twice at an accountant who minored in woodworking. He snuck a peek, despite himself.

She gave him a slightly apologetic look and turned the key, the Ford's engine rumbling to life. "I bet I'm not what you expected. You'll have to excuse my attire. I'd already asked for the day off to hike Cache Creek before the fall weather sets in. Duncan didn't see the point in sending someone on company time."

Carving and taking off weekdays from the office to hike? A cultural thing, or a Sadie thing?

Blake experienced his first dash of doubt since his plane kissed down on the tarmac runway. He wasn't mountain man material, and the upcoming winter loomed over him like an ominous, hulking giant. Friend or foe, he wouldn't find out until he was in the thick of it. He squelched his uneasiness, something he'd done many times since making the big decision to come north.

A few minutes south on a two-lane highway led them down into Jackson Valley with a dramatic drop in elevation, visible in the wide open space on either side of the road. A rocky, sagebrush-dotted hill sprung up on the right as the highway descended on a curve. On the other side, Blake spotted the sign for a fish hatchery, and then a great expanse of fenced land stretched all the way to the streets of town in the distance.

"The Elk Refuge," Sadie helpfully explained. One hand left the steering wheel to indicate the massive acreage beyond the fence. "You can take a sleigh ride out to feed the herds when they come down from the higher elevations for winter. It's pretty incredible."

Straight ahead, beyond the buildings that marked the beginning of town, a small mountain—small compared to the Tetons, at any rate— rose up. Two strips were cleared through the trees, as though someone had taken a razor to it. Blake lifted his chin toward it. "What's with that mountain?"

"Oh, that's Snow King, both the ski slopes and namesake resort. The *big* ski resort is about fifteen miles from here, a few peaks over from the Tetons, but this place works for the townies." Sadie gamely played host, all the while taking no pains to hide her curious glances and critical studies of him at every chance.

By now the rumor of his previous position would've moved through Avery & Thorp like wildfire. She was probably curious. Maybe he'd appease her some other day, but today all he wanted was to get somewhere quiet to call Quinn. For Seth's sake, to talk about his Purdue ambitions. And to hear her voice. And to give himself another reason to pity his fool self when he heard Jack's loud, happy voice in the background, gregariously living the life Blake had given up.

They cruised into town. Sadie took a right once they passed the famous town square with its four deer-antler arches, explaining how they were reconstructed each year. She pointed out the Cowboy Bar across the street, famous for its saddle barstools. And The Silver Dollar, named so for the bar inlaid with 2,032 uncirculated 1921 Morgan Silver Dollars.

"Great." Blake tried to nod with some enthusiasm but didn't quite pull it off. "If I want to get hammered, I have a number of renowned drinking establishments to choose from." The thought didn't lift his spirits any. *If it gets so bad I turn to the bottle, I'll give up and move back in with my mother.*

"Welcome to the Wild West." Sadie's tone had lost some of its amiability.

Blake let a few blocks of silence pass while he tried to force himself into a better frame of mind. If Sadie could be accommodating, he could manage a little interest.

Sadie's cheeks puffed out as if capturing unsaid words. Finally, she loosed a sigh, drummed restless fingers across the steering wheel, and regarded him again. No intake of breath to warn him, just a rush of words spoken precise and direct. "You're in Jackson Hole. You realize that, right? People save money their whole lives to visit this place. Don't let me kill your joy buzz over there, but you could be a little more impressed. If it's really so ho-hum, at least fake it for my sake. We locals have our pride."

He smiled at her forthright manner. Now, that bit reminded him of Quinn, which was a nice departure from her eerie likeness to Kira. "Sorry. Jet lag."

She nodded but didn't smile back. "Right. Anyway, we're here." She pulled into a hotel parking lot.

Blake squinted at the double doors, glass framed in glossy fake pine. "A hotel? That's what they call 'temporary housing' these days?"

This time she did smile, but it was back to the plastic version. "The room you have comes equipped with a kitchenette, a small living area, and a terrace, as well as room service. I'm sure it has everything you need, but if not, feel free to contact Mr. Perry at your earliest convenience."

Oh, right. Blake was going to call Duncan to complain about five-star accommodations. He bit his tongue as a reminder to keep it from flapping next time. He closed his eyes briefly and sighed. "Look, I'm sorry. I just left L.A. this morning, and I had this stupid idea in my head of a quiet place. I don't mean to be"—now, what was that word? The one Quinn loved to use…

"A jerk?" Sadie supplied without apology.

Prick, actually, but no need to fill her in. Uncomfortable with her unflinching stare, he shifted and opened the door to let himself out. "Yeah. That." He shut the truck door and reached for his suitcase. He walked around the truck so he could pass Sadie's window on his way toward the hotel lobby, meaning to utter yet another weak apology.

It buzzed as she rolled it down before he had a chance to rap his knuckles across the glass.

Her face seemed awfully near. Under those wide, inquisitive eyes was a straight, patrician nose, small on her face and sweeping thinly to a point above an uneven mouth. Her top lip was plumper than her bottom, giving her the perpetual impression of biting her lip. Kind of adorable.

Jackass. Quit looking at her mouth. He blinked rapidly, working himself out of the stupor with some effort.

"Duncan is going to take you house hunting personally to make sure you find a home you'll like. He wants you to be happy here. The suite is temporary, and as close to a 'house' as his secretary was able to manage. And if I know Nina—which I do—she did her very best."

The flush started at his neck and spread. Her total sincerity amplified his embarrassment. All the work and time he'd put into being a better man, only to still be an ass when it mattered. He mumbled his apology, even less substantial than the one he'd planned in the first place, and stepped away, head down.

"Duncan will send one of the file clerks to pick you up Monday morning. They'll take you to get your rental car. See you." She stuck a hand out the window in farewell, and the truck roared away.

Her ability to go from fake to sincere ruffled his feathers. Something about the stiffly polite act gave Blake the distinct impression he was being mocked. He watched her drive away and decided it was probably deserved.

Chapter 2

Sadie shook her head with reverence and poked at the dying fire. "You nailed it, Nina. Nailed it with the hammer of truth, forged by the gods on Mt. Seriously. This guy is so vanilla it hurts my teeth."

Vanilla with chocolate sprinkles, maybe, but she wouldn't go any further than that. Yes, his eyes were stunning, and yes, they'd run over her like melted honey, and *yes,* she'd felt the heat down to her pink painted toes.

Somehow, the heat in his gaze, the fire she probably only imagined, was in direct odds with Blake's demeanor. Distant, bland, cut-off. Affectations or a personality defect?

Nina made self-satisfied noises over the line. "Told you, honey. Stiff and formal, like I said."

"Yeah." Disheartened, Sadie slid the metal poker into the holder and dropped into the overstuffed chair closest to the ambient warmth. September nights were tricky in the mountains, some cool, some fair, some touched with the chill of upcoming winter. "The thing is, Nina, I saw a spark. I swear I did, and not just due to his crazy impressive jawline and those devastating eyes, both of which I was unprepared for, despite your warnings."

"I tried." Nina's tone took on a hefty dose of doubt. "Look, hon, a few quips an interesting man doth not make."

"I know, but I think maybe a little digging could unearth a real gem."

"Sure, and I bet Amanda is a bucket full of clever conversation behind her blank stare."

Sadie huffed and burrowed deeper into her chair. "You're probably right. Besides, we've already been over this. If I was into Blake—which I'm not, because he's a class-A jerk—there'd have to be something diabolically wrong with him. Thanks, Nina. You really help me put things in perspective."

Sadie smiled as Nina practically purred. "What else are friends for, sweetheart?"

* * * *

Blake settled into his new desk. It didn't feel like his yet, even with his sparse belongings decorating the surface. According to Kennedy, his inherited secretary who was weird and flirty and giddy in a way that gave Blake a headache, the previous auditor was an old man with something of a hoarding issue and rarely saw the pristine cherry finish of the fine wood desk.

A photo of Seth sat in one corner of it now. In the other, Blake's daily calendar and a small novelty canister painted to look like a red London telephone booth. A gift from Quinn after one of her return trips from London. She relocated there with Jack after they were married. Seth, too, although they'd all done their best to keep Blake involved in his life.

Blake picked up the canister, popped off the top, and tilted it toward his cupped palm. His wedding band slid out.

His *first* wedding band, specifically. Not the second one, from Kira. Or the third, from Emily.

This one, the plainest and cheapest by far, Quinn had given him on their wedding day, purchased from the local Wal-Mart jewelry counter because they were young, fresh out of high school, and just starting out. This was before Blake's success and client roster went to his head—and other regions—and before Quinn made it big selling her horror novels as Clementine Hazel.

Of everything he'd come to regret, walking away from Quinn reigned at the top of his list.

Three failed marriages. Only one that haunted him.

A light knock on his frosted-glass door made him look up to catch Kennedy poking her head inside with a shy smile.

"Hey, you. I thought maybe I should give you the tour. You came in so early this morning, no one was here to meet you."

He half expected her to follow it up with a bat of her lashes. He adjusted his tie—another gift from Quinn; another remnant of the past he clung to—and nodded for Kennedy to enter. She was right. He should meet his new coworkers, appease their curiosity, and get back to sorting through Henry Rupert's mess. The desk might be clear, but his files were a wreck.

Blake stood and rolled his shoulders. "I should've thought to introduce myself earlier."

"Oh, it's fine." This time she did bat her eyelashes, long false things curving severely over deep-set green eyes the color of an evergreen pine.

Her long face was framed by golden corkscrew curls that grazed her shoulders. Not his type.

Actually, he didn't seem to have a type. All three of his wives had been drastically different. Quinn, the tall green-eyed blonde. Kira, with her black bob and arresting deep brown eyes. Finally, Emily, the plain Jane of the bunch. Thick, brown hair and identical-hued eyes.

She and Quinn were unlikely sisters.

But sisters they were. Marrying Emily was probably Blake's second biggest regret. The only thing worse than screwing up his marriage with Quinn by having an affair had to be marrying her sister in some misguided attempt to make things right. Then again, perhaps marrying Kira, his mistress, ought to take the prize for the biggest mistake. Really, he could forget about having a list—he regretted each blunder with equal fervor.

He pushed the dismaying thoughts aside and followed Kennedy into the main office area, where the desks came together in a haphazard fashion. The nameplates he'd read this morning now had faces to match.

Pearl Harris, payroll clerk. No obvious relation to Opal Montgomery, the accounts receivable and payable clerk, whose desk sat adjacent. Pearl was in her sixties, at least, with tight, silvery purple curls worn close to her head. Opal was a black woman, close to Pearl in age, with a long ponytail of straight, glossy black hair and intense streaks of red highlights. They both looked at him, unsmiling, but turned friendly and accommodating at his polite introduction.

Kennedy's smile held a measure of pride, like she was showing off a model horse.

A Latina woman with flawless caramel skin strode through the office on her way to the front foyer with a lilac-colored folder. She was tall and curvy, with straight light brown hair falling past narrow shoulders.

"Catalina! One second."

The woman paused at Kennedy's frantic wave.

Kennedy indicated Blake with a showy motion. "This is Blake Cobb, our new audit director."

Blake offered Catalina a thin-lipped smile, hoping his embarrassment at the way Kennedy announced him like a local celebrity didn't show on his face. "A pleasure."

Brisk, Catalina took his proffered hand and smiled knowingly. Her eyes were a lighter hazel than his; more brown than green, and softer. "Likewise." In an undertone, she added, "You'll get used to her." She winked, cast a side glance at Kennedy, and resumed her hurried walk.

Blake smiled and hoped she was right. If he couldn't acclimate to his enthusiastic secretary, they'd have trouble. Catalina disappeared from sight.

A second later, a different woman appeared. Pale blond hair, long, straight, and gossamer thin, brushed their tips near a trim, swaying waistline. She entered his field of vision like a mirage.

The roiling sense of *déjà vu* threatened to suffocate him. At the same time, he had the odd sensation of floating.

Quinn.

She stood there with Kennedy, and her mossy green gaze zoomed in on Blake over a button nose and thin, wide lips.

No, not Quinn. But close. Similar enough to make Blake's skin tingle. First Sadie, the Kira doppelganger, and now this? Virtual look-alikes of his ex-wives were populating his new environment like vengeful poltergeists. Blake swallowed and loosened his tie a smidge, suddenly hot under the collar.

I thought Hell is for the afterlife.

Little differences began to stand out as he reflected on the woman's dizzying appearance. Her style, in particular, lessened the likeness by a degree or two. Quinn didn't really do skin-tight pantsuits that left little for him to guess in terms of measurements. Nor accessories so bright they made his eyes water. Blake pretended not to notice the Day-Glo purple heels that matched the large hoops in her ears, or the overly large rings glaring from every finger.

"You're our new auditor." The words were crisp and direct. So like Quinn. They were accompanied by a halfhearted lip curl that might've been a smile.

Blake tried not to stare, looking back and forth between the woman and Kennedy like he didn't know where to rest his gaze. "That's me. The new guy." *Idiot.* "Nice to meet you."

Kennedy chewed the inside of her cheek as she glanced at the woman, then back to Blake. "New guy, this is Amanda Avery. She's Mrs. Avery's daughter"—here Blake caught a hint of defiant delight in Kennedy's tone, as if Amanda being the boss's daughter would put an end to his sudden and apparent fascination—"as well as head of bookkeeping."

"Lovely." Blake felt like a dimwit the moment the word escaped, but Amanda seemed not to have noticed. In fact, she seemed rather blasé and distant. Busy, like Catalina, but not rushed.

She offered him a final twist of her thin lips. Again, possibly a smile. "Likewise." She strode away purposefully, leaving Blake staring after her like a dream he wanted to chase.

Kennedy cleared her throat and spoke stiffly. Her friendly, flirty demeanor vanished. "You've met nearly everyone. Reba Garcia is our receptionist. Nina Walsh is Duncan's secretary. We have two file clerks running around here somewhere. Xavier and Trish. Part-time, you won't see them often. Lyle Thorp works over the hill, in the Idaho office. Mrs. Avery keeps her office at our Alpine branch."

She abruptly ceased talking. She paused and tilted her head like a dog might lift an ear to a whistle. Her brow creased in mock inquiry. "Do you hear that?"

Voices. "Yeah..."

Kennedy rolled her eyes in a self-deprecating manner, her friendliness returning. "I forgot someone, but here he comes now. And, if I'm not mistaken, they're at it again. Meet Wes Black. Sadie's nemesis."

The voices grew louder, and Sadie burst into the bookkeeping parlor behind a reedy, raven-haired man, shouting at his back. She clenched a stack of colorful file folders in one hand. The other gestured wildly. "You're a thief, Wes. A slimy, underhanded thief."

Wes whipped around. His hair, long by typical office standards, was gelled back from a narrow forehead. "I haven't taken the account, Sadie. I only asked Duncan to consider me. You're not *senior s*enior accountant, no matter how much you wish it was a legitimate job title. I'm as qualified as you are."

Sadie's gaze narrowed. It pronounced her catlike features and prodded Blake into taking a closer look. She didn't have the regal, high-born features Blake admired in Amanda. Sadie had something infinitely more cunning. It tugged at him and made him curious.

"Don't forget," she growled at Wes, "I have the Kesh account. You'd think taking lead on the only billion dollar account in our entire firm would count for something."

Wes visibly calmed and held his palms up in supplication. "I'd be stupid not to ask for it, Sadie. I know you think I'm crap. I can tell by the way you shoot me down every chance you get. But I'm going to do my job, and if it means competing with you, so be it." He turned on his heel, went behind the frosted glass door caddy corner from Blake's, and slammed it shut.

Kennedy blew out a plume of air. "Well, Sadie, that's one way to say no to a date."

Sadie didn't smile. She rolled her shoulders. "I'm having to get creative. The bastard won't quit."

* * * *

Sadie stood in her office doorway with crossed arms and watched Blake linger near Amanda's desk, attempting conversation.

He seemed different, talking to Amanda. Open, smiling, gabbing away. Why was he interested in Amanda, whose facial expressions ranged from vacant to slightly less vacant, while Sadie attracted losers and a weirdo like Wes? Wes, who wanted to steal the new million dollar Castley account from right under her, knowing full well Duncan had it slated for Sadie, and ask her to dinner at the same time.

Behind her, Kennedy sat at Sadie's desk, filing her nails again. "Why can't I have a private office? Then I wouldn't have to hide from Duncan all the time."

"Don't you mean from Amanda and her bookkeeping minions?" Kennedy might sit clustered with the bookkeeping ladies, but she wasn't part of the team. Pearl was friendly, Opal was clique-ish, and both adored Amanda to an unnatural degree.

"I'd never hear the end of it if Pearl caught me tending my manicure, but you'll never hear anyone utter a word when she slides her Sudoku puzzle onto her desk." Kennedy huffed. "And it looks to me like Blake is about to become another Amanda Avery casualty."

Sadie couldn't disagree. The two of them talked in quiet conference. Amanda wore a small smile, a nice change from her normal blank glare. "Have I told you how vanilla Blake is? Vanilla-flavored vanilla."

"About three times, yes." Kennedy's voice perked up with optimism. "But he's still super hot."

Sadie was running thin on resistance to Blake. She'd spent about ten minutes chatting him up in the breakroom this morning. She sensed something more, something deeper, shimmering beneath his carefully cultivated exterior. She itched to scratch the surface. Which meant trouble, naturally. Best to talk herself out of her interest before it bloomed into infatuation. "Okay, but he's also older than Nina made him out to be. At least forty."

Kennedy's scoff rang through the room. "Your point? It's all about the older, mature man these days. Brad Pitt and George Clooney are still at the top of their game, even with all these new youngsters showing up on the scene."

Sadie rolled her eyes, glad Kennedy couldn't see her. "That's outside the point. I'm saying, he's exactly Amanda's type, isn't he? Quiet, boring, pleated."

"Pleated?"

Sadie turned around to give her friend a pointed look. "You're going to pretend you didn't notice his pleated slacks?"

Kennedy shrugged. "Whatever. Clothes aren't static, Sadie. They change. *Ha.* Get it? Like, change clothes?" She paused in her filing to slap her knee.

Sadie pursed her lips. "All the women in this firm, and I choose you for a best friend."

"I'd like to take credit, but even I can't deny it is slim pickings around here."

Sadie turned her attention back to the bookkeeping parlor, where Blake was giving Amanda a shy little wave good-bye as he walked back toward his office. The other hand he kept demurely in the pocket of his oh-so-creased slacks.

Even from across the room, past desks and lamps and bodies moving, Amanda's uniquely expressionless face stood out like a splotch of gray in an otherwise colorful, vibrant world. Her outfit screamed, all right, but in agony. The neon purple made Sadie want to scrub her eyes with a Brillo pad. Not that Amanda wasn't pretty. She was. A blah shade of blond hair, and eyes that Sadie was pretty sure were green, but might also be blue. Honestly, she couldn't meet Amanda's vague stare long enough to be sure. Amanda's conversational skills began with the weather and ended with obvious observations, so the vacant expression wasn't just an unfortunate physical attribute, like resting bitch face. It was more like a warning flag. *Beware! Attempts to unearth anything resembling a personality will prove fruitless.*

Given all that, the way Blake was acting like a teenage girl at a boy band concert had Sadie mentally scratching her head. "Why do you think that is?"

"Probably because you're a little on the catty side. Honest, hardworking, dedicated, but definitely catty."

She'd hardly noticed she'd spoken out loud. Turning back to her friend, Sadie put her hands on her hips. "I'm not catty. I'm sassy, which is right up there with lip gloss in terms of necessities. No, I'm talking about Amanda. Why is Blake drawn to *her?* Why not me? Or you?"

Kennedy harrumphed and brushed a runaway ringlet from her eyes. "Beats me. I'm the wrong shade of blond? I smiled, maybe, or gave some other indication I'm not a robot? He's clearly into robots."

They held the same basic opinion of Amanda, but Sadie was better at keeping hers to herself. "I'm going to do some recon."

At this, Kennedy gave her a steady look, her head tilted slightly to one side. "What, exactly, are you investigating?"

Fine question. With an answer Sadie didn't want to share. Because, as she stood there watching super-starched too-serious Blake try to woo blank-faced Amanda, Sadie's mind had wandered to the depressing list of her past relationships.

Losers, users, abusers, the lot of them. Those were the men she attracted and who were attracted to her. What was she supposed to do? Were there request forms she could fill out and submit for a list of nice men? Hell, a *boring* guy would do. Then again, maybe she ignored and mocked boring men the way she ignored and mocked Amanda.

What if, for once, Sadie didn't wait for the next loser to find her but went out and made a little effort? What if she actively pursued a nice, boring man like Blake, instead of being a sitting duck for the next deadbeat to come along?

She put on her best serious face—the one with slightly raised eyebrows and a near-frown that made her look weary and slightly bored of her own intelligence, and answered Kennedy's questioning stare. God forbid she catch on to Sadie's true motive. If Kennedy knew, everyone would know, and then the full extent of Sadie's desperation would become the new hot topic in the office, forever sullying her image. She had a reputation to protect for being an independent badass.

Besides, if Kennedy was already crushing on Blake, a likely scenario, she'd only take Sadie's interest as a personal affront. "Isn't it obvious? He might've let something interesting slip in his fawning all over Amanda, so I'll talk to her." As if it would be that easy. Were it anyone else, easy as pie. "As a potential runner in the bid for Duncan's job, I need to know everything I can about Blake Cobb."

Sadie inhaled, squared her shoulders, licked her teeth, and eyed her quarry. She could do this. She had until her feet carried her across the room to come up with a sincere, welcoming introduction.

"Hi, Amanda." Not what she had in mind, but simple.

Even caught off guard, Amanda's expression hardly wavered. Perhaps some slight widening of her eyes, but it could've been a trick of the light.

She had green eyes, after all. Sadie mentally added that to the tiny list of things she knew about Amanda. "I, uh, noticed you striking up a conversation with the new guy. What're your impressions of him?" She ended the question on a conspiratorial tone, hoping it would lure Amanda into a bout of gossip.

Instead, Amanda's mouth turned down. "He's nice."

Sadie couldn't blame her for frowning. Outside of work-related topics, she doubted she'd said more than ten words to Amanda before today. "That's good. I suppose we need someone to balance out Wes."

Amanda's frown deepened. "Wes is nice, too."

Sadie bit her lip and switched tactics. Wink, wink, nudge, nudge wasn't doing the trick. She stood up straighter and gave Amanda a concerned appraisal. "Are you okay? You seem kind of down. A little frazzled." Actually, she seemed as complacent as ever. Smooth as a stagnant pond.

Magically, Sadie had hit a mark.

Amanda inhaled deeply, her frown still fixed. "I appreciate that you noticed. Duncan has decided to double my workload."

Sadie tutted. "Geez, what's with that guy? Don't you do enough around here?"

"Exactly the point I made." Even commiserating, Amanda remained perfectly poised. No gesturing hands or rolling eyes. "I'm not certain it's my job to pick up Duncan's slack, although I understand the demands of his position. Still, I have my own responsibilities to see to."

Right. Because Mama Avery owned the firm, Amanda understood everyone's position. Yet she had no interest in filling any role more ambitious than bookkeeping, for whatever reason. Sadie had never bothered to ask. She was afraid inquiring now would open up a world of chitchat she hadn't come prepared for. On the one hand, she was on a time-sensitive mission. On the other, sometimes you had to go around your elbow to get to your ass.

"I understand," Sadie lamented. "What job is old Duncan trying to pawn off on bookkeeping?" Something boring to do with internal accounting, probably.

Amanda loosed a tiny sigh. "I'm supposed to take the new audit director to look for a house this weekend. What Duncan perhaps doesn't realize is I spend most of my free time in Alpine, and I hate driving the canyon more than I absolutely have to."

Cha-ching noises rang in Sadie's ears. Karma wasn't always a bitch. Sometimes she was really sweet and thoughtful. "I don't blame you. That canyon highway is just as treacherous as Teton Pass in the right conditions."

"More like the wrong conditions." Amanda's frown did a weird thing—it turned up a tad on one side.

It caught Sadie like a sudden strong wind. *Holy moly, did Amanda Avery just make a joke? What planet am I on?* "Ha. You're right. The wrong conditions. Okay." She licked her lips. "Um, so how can I help?

I'm free this weekend. I even know a place or two on the market. I could show Blake around if you'd like."

"Blake?" Amanda's face turned quizzical.

It was probably a good sign Amanda didn't recall his name. Especially if Sadie was serious about angling for a date. Although, *date* would be more aptly described as a *field study* in her new crusade to give the nice guy a try. "The new audit director. Blake Cobb."

"Oh, right." Amanda paused and seemed to think it through. It was hard to tell, her face as blank as ever. Finally, she met Sadie's gaze. "I couldn't express how much I'd appreciate it."

Ain't that the truth. Sadie gave her an aw-shucks smile. "Glad I can help you out."

Chapter 3

Blake tried really, *really* hard to keep his disappointment in check when Sadie's familiar red Ford pulled into the curved drive of the hotel lot. He felt stupid now, looking at the charcoal gray slacks he'd pressed to perfection in preparation for spending the day with Amanda.

Instead, he got Sadie, Kira's long-lost sister.

She pulled up to the curb, and Blake hopped in to be greeted by a winsome smile. The ball cap hadn't made a return appearance, but Blake was learning Sadie's personal and professional styles didn't occupy the same sphere.

At work, she wore three-inch, black peep-toe heels like she'd been born in a pair, and slim black slacks with bold silk shirts, sometimes tucked with a decorative belt but more often left long like a tunic and enhanced with one or two eye-catching pieces of high quality jewelry. A thick gold cuff on her wrist or large cubic studs in her ears that peeked and glinted with every tilt of her head. No neon purple hoops for Sadie.

Her weekend apparel had a more playful, practical flair—cut-off denim shorts, a beat-up pair of Nikes sans socks, and no jewelry, with the exception of tiny silver hoops. To replace the ball cap, a red bandana was wrapped around her head and tied at the top, pulling the hair back from her face. An overly large pair of round white plastic sunglasses completed her look. She reminded Blake of a ladybug.

He buckled his seat belt. "Thanks for taking me house hunting. I appreciate it."

Sadie nodded but made no move to put the truck into drive. Instead, she smiled wider. "You were expecting Amanda, I know. She spends most weekends with her mom in Alpine. You know, Mrs. Avery. I'm sure you've met her."

"Telephone interview, actually." He glanced over his shoulder. No oncoming traffic. "Are we going to go or what?"

She tilted her head. "You don't want to change? Jeans and a T-shirt, maybe? We aren't doing anything today that requires…" Her hands finished the sentence as they waved, fingers wriggling, in the direction of his lap.

Heat suffused his face. For the sake of his pride, he wanted to tell her he dressed like this all the time, *thank you very much,* but the thought of a pair of loose Levi's and an old band shirt sounded too nice after a week of slacks and button-ups. He opened the door without a word.

Fifteen minutes later, they were cruising south down Broadway, the major four-lane highway that cut through the valley and ran the length of town. He'd spent the night in his hotel room scouring a map of the city, but there hadn't been much to scour. Few main arteries and a smattering of gridded residential areas made up the bulk of the small town.

Sadie pointed to a busy intersection as they passed, a small highway forking to the right. "Highway 22. Stay on it, you'll end up in this tiny speck called Wilson, the cutest, quaintest town around. Beyond it, Teton Pass, which takes you over into Idaho. Not for the faint of heart, that pass. Eight thousand feet doesn't seem like much."

Blake nearly interrupted her there. He didn't know a soul who'd call eight thousand feet *not much.*

"But after a two thousand foot climb in a metal box on the side of the mountain, it's pretty damn intense. Every year, some idiot flies right off one of the switchbacks. In Wilson, if you hook a right on Moose-Wilson road, you'll end up in Teton Village, with world-class skiing, high-end restaurants, and some very exclusive gated communities."

Blake wouldn't mind exploring his new landscape, but he could think of better company. The polished wooden beams of downtown turned into average buildings and businesses. A familiar sporting goods store and a dollar store whizzed by. Then an Albertson's off to their left, and as they rounded a curve, Kmart came into view. "Where are we headed? Are you taking me to the bad side of town?"

Sadie didn't take it for a joke. "There is no bad side of Jackson. I'm taking you to a subdivision outside the city limits called Rafter J. It's gorgeous, and you'll have an open, unobstructed view of the mountains on either side of the valley. Plus, if you're the hiking type, High School Butte is a hop and skip away. Flat Creek Trail, too. It's paved, great for biking. And, of course, this mountain here"—she pointed to the one rising beyond the Kmart—"is the backside of Snow King, the ski slopes here in town. Jackson sort of wraps around it like a C. Trails all over it. You can climb right to the top."

If he didn't come clean now, she'd never stop. "Look, I don't really hike. Or ski, or do much outside of hitting the gym a few times a week."

Sadie looked away from the road to gape at him. "What the hell did you move here for, then?" She didn't wait for his answer but gave her attention to the road and snorted. "The cost of living is through the roof, and houses have a median dollar tag of a cool million bucks. We're isolated, cut off on nearly all sides by mountains, and while it's awesome to be the 'Gateway to Yellowstone,' it's a good hour away and closed almost half the year. So, really, why here?"

"For all the reasons you just said." Blake wanted to bite his tongue. He didn't owe Sadie an explanation, but something about her made him want to give her one, in a defensive, insecure way. Now, why could that be?

Oh, yeah. The whole Kira thing. So far, Sadie's personality was pretty much in line with what Blake might've expected from his ex-mistress, especially the edge of condemnation and judgment in her exasperated voice.

When Sadie's lip curled, he tried again. "It's not your business, but I came here for solitude and a job suited to my résumé. Like you, I deal in millions. There aren't many small mountain towns with a year-round population of less than ten thousand people and that sort of financial profile."

Sadie started to reply and stopped. Her mouth clamped down. They passed a couple of hotels and a pet supply store. "You're an auditor. What's it matter if the client roster is high-end when you deal with internal accounts?"

The truth? His paycheck. Avery & Thorp paid nearly four times the amount some of the others firms offered for the same position. Since Quinn had taken her best-selling novelist income with her in the divorce, Blake was left on his own to uphold his high-finance lifestyle. Much as he'd grown as a person, he still had expensive tastes, thanks to a solid couple decades spent indulging them. He refused to feel bad about liking money. Nothing wrong with making it to spend it.

And it wasn't like he didn't have bills. He'd be accountable for half of Seth's tuition the following spring, and he doubted Purdue offered discounts for the privileged.

Blake decided he was done answering Sadie. In fact, he needed to cut the head off the dragon now, before it had a chance to grow bigger teeth or thicker scales. "What does it matter to you why it matters to me? How about we just look at houses and stop talking about work."

A half-shouldered shrug. "Fine. We can talk about other stuff. You have any interesting hobbies or character quirks? What do you for fun? Knit? Volunteer? Collect vintage spice racks? Starch your pants while you listen to NPR?"

"For fun, I..." Blake paused mid-breath. In one rapid-fire round, Sadie had him pegged. He was boring. Dull, mundane, humdrum. Lifeless. The realization stung, then settled heavy in his chest. No wonder Quinn didn't want him. He'd never had a chance up against someone like Jack, had he?

He shifted uncomfortably and gazed out the window. "I, uh...Well, I read."

Sadie slowed to turn onto a sloping road that dipped into the valley on the right. A creek bed snaked between houses and clusters of aspens and cottonwoods. The road followed the same curving pattern as it turned toward the sprawling neighborhood. The houses weren't built on a typical grid system, something Blake had noticed was the norm for Jackson; more like they sprinkled across the valley in a random pattern, with lots of open space and a substantial number of cul-de-sacs.

"What do you read?" Sadie had slowed to a near crawl, the speed limit having dropped down to twenty. "Romance? Sci-Fi?"

He didn't think *my ex-wife's novels* would earn him any points. "*Business Weekly.*"

Sadie sighed with such obvious disappointment; Blake felt it right in his pride. Good thing he wasn't here to entertain anyone.

After a few more curves, they passed over a charming wooden bridge, like something out of a fairy tale, and Sadie pulled up to the curb in front of a huge, white clapboard house with two stories, a looped gravel driveway, and landscaping fit for the cover of *Home & Garden* magazine.

"I hate it." He couldn't have handpicked a better visual representation of the cookie-cutter life he was desperately trying to leave behind.

Sadie's head whipped around so fast, Blake winced. "What do you mean, you *hate* it?"

"Okay, hate's kind of intense. I only mean it's not much different from my place in L.A. I can't see the mountains through the stand of Douglas firs. There's nothing rustic about it, no charming mountain-type features. It's not a log home. It's on flat land. It's also huge. I'm one guy. At most, I need a guestroom for when Seth visits."

If Seth ever visited.

She chewed her lips, and her smoky gaze traveled over his face like he was some alien species.

Blake squirmed in his seat and wished he was with Amanda. Reserved and poised, she could've easily been Quinn's sister. More so than Quinn's *actual* sister, Emily. He didn't like to think about that, though. He'd rather think about Amanda and how he'd eventually pry her out of that cool, confident shell. Finally, frustrated with both the house and the current company, Blake huffed. "Look, it's not a big deal. If this is what's available, I'll take it."

Abruptly, as if coming to some internal decision, Sadie dropped the truck into gear and shot away from the curb. "You want a mountain? I can give you a mountain."

Blake swallowed. What had he done? Rather than backtrack, he accepted his fate and promised himself he wouldn't blame Sadie if she landed him a ramshackle cabin perched high on a mountain cliff. He'd literally asked for it.

Blake refused to give into surprise when Sadie took him back into town, right through the heart of downtown, this time staying due east once they hit the square, and on toward where two mountains ridges seemed to draw to a close.

She took a few winding roads, which grew thinner and less maintained the closer they drove toward the gathering ridges, and took an abrupt right onto what appeared to be a narrow gravel alleyway.

Except, it wasn't an alley. It was a road, evidenced by the faded road sign naming it Brewster's Lane. It shot up the side of the mountain— not far from Snow King Ski Resort if Blake's internal compass was functioning properly—and made a razor-sharp switchback before angling up and out of sight, blocked by a wall of thick, towering pine trees.

She was messing with him. Trying to get a rise out of him. A little payback for saying the last house wasn't good enough.

Why hadn't he said, "Sure, it's great," and been done with it? He'd be collecting his things in his rental car and pondering furniture right now. Then again, why should he let Sadie's talent for making him uncomfortable cause him to lose sight of what he'd come here for? He wouldn't play along in the head game. He wasn't going to complain or object. He'd see the house on the side of the freaking mountain, he'd tell her thanks but no thanks, and they'd move on. Worse case, he'd choose the first house, after all. Like an episode of *House Hunters.*

He bit back a groan as the truck climbed. *I did this to myself.* The story of his life.

They traversed two more switchbacks before the road widened and a few houses cropped up. The fronts were poised on high stilts so they sat even on the mountain face, with parking spots either carved into the mountainside or paved patches beneath the foundation of the house. The third turn was softer than the other two, rounded in a flat semicircle, framed by patches of tall grass and low shrubs.

There, sitting perfectly flat on a small strip of even ground, a small log cabin. Nothing too special. It sat back far enough from the gravel road so two vehicles could park parallel without impeding traffic. It faced north, thick pines filtering a killer view of the town far below. Two small windows flanked the front door, painted a dull red to match the battered shutters.

The deal slid neatly home when Blake spotted the nifty yellow *For Rent* sign staked into the ground. "Stop."

Sadie hit the brakes, jostling them both against their seat belts. "Why? What? Is it a bear? Did you see a bear?"

"Right there." He pointed. "The place for rent."

She squinted past him, through his window at the sign, then turned an incredulous glare to him. "*That* place? No, no. Listen, there's a place a little farther up, okay? It's got three bedrooms, in case you have family come visit, a big stone fireplace, and a top-notch kitchen. Also, the rent sign isn't handwritten."

Blake opened the door and got out, drawn by a subtle tug of a deep secret desire realized. This was the place he'd seen in his daydreams of a simple life lived with simple pleasures. It was as far from the game as he could get. A place to hide away and rediscover who he was, rather than obsessing about the jerk he'd become. A place to heal.

"It's perfect."

* * * *

Sadie retrieved her jaw from its unhinged position and blinked.

Blake morphed before her eyes. His face alighted with childlike wonder, a genuine smile—the first she'd seen—played across his lips, and he bounced on the balls of his feet as he approached the cabin. In his fascinated stupor, he hadn't bothered to close the truck door.

She climbed out and came around to shut it. Blake peeked through windows of the cabin, his smile growing with each inspection, even as he wiped away dirt from the panes with the side of his fist.

She didn't get it. She found the cabin unimpressive and bleak. Blake made great money. He could afford something with more creature comforts. The other house had a big balcony with Adirondack chairs already set up, ready for prime coffee sipping.

His life. She pulled her phone from her pocket.

Blake glanced at it. "If you're calling my therapist, tell her the jacket's not necessary this time. I promise I haven't lost my mind."

Oh, wow, a joke. Sadie thought back to the last week. She hadn't witnessed any signs of an actual personality inhabiting Blake...until now. In fact, he was alarmingly similar to Amanda. But maybe he wasn't dull and boring, after all. Maybe the guy was depressed.

Sadie cocked her head and peered at Blake. "I bet she's been burned by that one before."

He turned his delighted smile on her, and Sadie's skin warmed. "I guess she can bring it along in case."

Sadie shook her head. Damn if this guy wasn't getting to her.

Blake looked back at the cabin and kept talking, as much to himself as to her. "I know, it seems crazy. Because I'm...whatever the hell I am." His voice lowered some, and his usual starched tone colored over the small bit of happiness he'd had for a minute there. "I was partner in my old firm. Success never once made my life better, though. Ambition to be the best, to have the best—it only made me lose sight of my values. And when I lost those, I lost just about everything else. Ambition used to be a quality we frowned upon as a society, you know that? And I can see why. It's why I have to step back and find a little humility. I can't just think about it. I have to live it."

An ambitious player in the game, Sadie took the dig personally. "Sounds to me like a personal flaw. Not everyone who achieves success, or has the ambition to strive for it, loses sight of their values."

The stricken look on Blake's face made her want to recall the words. She hadn't meant it as an attack. A little paler than he had been a second ago, he nodded but said nothing. His awed, happy expression darkened.

Sadie felt it right in the gut. "Look, Blake, I didn't mean—"

"Who were you going to call?"

She bit her lip. Blake had revealed depths she wouldn't have guessed at. A past riddled with regrets and loss. She wanted to pry him open and steal his secrets; make him sing like a canary. But not today. She'd unwittingly compelled him to close the window, and now she'd have to wait for another opportunity to delve into his layers.

"The landlord." Sadie hooked her thumb toward the sign. "There's a number scrawled across the bottom."

The wait for the old man who'd answered on the first ring was one of the most uncomfortable stretches of time Sadie had ever suffered through. Blake's mood had fallen into dismal territory, and Sadie had no idea what to say to fix it. Finally, a dusty little pickup meandered up the hill and pulled in behind her Ford.

A round, gray-haired man with a tremendous scraggly beard and thick glasses approached. "Dale," he grunted by way of introduction. "You want to see inside the place?"

Since he'd addressed Sadie, she pointed to Blake as he rounded the far side of the cabin, having inspected the whole exterior. "He's your guy."

Dale followed the line of her pointing finger. His face fell a little.

Sadie didn't blame him for doubting the sincerity of a renter who looked like Blake. With his perfectly smooth face, stylish salon-grade haircut, and jeans that looked like they were purchased brand new this morning, he looked like money itself. The smooth vanilla type usually preferred the landscaped yards of the Aspens, an upscale community of condos near Teton Village, or a swanky downtown loft.

She waved Blake over. Dale launched into an introduction and unlocked the cabin for him to have a look around. "Two small bedrooms. Partially furnished, so you'd probably want to pick up a few things. Dishes, things like that. Kitchen's there." He pointed to the left. He stood just inside the door and let Sadie and Blake move past him into the cabin.

It wasn't so bad. Cupboards lined the far wall, and a small square table was shoved into the corner next to the fridge. Not much counter space, but did Blake cook? Probably not. He struck Sadie as a takeout kind of guy. A faded green sofa backed up to the kitchen, serving as a barrier between it and the living room. Which was tiny; just large enough to squeeze in near the only heat source Sadie had spotted so far.

She smoothed a hand over the uneven mantle fixed over the wood-burning stove, pleasantly surprised when her hand came away clean, and turned to Blake, who was opening cupboards in the kitchen. "You'll need firewood to get through the winter."

On the right, two identical doors led to the two bedrooms, also identical in both size and shape. The sofa faced the bedrooms, which left just the small stretch of wall between the two doors to stick a television set if Blake were so inclined.

She expected the inside to be a let-down. Sparse hardly covered it. "What do you think, Blake?"

He'd moved over to study the wood-burning stove. When he faced her, she was struck by the simple happiness there. Her mind whirled back to Nina's first description of Blake. So very good-looking. And so, he was. More so without inner troubles clouding his face. For now, he seemed to have escaped their grip.

This close to him, the individual colors in his eyes stood out with the starkness of a child's crayon drawing. Green like summer grass at its lushest, with a swirl of amber dancing through the middle. The lines at the corners spoke to his age, as well as the scarcity of his smiles. A lively twinkle replaced his usual somber stare, and it was enough to stop Sadie in her tracks, like someone had hit the pause button.

Their gazes seemed caught together. He didn't look away, and Sadie couldn't if she wanted to.

Finally, he blinked, breaking the spell. "It's exactly what I want."

A few minutes later, the details sorted out, Dale led them to his truck, where he'd thoughtfully brought along a rental agreement.

He added an indiscernible squiggle beneath Blake's neat signature. "You have any problems, call and I'll take care of it. One last thing. The cabin's called Fox Watch. There's a den of foxes somewhere nearby, which is odd because they usually den down near the creek beds in the valleys, ya know. You'll probably see one, but I always advise renters not to attempt to engage. After all, they're wild animals, protected since we're in a national forest, and probably on edge to begin with, since they'll have young nearby during certain months. So, keep an eye out. And use good judgment."

Dale lumbered away, waving over his shoulder without looking back, and Blake hit Sadie with his full, unhindered smile, once more jolting her into a new level of awareness. "Fox Watch. That's cool. Sounds like something Quinn might like."

Quinn, huh? Could be a man. Could be a woman. Sadie wouldn't find out without asking. "You need any help getting moved in?" An easy excuse to hang out and worm a few details from those tight lips.

He paused and studied her.

She didn't squirm under his scrutiny, but she didn't particularly enjoy it, either.

Blake's features settled once more into their normal flat state. The shades drawn, the hood down, and the door shut. "I think I've got it, thanks."

* * * *

Sadie gulped wine, well past the sipping point. "I mean, what the hell is wrong with the guy? You know me. I'm not abrasive. Or offensive. I'm as chill as f—"

"Forget Blake," Kennedy chimed in. "He's hung up on Amanda, anyway."

Sadie relaxed back into her pink chenille throw blanket. She had her favorite slippers on, a fire roaring in the massive stone fireplace, a comically large glass of wine in her hand, and her favorite people huddled nearby on the sofa. So, why was she so damn grumpy? "We were doing great today. He found that stupid cabin, and it was like another person emerged. Then, *bam!* He looks at me like I'm some kind of offensive *thing* and doesn't want anything more to do with me. What if it's that crappy comment I made about ambition? Of course, I'm sorry for whatever he did to himself on his climb up the ladder, but not every successful person in the world has a crumpled heap of bodies and burned bridges behind them."

Nina sipped delicately from her glass and tucked her feet neatly beneath her. "Kennedy, you're his secretary. Didn't you learn anything last week? Aren't you taking his calls?"

Kennedy studied her freshly painted fingernails. "The only personal call he gets through the office is from his son, Seth, who I've gathered is attending Purdue next spring because he stalled and missed the fall deadline."

Sadie nodded. "Maybe he has empty nester syndrome."

Kennedy groaned. "Do we really care? Again, Blake likes Amanda. I bet he'd have taken *her* up on the offer of help." She directed a pointed look at Sadie.

Sadie narrowed her gaze, but Kennedy probably had it right.

Kennedy said, "You're kind of obsessing, Sadie. You're supposed to be finding out if he's after Duncan's job, not trying to be his girlfriend."

Secretly, Sadie was attempting both. She was definitely developing something of a crush on Blake. Surprising, given how normal he seemed. Did he have a deep, dark secret like all the rest of the guys she gravitated toward? And just what about Blake drew her in? Boring, staid Blake. Could it be that he hardly looked at her, let alone with any sort of mutual attraction? What the hell did that say about *her?*

That I'm abnormal, or I'm like every other woman on the planet? Say no to the dude who wants you, pine after the guy who doesn't.

But the last person she wanted to know all this was either one of her friends, sadly. Kennedy was prone to attention-seeking and wouldn't appreciate Sadie moving in on the new office hottie, and Nina didn't corral her gossip for Sadie's ears alone. In fact, she was quite friendly with Reba, who'd tell anyone anything.

Sadie decided a pinch of honesty might go a long way. "I know. And you're right. But today, I saw a side of Blake I don't think he even realizes exists. He's so somber and serious all the time, but today was like a glimmer of someone else shining through. Someone different. He's clearly troubled. I think he's depressed. I really do."

Nina shrugged.

Kennedy rolled her eyes. "So, help him out. Convince Amanda to go on a date with him. That'll perk him right up."

Sadie wiggled her toes and ignored Kennedy, even though she suspected her insightful best friend had nailed it. Blake definitely had Amanda on his mind. On the way back to the hotel that afternoon, Sadie had attempted to mine details from him about his life. He'd somehow turned it around, and instead, she'd spent the drive fielding questions about Amanda.

But she wasn't ready to give in, not when she hadn't really tried yet. "You're right. Blake does need help." She drained her wineglass and smacked her lips. "So, I'm going to help him. Whether he wants it or not."

Her cell bleeped from where it rested on the arm of the chair. She plucked it up and stuck out her bottom lip in an exaggerated frown. Wine did weird things to her. "It's Amanda. Why is she calling me?"

Her friends shrugged.

Sadie answered, still watching her friends quizzically, hoping one of them might offer up a theory at the last second. "*Hey.* Amanda. What's up?"

"Hi, Sadie. I wanted to ask how it went today. I really didn't feel comfortable delegating Duncan's task to you. I didn't stop to think you might've had Saturday plans of your own."

Sadie struggled to sit up. Eventually, her feet would find the floor and she'd make it to the wine bottle for a refill. "Oh, no trouble. I offered, after all. Besides, it turned out great. Blake found a little cabin up Brewster's Lane he really seems to love." She checked her watch. "By now, he's probably settled." Her gaze traveled over to Nina and Kennedy. She had an opportunity to keep them off the scent for a while yet. She gave them a flashy wink and dropped into a conspiratorial tone for Amanda. "You could, uh, maybe give him a call. I bet he'd appreciate that."

"No thanks."

No pause, no stutter. Zero interest in Blake. Sadie magically refrained from unleashing a goofy, happy grin.

"I only wanted to thank you again, Sadie. I appreciate you stepping up to help me out."

Sadie's feet hit the floor, but she sat there a minute. Not ten words to the woman in weeks, and now this? Maybe, like Blake, Amanda had a personality, too. It was just buried so deep she had to poke and prod to get it out of its hole. "Sure, Amanda. Anytime."

The call ended, and Nina raised her eyebrows at Sadie. "Since when are you and Amanda are on weekend terms?"

"Since now?" Sadie shrugged and padded into the kitchen area. "Maybe she wanted to make sure I didn't screw up, so Duncan couldn't put the blame on her for anything."

"I'd be worried, too. You're Duncan's pet. Everyone knows that." Kennedy had officially slurred her first word.

Sadie shook the empty wine bottle and set it in the sink. They were definitely done with wine for tonight. "Duncan and I keep it twelve degrees of professional. Everyone knows that."

That seemed to shut Kennedy up for the time being.

"And anyway, if Duncan was *really* my friend, I'd know a lot more about Blake by now."

Chapter 4

Kennedy was starting to push Blake's buttons.

And not the good ones. Every day, she found some new excuse to come in his office, lately with the habit of closing the door behind her, which Blake disliked for several reasons. In his past, he'd closed his door for two kinds of visitors—clients and his mistress.

Kennedy found all sorts of interesting ways to catch his eye, including, but not limited to, bending over in strategic places to pick up something she "dropped," bending low over his desk to offer him a view down her blouse, and asking his plans for the weekend. To which he always replied he was busy.

Thank God she'd never asked with what, because the answer was usually to practice fire-starting skills and try to make friends with the fox who lived near his cabin. Blake had named him Eric, after a character in one of Quinn's recent novels, who he secretly suspected was loosely based on him—blond hair, hazel eyes, and a penchant for being a self-serving prick.

No offense to the fox. Blake only meant it as an homage to Quinn, and a reminder to himself.

And was it just him, or did Kennedy's outfits get a little more revealing with each passing day? It didn't seem terribly convenient to attempt to get his attention this way, given how the weather had turned. October had come in like a whisper and turned to a roar about two weeks in. A mild month in California, it was a different animal in these parts. And still, everyone assured him real winter hadn't started yet.

It would really help if he could start a fire. He purchased tiny bundles of firewood at the gas station on the way home and burned through most of it trying to keep warm through the night.

He compared it to when Hunter was born. Thinking of Hunter still brought the dull edge of an old pain front and center. Hunter was Kira's son. For the first several months of his life, he'd been Blake's, too, until Blake learned he wasn't the father. But for those first few months, when he'd been none the wiser and reveled in having another son, Blake had been up and down all through the night to feed and change Hunter.

Tending his meager fire was a lot like that. And it took him no less than an hour just to get it started most nights.

Sadie seemed too busy lately to bother with Blake. Relief warred with disappointment every time they passed one another in the hallway or the lobby. She'd smile, a lovely genuine thing that cast Catalina and Amanda's lukewarm greetings in a pale light.

He did his best to ignore how it made him feel, her smile. It was a little perk, a surprise pick-me-up. She had some kind of magnetism, and as often as Blake's gaze sought out Amanda, it often found its way to Sadie. He watched her professional hand at dealing with high priority clients, and how deftly she snuck Kennedy into her office to gossip.

Occasionally, she had the uncanny talent for catching him at it. She'd turn her head suddenly, and their gazes would lock. He had to wonder if she sensed his attentions on her, or if she suffered from the same staring problem he did. Sometimes, she smiled. He'd smile back. Other times, her face hinted at more somber thoughts. He'd have paid to know what they were.

Then there was her reaction to Wes. A wild animal came to life behind her bright, silvery gaze when he entered the scene. Blake had spent the last several weeks observing her feud with the greasy-haired Wes. It interested him. Blake couldn't say if it was because Sadie was an intriguing study all her own, or if Wes's love/hate relationship with her fascinated him. Wes wanted the new Castley account, but he also wanted Sadie, who wanted the same account.

Would Sadie eventually give in and date her rival? Would Wes choose between his ambition and his crush on Sadie? Was Sadie's hostility fueled by ambition? Or passion?

He'd find out today, when Duncan announced who'd won the account.

A gentle knock sounded on Blake's door a few minutes before noon. It took a great deal of willpower not to drop his head directly onto his desk and hope it hurt enough to block out the sound of Kennedy's voice.

Kennedy beamed. "Hi there. You snuck right past me this morning!"

He gave her a thin-lipped smile. "That's me. Sneaky McGee."

Her giggle was a tinkling girlish variation of her normal laugh, which he only ever heard in his office, for his benefit. Her normal guffaw was much hardier, and not so pretty. "You're so funny. Anyway, I thought I'd better remind you of the time. Wouldn't want you to miss lunch." She gave him a small, secret smile that made his hackles rise.

An invitation. Blake ought to know. Once upon a time, he'd taken a woman up on it. "Actually, I was just leaving." He rose and grabbed his black suede coat from the coat tree in the corner of his office before brushing past Kennedy.

She followed close at his heels. "Really? You sure? Actually, I was going to ask you—"

Blake whirled on her. "I have plans." His mind raced. "With Amanda."

Before she could question him further, he sought Amanda in the bookkeeping parlor. She had her head down, working with her usual single-minded steadiness. He started toward her and checked back quickly to make sure Kennedy had stayed put.

She had, looking sad with the downturned lips of frustration. It probably wasn't the best idea to piss off his secretary. But, at the same time, if she didn't find the line, he'd have to ask Duncan to point it out to her.

Talk about awkward.

He slid his hands into his pockets when he approached Amanda's desk. "Hey."

She didn't startle but looked at him with a perfectly blank face he couldn't have read if his life depended on it. Was she irritated by the interruption? Happy to see him? Indifferent?

"Hi, Mr. Cobb."

"You can call me Blake."

"Okay. Can I help with something? If it's a payroll concern, you'll want to speak directly with Pearl Harris. I can point her out if you're unsure."

"Oh, no. No, I don't have a payroll concern. I, uh… See, I wondered if you had plans for lunch. I thought maybe you'd have lunch. With me?" Should he say please, or would it sound desperate?

His neck heated. He didn't recall this being so difficult or awkward. His recollections of his high school relationship with Quinn seemed to come back to him like a perfectly scripted movie. Words spoken with ease, kisses achieved with little effort, everything he wanted placed ever so obligingly into his waiting palms. Kira had pursued him with a sexual aggression that was reminiscent of a different type of movie. With such little life experience, having been with Quinn since the beginning, it hadn't once crossed his mind to fight the pull, let alone take a hard look at the distinction between love and sex. And Emily had simply wanted him when no one else had.

They'd all come to him. He had no idea how to properly pursue a woman.

Amanda didn't help the situation. She could at least smile pityingly. Offer a tiny hint to give him an idea of what was going on in her head, or prepare him for rejection.

"No, thank you. I brought lunch from home." For a second, her gaze wavered and she seemed uncertain of what to say next, as though something were owed to him. "Turkey on whole grain seed bread. No mayo, with sprouts."

Before he could figure out a response that didn't make him look or feel like an idiot, a tap on his shoulder made him turn around.

Sadie's heather-hued eyes were alight with mischief.

The queen of zippy one-liners had witnessed his spectacular fail. Fabulous. Like he needed any more reasons to hide in his office. "Can I help you with something?"

Her grin widened. Her hands clasped together in front, reminding Blake of a child with a secret. "Oh, just thought I'd rescue you, that's all. Since Amanda is busy"—she glanced past Blake's shoulder to give Amanda a wave in the form of wiggling fingers before looking back at Blake—"how about I take *you* to lunch?"

His eyebrows rose on their own accord. "You want to go on a date with me?"

She blinked but didn't appear surprised. "Oh, I'm sorry. I didn't realize you were asking Amanda out on a date." She performed a solemn nod for her audience, which had grown to now include Amanda, Reba as she passed through on her way to the break room, and Wes, who watched from his office doorway. He rested against the jamb with crossed arms and an indiscernible look on his patrician face.

Blake came close to pulling his collar away from his neck in a cartoony gesture of nervousness. Sadie's entertained expression said she knew it, too. "Uh. No. Not really. Not like a *date* date." He turned to glance at Amanda with a nervous smile but needn't have bothered.

Her attention was once again trained on the work at her desk.

Blake sighed and gave Sadie a flat glare. "Fine. But you're buying."

* * * *

Sadie's mouth almost hurt from the effort of wrapping it around the massive burger. She'd taken Blake to the famous Billy Burger's only to have him order off the menu from the fancy-pants Cadillac restaurant instead.

A genius concept, really. The famous Cadillac Grille was split down the middle, separating the upscale dining area from the retro-style bar. Billy's, attached to the restaurant front, hit full capacity with fifteen

people. It took a stroke of luck to get an empty seat. The simple solution
had been to combine the menus, so that even if there was no chance in hell
you could squeeze into Billy's, you could still get one of their humongous
burgers and fresh waffle fries.

Sadie licked ketchup from her thumb and mumbled around the wad
of food in her mouth. "What's with you and Amanda? You're crushing
pretty hard on a woman you don't even know." If a direct hit couldn't
draw him out, Sadie was at a loss. She might have to give up on Blake,
no matter how stunning his eyes were against the hunter green button-
up he wore today.

He stabbed at a pork dumpling like it deserved it. A deep sigh escaped
shortly after, and he seemed to come to some kind of internal decision.
Shoulders squared, he looked at Sadie dead on. "You're really nosy. And I
don't like it. But you know who else is nosy? My ex-wife's new husband,
and I've learned from having that guy in my life the last five years, there's
no defense against people like you and him."

Interesting. Finally, they were getting somewhere. Sadie scooped
ketchup onto a waffle fry and used it to motion Blake to continue before
plopping it into her mouth.

He dropped his fork as though it disgusted him.

He must have some intense history if it made him lose his appetite
to think about.

"Amanda reminds me of my first wife. Okay? They're practically
identical. Besides physically, they share the same polished reserve and
poise, which I find attractive in a woman. There. Now you know."

"*First* wife? How many times have you been married?"

"Three." He shook his head. "I don't want to talk about it."

"Fine." Sadie sat back and dropped the fry she'd been about to eat.
"You should know I'm picking you up Saturday morning. Don't ask
me what for or where we're going. My only warning is that you attire
yourself in the exact opposite fashion of how you're dressed now. We're
going to get dirty."

A slight blush crept up from Blake's collar.

Aww... I think I flirted. The only problem was her own face heated.
What were they, twelve? Sadie went back to her burger. "Tell me what
happened with your wife. The first one. Divorce?"

Blake inhaled deeply and directed his gaze at the tabletop. "I had an
affair with a woman named Kira. For five years. Quinn found out. We
divorced. She eventually moved to London, met her new husband, and
gained primary custody of our son, Seth. Not long after the divorce, Kira

got pregnant. We married, making Kira wife number two, and had a son together. Sometime later, I learned I wasn't Hunter's biological father. Next came my second divorce. Obviously, she took Hunter. If you're counting, that's one mistress, two wives, two sons, two divorces, and a partridge in a pear tree."

Ah. The mysterious Quinn he'd mentioned. Dumbly, Sadie chewed her thumbnail. That was some serious, *serious* baggage.

He raised his eyes to hers. "There you have it. I'm pining after a woman who reminds me of my first wife."

Sadie thought back to the last time she'd heard the name Seth. "How's your relationship with your son? The, uh, real one." An awkward personal question, but Sadie needed a minute to mull over the wife stuff. So far, he'd mentioned two. The third remained unaccounted for.

"Fair enough, given our history. He starts college in the spring."

"I recall. Headed to Purdue."

Blake lifted one shoulder. "Probably. Quinn wants him to go to Oxford. She lives in London most of the time. Goes back to L.A. occasionally for work stuff." With his elbows resting on the table, Blake regarded Sadie from behind hands locked together. "Are we done with my history yet?"

Not by a long shot. Curiosity niggled at her, like a rabbit with a lettuce leaf. But also, something sour lurked in her stomach. Blake was a cheating douchebag. But of course, right? Because the universe had long ago dictated Sadie couldn't be attracted to simple, kind men. At least Blake had the redeeming quality of remorse.

She supposed her most burning question had to do with the mistress. "If Quinn's so wonderful that you're drawn to Amanda because of their likeness, what the heck was so great about this Kira lady?"

Blake didn't seem to mind the question. He even picked up his fork again. "Ambition," he said, almost curtly. "Quinn and I were both accounting majors in Los Angeles, where money is king. But when she had Seth, her priorities changed, while mine didn't. She was content to be a stay-at-home mom and wrote to pass the time. It turned out to be a lucrative endeavor, but by the time she had any success at it, I lived in a different world. My clients were movie stars, bankers, and politicians. I wanted to go to the top of the top. I met Kira on the way, flying up the same ladder. She was everything I imagine Quinn might've become if it weren't for Seth. I came home to a wife who was bored to tears by my talk of the office, while I didn't really have an interest in what Seth had chewed on that day. Or the words he learned to say."

Blake paused and stared off into the space beyond Sadie's shoulder. Sadness and simple longing filled his expression until he blinked it away.

An ill feeling crept through Sadie. Blake wasn't pulling any punches— the picture he painted did him little credit. At the same time, her heart went out to him. The lines that were always on his face were deeper now.

She guessed he spent a lot of time in this headspace, contemplating a past he was ashamed of, apparent in the way he could hardly meet her gaze.

After a short silence, an abrupt dry laugh croaked from Blake. "I'm not innocent, by any means, but Kira... That woman is like no one I've ever met before or since. Ambitious to a fault. Manipulative."

His hazel gaze flicked over Sadie, hard and distrustful, before dropping to his plate.

Her skin broke out in goose bumps. What the hell was *that?*

Blake turned his attention to his food, without touching it. "Weirdly, Seth actually was the one who found out about Hunter. And yet, it was months before anyone clued me in." Blake's lips twisted sardonically. "Quinn's sister, Emily, did the honors. Since I'm telling the story, I should go ahead and mention she was wife number three. Divorced three years ago. She's remarried now to some surfer dude she met in Honolulu."

Sadie suddenly found she was the one unable to keep eye contact. For someone he claimed to love, Blake had done a real number on Quinn. First, an affair. Then he marries her sister. *I sure know how to pick 'em.* She brushed crumbs from her fingers. "I have good news for you, Blake."

His eyebrows rose. A hint of something close to exasperation or even despair glinted behind his green-gold stare.

She looked away. "We're definitely done with your history."

* * * *

Sadie turned onto Brewster's Lane with a quick peek at the dashboard clock. Hopefully, eight wasn't too early on a Saturday morning for Blake. But the drive out to Cliff Creek took time, not to mention the actual cutting and chopping to get the wood to fit in her truck bed. Her back hurt just thinking of the splitting that came later. She'd leave that part to Blake, once she gave him a tutorial.

Her cell phone buzzed, and she grabbed it with her right hand, while using the left to smoothly navigate the first switchback.

"Hi, Kennedy. Sorry, can't hit yard sales this weekend. I have plans."

"Yeah, I heard."

Her voice was like a frosty breath in Sadie's ear. "You okay, Ken?"

"Sure, I'm fine," Kennedy began, with blatantly false lightheartedness. "Just seems weird to me. Last weekend, you weren't interested in Blake in *that* way. Yet, you've been his new little best friend ever since."

Torn between irritation and a hint of guilt, Sadie exhaled through her nostrils. "I took him to lunch on Monday, and I told you last week I was going to offer to help him out. Which is why I'm taking him out to cut firewood. He mentioned spending a fortune on those little bundles at the grocery store, trying to learn to make a decent fire before winter. Anyone in the office could've offered to help him out. Besides, why do you care?"

"Isn't it obvious?" Exasperation swept Kennedy's cry into the realm of petulance. "Monday, I'd been two seconds from asking him out after Amanda shot him down, but you zoomed in like Superwoman and snatched him up. All I have to do is show an interest in someone for you to suddenly be keen as hell on them. Wes is a perfect example. What's your deal, Sadie?"

"Whoa, whoa, whoa." Okay, she might cop to Blake, but Wes was a different matter altogether. "You're mixed up, Ken. The thing with Wes is…" Crap. Sadie clenched her teeth. "It's complicated. And it's long over. You want him, he's up for grabs. As for Blake, I've told you, my goal is to find out if he wants Duncan's job. That's it."

Kennedy's tone fell into tired dejection. "Yeah? Well, Wes called looking for your number again. He said you keep deleting it from his phone."

Sadie grinned. "Eventually, he'll quit leaving it in the breakroom."

"This time it was important. But I think I'll let you call Wes yourself. Maybe you can go back to pretending not to flirt with him under the guise of not wanting attention instead of pursuing Blake, with whom I've made my interest clear."

Crap. It's last summer all over again.

The same thing had happened when a cute young guy from Utah had moved in next door to Kennedy mid-summer. Her best friend had crushed hard on the guy for months, who ended up asking Sadie out. The circumstances incited pity for her friend but also incurred a fair amount of frustration and irritation—Sadie would have said yes if it hadn't been for Kennedy's irrational anger that he'd dared to ask, and the not-so subtle hints that Sadie had enticed him to do so.

The kicker was that if Kennedy knew the gritty details of Sadie's past with Wes, she wouldn't be so blasé about her crush on him. But it was Sadie's own fault the whole office thought of their past relationship as a mere fling.

"Look, I don't flirt with Wes. We have history, and it shows. That's all there is to it. Concerning Blake, you can't claim every man who randomly shows up in our lives, okay? What if I like Blake, too? I don't owe you first shot, Ken. And I definitely don't have to let you treat me like crap for hanging out with him."

The silence told her Kennedy had hung up. Wonderful. She ended the call and immediately dialed Wes.

"Hello?" He answered on the first ring, deep and slow as usual.

The one and only thing she would ever admit—and to herself alone— was the attractiveness of Wes's disembodied voice. "If you memorized my number, you wouldn't have to spaz and call every other person in the office to get in touch with me."

"Yes, but if I did that, you'd probably change it just to be difficult."

She almost laughed, then recalled Kennedy's accusation. She wasn't *flirting*, she simply forgot and slipped into old habits occasionally. Such as laughing at his lame jokes, which she vowed to never do again. "What's the big story?"

"Duncan sent out a company-wide e-mail this morning. When I didn't hear from you, I had to wonder if you've seen it. I'm not sure if you're still refusing to check your office e-mail on the weekends."

Sadie pulled up behind Blake's rental—when was he going to get his own car?—and set the parking brake. "Yeah, well, I have a life, unlike the rest of you."

"He announced his exit from Avery & Thorp. He and Zoey are going back to Salt Lake City in the spring. She's pregnant, so there's no way they can pull off the move before winter hits."

So, Nina had gotten it right. Duncan was leaving behind the coveted chief accountant position. And Sadie's number one obstacle was on the other end of the line.

He seemed to know it, too. "I guess this means no more games, huh? I know you're going after the promotion. As am I."

At that moment, Sadie caught sight of Blake, and something in her chest squealed with delight.

He crouched barefoot on the ground, pine cones and rocks scattered across the dirt and grass. In lieu of his usual starched slacks, or even the new-looking Levi's he'd worn last weekend that still had their store creases, he wore a faded pair of jeans she'd bet anything he never wore in public. They rode low on his hips, which dipped into hollows she hadn't imagined he might have. Shirtless, a fine sprinkling of blond chest hair glinted from the dappled morning sun shining through the pines.

Sunbeams fell over his hair, reflecting like a halo. Sitting back on his heels, Sadie had a swift urge to climb right onto to those steady thighs.

Oh, damn. I'm in so much trouble. It'd be easy to put a swift end to a crush, given Blake's horrid relationships of yore. But if she dipped too low into the vat of physical attraction, there'd be no digging herself out of that hole.

He stretched out a hand toward one of the trees. A black snout rimmed with red fur cautiously peeked out.

"Wes, I have to go. We'll have to talk later."

"Lunch on Monday to discuss this new development?"

The snout emerged another inch, and the black spread into bright orange. Blake was squatted on his heels, about to feed a wild fox something from his bare hand. The idiot was going to get rabies. "Fine. That's fine. Gotta go." She hung up and dashed from the truck.

Blake jumped at the sound of Sadie's truck door slamming closed.

By the time she reached him, the little red snout had disappeared, and Blake stood shirtless and sullen, looking at her like she'd broken his favorite toy. "What the hell was that? Didn't you see how close I was?"

She swallowed and forced her gaze to meet Blake's dead on and not wander over his collarbones. God, his bone structure was ridiculous. "Did you forget what Dale said about approaching wild animals? This isn't L.A. There's more to worry about than stray dogs around here."

He blinked against a streak of sunlight that fell through the trees in a line across his face. "We have mountain lions in Los Angeles. Don't treat me like I'm ignorant."

"Don't do ignorant stuff," she shot back, frustration from several sources taking control of her mouth. "Ever try to approach a mountain lion? A fox might not try to feed you to its cubs, but their bite can be nasty, like any wild dog. Rabies could be the last of your problems. Literally."

Blake pressed his lips together like he wanted to argue more but wouldn't. He dropped his gaze and pushed his big toe into the dirt. "Yeah, it's kind of stupid, isn't it?" He let go a sad, tired exhale and looked around, like he couldn't meet her gaze. "It just seemed like something Jack would do." He snorted, a self-deprecating laugh.

"Jack? Who the hell is Jack?"

A pained expression took over his face. "Quinn's husband. I mentioned him. He's one of those guys, you know. Cool by virtue of their lack of awareness of their inherent coolness. If that makes sense. Cool because they don't know they're cool. The kind of guy who'd make friends with the fox in his yard." Blake shook his head and stepped back, headed for his cabin. "It's nothing. It's stupid."

Pity wrapped around Sadie's heart. Blake seemed like two people to her—an obscenely good-looking success story but also lost, insecure, and wholly unaware of his true nature. He wasn't the guy he used to be, obviously. His personality seemed at odds with his history. At least he'd exuded a certain self-disgust and remorse when he'd talked about it. Maybe he didn't know who the hell he was now, caught between his old self and the person he strived to be instead.

Which would make it close to impossible for Sadie to figure out who he was. "Should I wait in the truck while you get ready?"

Blake made it to the front door and held it open. He finally allowed himself a glance at her. "I made coffee for two." He stepped inside, then quickly looked back at her. "And his name is Eric."

Sadie reached the door. "I thought it was Jack?"

Blake smiled, and her stomach fluttered. "No. The fox. His name is Eric."

Chapter 5

Sadie tucked her hair behind her ear. "You're up, Lambert."

Blake politely cleared his throat and leaned against the truck, angling his head against the cloudy sky to look at Sadie through the dark lenses of his retro sunglasses. Dark enough, he hoped, for her to not notice how his gaze kept returning to her bare legs.

To be fair, they were literally in his face. And the way she kept bending over the chainsaw, a lightweight model suited to her small frame, checking this and that, made it even harder to stay focused on what she was saying. "You call your chainsaw Lambert?"

She looked down on him imperiously and replied straight-faced. "That's his name. What else would I call him?"

If she wanted to name her chainsaw Buzz McChoppy, it was no business of his. He sensed more to the simple defensive reply, but it was hard to gauge Sadie's current mood.

She'd been a little muted since they left Fox Watch. It made the long drive out to wherever the hell they were mildly uncomfortable. He'd had the view to keep him occupied. Looming rocky cliffs, a rapid, rushing river. Anglers knee-deep in the water whipping their lines across the surface as they fly fished.

Blake scratched his chin. No good. He had to ask. "Everything okay with you?"

She ignored him, hopped down from the truck bed, and hefted the chainsaw, only to lay it on the ground at her feet. She leaped back up to rummage through the diamond-plate toolbox and yank out two pairs of safety goggles and work gloves, then set them aside. The last item she retrieved was a folded pair of thick canvas pants she deftly unrolled and shook out.

She hopped down with her arms full and shoved goggles and gloves into Blake's chest, which he grasped a second before she let go. "Wes called me this morning." She laughed. "So did Kennedy, but that's a whole different pile of steaming crap."

He grappled with the items she'd handed him. "What did Wes want?" *Besides the obvious.* His gut reaction to Wes's not-so-secret desire ran dangerously akin to jealousy. He studiously ignored this.

Sadie slid her legs into the heavy duty pants. She waited until she'd hitched the first strap onto her shoulder. Then she ceased all movement to stare at Blake like he'd said something offensive. "Duncan's leaving."

The announcement fell a little flat for him. But the way Sadie glared at him, like waiting for something...

An old memory of Kira, like a flashback from wartime, hit him in the solar plexus. This feeling of uncertainty, this tense guesswork of "name that mood" before he became a target basically summed up their entire short marriage. Every time Sadie started to seem appealing, something about her broke the surface and reminded Blake why his instincts had gone haywire at first sight.

"And?" He made sure to put a good deal of annoyance in the succinct question.

Sadie blinked. "You want the job, don't you? That's why you're here."

Stunned, Blake nearly laughed, but his ire outgrew his mirth. A realization dawned, something he ought to have caught on to sooner. Suddenly, Sadie's helping hand made a little more sense. "Is that was this is all about?" He held out the goggles and flopped the gloves around for emphasis. "You helping me out? Taking me to look for a place, lunch last Monday, teaching me the ways of the mountains? You're trying to find out if I'm a threat to your stupid ambitions."

Exactly like Kira. Down to the ulterior motives for everything. Blake felt sick with himself for liking her, being drawn to her. Talk about old habits dying hard. He couldn't kill this one with a machine gun.

She paused in hooking the final strap into place. "Since when is it stupid to desire success?"

Since it had destroyed his life and cost him everything that mattered— things he'd had in his possession all along and been too ignorant to see. "This'll be the last time I ever explain myself to you or anyone else. If I want Duncan's job, it's mine for the taking. I became the most qualified person in the firm the moment I stepped through the front door of Avery & Thorp. But I took a step back in my career for a reason. I definitely didn't come all the way out here to climb the very ladder I've owned the last ten years of my career. Do you want me to carve a tiny replica out of pine and hand it to you in a symbolic gesture that it's all yours and I'm not interested?"

"You can carve?"

"No, but maybe that'll be the next thing you offer to teach me out of the kindness of your suspicious little heart."

A grin cracked one side of her mouth. "I'm sorry."

It was Blake's turn to stare. Kira's apparition had disappeared, and only Sadie remained, looking a little abashed and a tad amused. "You're right to snap at me. I basically accused you of lying to me when you said you weren't interested in the rat race these days." She glanced away and tucked a strand of black hair behind one ear, revealing a tiny glittering stud.

Who wore earrings to go chop down trees? Blake snorted a quiet laugh and ran a hand over his rough cheek. "Look, I know what it's like to have a fierce drive burning you up inside. Rest assured, mine has sputtered out. Wes is the only person you have to worry about standing in your way."

Sadie's grin faded as she held out a hand for the goggles Blake still had crushed to his chest with one arm.

He handed them over, along with a pair of gloves, and donned his own. "What's the deal with you two, anyway?"

"Nothing. We don't have a deal. C'mon, let's walk up over this ridge and check out the meadow on the other side." She headed that way, hefting the chainsaw in her gloved hands. "We're looking for dead standing trees, or ones recently fallen. You definitely don't want green wood. I mean, it's fine if you've got time to let it season—dry, that is. So, if you wanted to get a good stack for next year, we could. But for firewood you can burn tonight, we need stuff with a low moisture content. I'll loan you my woodcutting axe until you can get down to the hardware store and pick one up."

Blake scrambled up the hill after her. His flat tennis shoes slipped on the thick reeds of grass. He needed to pick up a pair of sturdy boots while he was at it, eying Sadie's thick-soled boots with deep treads. "Why do I need an axe if you have a chainsaw?"

She glanced over her shoulder. The twist of her body, even in the shapeless drab coveralls, was overtly female. "This is but the first step, my handsome apprentice. We cut a tree down into thick logs. Then we use an axe to split the logs into firewood that fits into your tiny stove. Usually, I pay my neighbor's kid to chop mine for me, but it's for the best you learn how before hiring it out. Once you've got a good supply, I'll teach you how to properly start a fire so you don't freeze to death over the winter."

"Handsome, huh?" He looked up in time to catch the blush on her cheeks before she faced forward again and crested the small ridge.

"It's the scruff," she said over her shoulder, her face out of view. "I have a thing for scruff. Not a full beard. That's far too mountain man, even for me. But a hint of roughness over a smooth surface holds a certain appeal." She stood next to a fallen tree, set the chainsaw on the ground, and glanced at him through the thick goggles. "Don't you think?"

With a sharp tug on the pull-string, Lambert roared to life.

She struck a mesmerizing figure—earrings glinting, calling his gaze to the shape of her jaw and the slope of her neck, rough coveralls conforming loosely to her feminine shape, goggles wrapped across her eyes, her mouth caught in a slight grimace of strain as she muscled the chainsaw into place, the biceps on her small arms flexing, and her legs braced on either side of the fallen tree as she deftly went about the task.

Yes, actually, he did agree. Definitely, a certain appeal.

Later, while they loaded the heavy barrel-sized chunks of dissected wood into the truck, Blake mused aloud, "I don't know. I find a little grit beneath a polished exterior equally alluring." He avoided meeting her gaze but didn't miss the small grin that crept across her lips.

* * * *

Kennedy's attitude had done a one eighty since last week. She dropped two bright orange file folders onto Blake's desk, her mouth a flat, unpleasant line and her eyes hooded.

Blake cleared his throat before she could disappear. "Is there a problem?"

She stopped abruptly but didn't turn around. She kept her hand on the doorknob. "No, sir. Everything's peachy."

Why did women do that? Pretend everything was gravy when it clearly wasn't? "Have a seat please." The words formed a request, but his tone pulled rank.

With a moan, Kennedy turned around, issued a massive eye roll, and slumped into a chair across from Blake. "What?"

It came close enough to snappish to test his patience. He sat forward and folded his hands together. "Ms. Hale, I would suggest approaching this conversation with a different attitude."

Her shoulders squared, and surprise widened her eyes.

He had her attention now. He wished it hadn't come at the cost of implied threats. "I've never had a secretary I didn't highly value. A good secretary makes all the difference in the world, and if you don't think so, ask me or Mr. Perry to go without ours for a day. You're good at your job. After what I've seen from the mess Henry left behind, you were instrumental in keeping major mistakes from happening on his end. I'm sure he'd be grateful if he realized to what extent he relied on you."

She said nothing but seemed to freeze, like she'd been caught at something.

"If you have an issue with me, I'd appreciate you coming to me directly. If you aren't comfortable doing that, take your concern to Duncan and allow him to mediate. I have to know what the problem is before I can find a solution. And there must be a solution, because you and I need to work together as an effective team."

Kennedy's eyes grew wet and her lips trembled.

Oh, no. Crap, crap, crap. He hadn't meant to make her cry. He'd just wanted to get her out of her funk. "I didn't mean—maybe this is an issue for Duncan. I'll get him in here."

Before Blake could reach for the phone, Kennedy waved him away and shook her head. "No, no, it's fine. I'm okay." She ran a pinky beneath her eyelashes, smearing her eyeliner in the process. "Just no one's ever noticed before! Henry, that old toad. He was a walking disaster. He couldn't see well, and I was over his shoulder constantly, making sure he had correct figures. I even had Amanda question me on the Wite-Out supply because I burned through it like you wouldn't believe. And I couldn't tell anyone. Not without hurting Henry." She sniffed.

Blake opened the bottom drawer of his desk and pulled out an unopened box of tissues. He handed it to Kennedy, who took it with a trembling hand. "You wanted this job, didn't you?"

She dabbed beneath her eyes. "Did Sadie tell you? Or Duncan?"

"Neither." Blake reclined, more at ease now that they were conversing with words instead of sobs. "You've might've gotten it had you been honest with Duncan about how much you covered for Henry."

She pulled a tissue from the carton and dabbed at her eyes. "Not likely, but I appreciate you saying so. It's too much of a leap. But maybe when Sadie gets Duncan's spot, I can squeeze in next to Catalina, huh? I've been taking classes. Even bookkeeping wouldn't be so bad."

Bookkeeping, huh? "Maybe I could talk to Amanda for you—"

"Why her?"

"She's head of bookkeeping. Who else?"

Kennedy tilted her head. "You know what I'm asking. Don't play dumb."

He peered at his secretary. A little too astute for his tastes, but he didn't see a way to dodge it since she'd come at him so directly. "I guess Sadie isn't the only one who's noticed. Amanda's my type. That's all."

"Not Amanda."

Suddenly, Kennedy's deep green eyes held depths Blake didn't want anywhere near.

"I'm not sure what you mean."

She seemed to recall Blake's warning about her attitude just shy of executing another eye roll. Instead, she inhaled and pressed her lips together. "Sadie has a history of being interested in men the moment I express a hint of attraction, or, in Wes's case, keeping her nails dug in to prevent him from moving on. It's a hobby of hers." She lowered her lashes, and a coy smile spread over her mouth.

Blake couldn't decide which side of Kennedy he disliked the most, because so far they were all annoying and problematic. He fought against another weary sigh. He didn't need to piss her off again. "Kennedy, I'm flattered, but you're my secretary, and—"

"Not if I get promoted. What would be the difference between me and Amanda then?"

Looks? Personality? Amanda might be on the flat side, but he'd rather be bored than constantly on the defensive.

"I'm sorry," he said, as plainly as he could state it. "I like Amanda. I'm not interested in you or Sadie." At least, he wasn't interested in Sadie romantically. She was fun to be around, fun to flirt with, but with her similarities to Kira, Blake only saw disaster in that direction.

Lumping Kennedy with Sadie seemed to take some of the sting out of the rejection. Her chin jutted out, and she ran her index finger idly across the surface of Blake's desk. "Well, I suppose you feel how you feel."

Blake scratched his cheek and considered Kennedy. She had more to her credit than her secretarial position implied.

Before she disappeared through the doorway, Blake halted her. "Hey, one last thing. What, exactly, is the deal with Sadie and Wes?"

Kennedy shrugged. "I guess you better ask one of them." She glanced out the door and into the bookkeeping parlor. "But you might want to wait. Duncan's about to announce he's giving the Castley account to Catalina. Wes said he'd hoodwinked Sadie into a lunch date today, but it wouldn't surprise me if they spent it at Emerg-A-Care getting their bruised egos tended to."

Blake thought back to his conversation with Duncan about plans for the new high-dollar account both Sadie and Wes were hot to get their hands on. "How did you know about the Castley account?"

This time, she let the eye roll fly. "I'm your secretary, Blake. I know everything you know."

It struck him she might know a few other things, too. "May I ask how well you know Amanda?" At Kennedy's playfully tilted head and amused grin, he balked. "Never mind. It's nothing. She'll come around once she gets to know me." He hoped.

Kennedy's grin turned pitying and made him doubt it. "Tell you what, boss. You buy me lunch, and I'll give you everything I've got on Amanda." At his obvious consternation, she groaned. "Not like a *date*. I get it, you're not into me. Let's move on. Grab your coat and meet me in the lobby in ten. I'm going to make sure Sadie and Wes leave for lunch without killing Duncan. None of us have time for a murder trial."

* * * *

"You realize this is all your fault, right?" Sadie ripped into the rib with relish. It felt good to tear something apart with her bare teeth, even if it was already dead and slathered in barbeque sauce.

Naturally, Wes would take her to Bubba's the day she wore her favorite white smock with the lemon yellow cap sleeves. He was too meticulous and neat for it to have escaped his notice. And, damn him, he knew she wouldn't turn down spareribs. They were her weakness.

Of course, *he* wouldn't do something as undignified as order the ribs. He took a fork to his delicate steamed trout. "I asked for a shot at the Castley account," he responded irritably. "You're the one who blew up all over Duncan for considering me. I think you screwed both of us."

Not for some time, pal. She snatched her cloth napkin from the table. "And I think you were never in the running. Honestly, I don't have time for another account of that magnitude. There are too many demands on my time as it is. And you're underqualified." She held up a finger smeared with sauce to hold him off. "Don't forget, I was doing this job long before I got you hired as the junior accountant, Wes. Toot your horn all day over how quickly you were promoted, but I'm the better candidate for Duncan's position."

Unruffled, he took a piece of fish cleanly from his fork with his teeth. His black eyes stayed unnervingly locked on to hers. "We don't have to be enemies."

"Yes, we do." Sadie scrubbed her fingers and took a deep breath. She couldn't believe she'd let him talk her into this. "People don't change. You were a controlling, manipulative jerk when we were together, and you won't magically become someone else if I go out with you again. You'd be the same guy, I'd be the same girl, and we'd have the same problems."

"I disagree."

His lazy blink made her want to toss her iced tea in his stupid face.

"Case in point." She threw her napkin down and stood. "Now, quit asking me out. And quit tricking me into lunch dates while you're at it."

"You wouldn't be here if you didn't want to be."

She didn't get a chance to deliver a scathing reply, because Blake and Kennedy walked right up on their table.

For a second, awkward silence ruled. Then Blake gave them each a flat smile. "I guess it's a day for working lunches."

From behind him, Kennedy's arms crossed. "It's not unusual for these two to go from threatening to rip each other's arms off to casual dining."

Her stony stare reminded Sadie of her accusation Saturday morning. Sadie had half a mind to lay it all out there, put every last sordid detail of her history with Wes on display. See what Kennedy had to say then.

Her best friend wasn't the only one throwing shade. Blake's eyebrows were drawn in confusion, and Sadie recalled him asking what was between her and Wes. Well, just because Blake had spilled his guts didn't mean she owed him her own embarrassing story—the one where she'd let Wes sleep his way into Avery & Thorp, then proceed to treat her like his most favorite possession.

"May I have a word?" Sadie didn't wait for a reply but stalked past Blake, grabbed Kennedy's arm, and tugged her toward the women's restroom.

Kennedy came willingly, even if her small pout as Sadie pushed her through the western-style swinging doors said she'd didn't appreciate being forced into an impromptu powwow.

Inside, Sadie turned and leaned against one of the two pedestal sinks. "We're best friends, Ken. Be honest with me here. Do you seriously believe I'm interested in Wes? After everything I went through with him?"

Kennedy's put-upon expression fell away and left an unsubtle mark of near-pity on her face. She tilted her head, and one fat golden ringlet flopped over her shoulder. "No. Not really, I don't. But I *do* think you tend to keep certain connections." She shrugged one shoulder. "I didn't mean what I said the other morning. I don't think you're pursuing Blake because you saw that I liked him. Maybe you saw what I saw, or you're curious, or whatever."

Keep certain connections? What the hell did *that* mean? "You're saying I keep Wes within arm's reach because…"

Indignation made her voice high. "Because it sucks to be alone. Because we're women, and hope springs eternal. Take your pick. Look, I've had a thing for Wes ever since your little fling didn't work out. You could've moved on, but instead, you keep him like a puppy on a string.

Do something about it or cut him loose, Sadie. Fair is fair. There aren't exactly a load of eligible bachelors around the office."

It took Sadie's entire wealth of self-control to keep her mouth closed. Fling didn't come close to describing her relationship with Wes, but Sadie had been the one to decide how the story would go. Now, she had to commit to it.

"Besides," Kennedy went on, eying her nails, "Blake and I cleared the air this morning. I might've come on a little strong, and he told me under no unclear circumstances he's not interested in me. Or you, for that matter. He's all about Amanda."

Sadie chewed her lip. She hadn't really expected Blake to like her or anything, but it still rankled a bit to come second to Amanda in any arena. "Amanda reminds Blake of his first wife. The one he's still clearly very much in love with, despite her being remarried and mother to a young toddler."

Kennedy's eyebrows rose. "Wow. You two really have done some chatting."

"It's like pulling teeth. Don't expect to get much out of him."

Her friend made a shooing motion with her hands. "Oh, I'm not here to sink my claws into Blake. I respect he was honest with me. And anyway, he's not my type. He seemed nice and he's terribly attractive, so I figured why not? I'm actually here to help him snag Amanda. If you can't conquer the captain, might as well join the crew, am I right?"

Fantastic. Sadie had a mighty crush on Blake, and her best friend led the campaign to help him hook up with another woman.

If Blake had shown the slightest interest in her, Sadie might've come clean to Kennedy. Instead, recalling Blake's dewy-eyed expression when he talked about Amanda, Sadie decided she wouldn't make an obstacle of herself. It was the right call, but her heart disagreed. The potential between her and Blake sizzled like bacon fat in a hot pan every time they were together. She'd fight for it, but not one-sided; not if Blake wouldn't fight, too.

Some things weren't meant to be. "Good luck with that, Ken. If there's a trick to getting in close with Amanda, I'd love to know what the hell it is. She's as closed off as a museum exhibit and less approachable."

Another tiny shrug, this one accompanied by a close-lipped smile and a far-away gleam in her best friend's forest green gaze. "Oh, I don't know about that. My powers of observation are fairly keen, and I've observed quite a bit in my time on the outskirts of the Bookkeeping Club. I may have an idea or two."

Sadie watched her go with a pang.

Chapter 6

If she didn't have makeup caked on and eyeliner painstakingly applied, Sadie would've splashed her face with cold water after Kennedy left the ladies room to do some magical voodoo that would supposedly unlock the mysteries of Amanda Avery.

Sadie hoped for Blake's sake there were, in fact, mysteries to unlock, because, otherwise, he'd spend the rest of his life bored to tears.

Her cell phone buzzed from the pouch pocket of her smock. Did she love it for the cheery yellow sleeves or the convenient pockets? The mundane bumbling of her brain came to an abrupt halt at Amanda's name on her cell phone's screen.

Did she sense Sadie thinking about her? Was she in one of the toilet stalls? "Hello?"

"Hi, Sadie."

"Hello." Sadie waited, apprehension deep in her chest.

"I'd like to invite you to dinner."

Sadie's mouth flopped open. She promptly shut it, only for it to gape open again. "Uh…um… Like, for a work thing? Or…"

"No, this doesn't involve the office. It's a personal invitation."

Sadie's eyebrows shot up. "Right." *Makes about as much sense as anything else that's happened today.* "Um, I'd love to. I guess." How bad could it be? Amanda might very well be part of an interoffice power couple if Blake had his way. It couldn't hurt to make a few friendly ties. Or, more realistically, keep tabs on Blake's progress from an insider's perspective. Out of sheer curiosity, of course.

Amanda's voice adopted a distinctly cheery note. "Fabulous. I won't ask you to come out to the ranch in Alpine, so I'll cook for us at my condo in town. Can I pick you up Friday night?"

Since she'd made it a question, Sadie saw her chance to decline. Things were moving a bit fast. She'd expected to go out somewhere, not have a home-cooked meal. Forget boring, Amanda was *weird.* "I'll drive myself. I usually change into something more casual at the end of the day." She paused, giving Amanda a chance to interject. Not a peep. "If that's all right?"

"Of course. I should've thought of that. We can make it a casual affair." A small laugh. "It'll be fun."

"Sure, it will," Sadie agreed, torn between confusion and curiosity.

They ended the call, and Sadie stared at her phone, as perplexed as she'd ever been. Amanda was reaching out, and Sadie had no clue why. She guessed by this weekend, she'd have her answer.

* * * *

Blake spread his paper napkin over his lap and pointedly ignored Wes a few booths away. He didn't have to worry about it for long. Sadie exited the bathroom a minute or so behind Kennedy, snatched her purse from the booth, said a few heated words to Wes, and promptly strode toward the exit.

Something was definitely going on between those two. He struggled for a moment with his instincts to go after Sadie. She was like a gnat in his ear, a constant low hum he couldn't quite ignore. If only his instincts had ever proven a reliable guide. Was it instinct or simple attraction that drew him to Sadie? His history pretty much told the story. He had to quit reacting to those initial gut feelings and follow his brain for once.

Before him sat Kennedy, the woman with the answers to all his questions.

Kennedy perused the menu and grinned at Blake. "I'll take the salad bar, with a side of fries. Can't get by without a carb at lunch. No clue how Reba does it. Fruit and a limp homemade salad every day. I know it's healthy, but that can't really be good for you, can it? Not spiritually."

Blake ordered an iced tea and the pulled pork sandwich and waited for Kennedy to slip from their booth and return shortly with a heaping mound of cold-cut veggies piled high onto a thin bed of lettuce, with chunks of chicken, ham, olives, and bits of hardboiled egg. "What can you tell me about Amanda?"

Kennedy plucked an olive from her plate. "Straight to the point. Yes, let's talk about Miss Avery. First, I have to ask, are you *sure* about this? You've seen how she dresses?"

He tugged on his tie. It seemed a little tight around his neck. "Hard not to notice."

Today, Amanda wore a glowing orange wrap-around skirt with matching pumps and a blood-red blouse. Lots of bold African-inspired jewelry completed the head-turning ensemble.

"Says she's a risk taker, doesn't it?"

Kennedy's searching stare turned flat. "Bookkeeping says *risk* to you? Look, I'm only making sure, because my theory is that her clothing is her way of making up for her lack of other attributes. She's not open or particularly friendly. Opal and Pearl adore her, but only in her job capacity. No one really knows Amanda outside of work."

"Could it be because of her personal ties to the firm? Maybe there's some kind of conflict of interest." He sipped his tea. "The standoffishness. Not the clothes." The clothes defied theory.

"You have the current high score in wishful thinking. Congratulations."

A waiter brought Kennedy's fries to the table, along with Blake's sandwich.

"I'm as sure as I can be given how little I know about her."

Kennedy went straight to dipping her fries in the metal container of ranch dressing on the side of her salad. "You asked for it. First, Amanda is privy to certain information, which is why she sticks to bookkeeping. Imagine, if you can, how Sadie or Wes might act around her if they thought she had an inkling of who was to replace Duncan as chief accountant. And anyway, if she went after anything juicier, Mrs. Avery would be accused of favoritism every time Amanda was handed a major account. As long as she works at Mommy's firm, she sticks to a position of little to no drama. I heard it from Reba, who heard it from Nina, who picked it up from Duncan, that Amanda has Mrs. Avery's blessing to work for another firm if she ever decides she wants more. Which, from what I gather, she doesn't. At least, until little Avery inherits the position."

"What's any of that got to do with me?" Blake picked up his sandwich and leaned carefully over his plate before taking a bite.

"Think, Blake. Amanda's prone to certain assumptions. I would be, too. She'll think you want information if you get cozy. Especially since everyone thinks you're dating Sadie."

Blake nearly choked but managed to get the wad of pork and bread down with a swallow of tea. "Excuse me?"

Kennedy returned to picking through her salad. "Well, yeah. You guys have been to lunch together a bunch of times. Hung out a few weekends now. Basically, if you're spending time together off the clock, everyone's going to assume you're involved."

He set his sandwich down. "So, you think Amanda avoids me because she believes I'm involved with Sadie and, therefore, only after information when I try to talk to her? Like finding out who's getting Duncan's job? That's stupid."

"Could be you want to find out for yourself. Another perfectly reasonable assumption for her to make. It makes sense you'd put your name in the hat for Duncan's job."

Exasperation stopped him from picking up his sandwich again. First Sadie, now Amanda. He guessed it made a certain sense. New guy with an impressive résumé shows up, takes over a position he's overqualified for, and not long after, the chief accountant puts in his notice? "For the record, my name's not going anywhere near the hat."

Kennedy's golden eyebrows wrinkled together. "It's not?"

He shook his head. "Nope. Amanda is wrong about me on both counts. All I have to do is explain."

Kennedy shrugged like it was the simplest thing in the world. "Basically." Then, her gaze drifted to his with something like an apology. "And maybe quit spending so much time with Sadie. Unless you *are* dating her."

"No. No, of course not." He went back to his sandwich. Finally, some progress. He was going to have a fair chance at asking Amanda out. There was a niggle of guilt when he imagined Sadie's face the next time she offered a helping hand and he had to decline for the sake of keeping the office gossipmongers at bay…Well, she'd understand.

"You're right," he told Kennedy. "Sadie has enough to keep her occupied, doesn't she? Between Wes and her bid for the promotion."

"You mean between Wes and Wes? Yeah, I'd say she does."

* * * *

Blake checked his watch for the tenth time in the same five-minute period. Should he ask Amanda out at eleven to give her time to prepare? Or right at twelve so they could leave straight away?

He paced in front of his desk. Probably eleven. That way, if she said no, despite his best efforts to assure her no strings were attached to his offer, he'd have time to come up with other lunch plans. He shook out his hands. Why was he so nervous? Something about the way Amanda kept her thoughts and reactions so neatly buttoned down poked and prodded at Blake's insecurity. He preferred Quinn's generally direct approach but didn't miss the sarcastic bite that often came with it.

Well, they weren't alike in *everything.* Of course, Amanda wouldn't be exactly like Quinn. That'd be too weird, anyway.

He checked his watch again. He'd better ask now, before Amanda made other plans. He opened his office door far more deliberately than the act warranted and approached Amanda with an auspicious smile.

"Hey, Amanda. May I have a minute?"

She glanced at him and blinked her pale eyes. "What can I do for you, Mr. Cobb?"

"Um, Blake is fine, actually." Not a great start. Blake clasped his hands together and wished she had a less exposed work area. "It's something of a private matter. It's been brought to my attention you may have some incorrect assumptions regarding my intentions concerning Duncan's resignation. I'm not interested in the job. Just so you know."

She stared at him blankly.

He checked a sigh. He'd chock it up to failure and try again another day. Before taking his leave, he squeaked in one last comment. "Also, I'm not involved with Sadie. She helped me get firewood. It wasn't a date or anything. I, uh, would actually like to take you to lunch today. You seem pretty busy, though. Sorry to interrupt."

He turned to leave when her hand flew out and grasped his sleeve.

"You and Sadie aren't dating?"

"No. She, uh, helped me out, that's all. My new place has a wood-burning stove, and she kind of gave me a crash course in how to operate it so I don't die of hypothermia this winter. I have plans to spend Christmas in L.A. I'd hate to miss them." Great. This was going great.

Amanda cocked her head. "And you won't be applying for the chief accountant position?"

"I have no intention of doing so, no."

A bona fide smile blossomed and lit up Amanda's whole face in a way he hadn't seen yet. She didn't quite meet Quinn's caliber, but when she smiled like that, she came very close. "I think lunch would be okay."

Blake beamed. "Great. I'll meet you in the lobby at noon."

Amanda surprised him by standing and reaching for her purse and jacket. She folded her long coat over her arm and leaned in close to Blake. "I've known for a while who Mother and Duncan are considering for the job. Since you're not in the running, I wouldn't mind discussing it. If you can keep a secret. You won't tell anyone?"

Blake hesitated for a fraction of a second—long enough to ask himself if he could keep a secret. Considering his past, he had to admit with uneasy acceptance that if there were anything he excelled at, it was keeping secrets. "Actually, Amanda, I'd just as soon not know."

Amanda gave him that smile again and took the arm he offered.

He smiled back. He imagined Sadie and experienced the slightest brush of something that might've been regret before his elation took over. Things were finally falling into place.

As they walked toward the lobby, Blake caught sight of Sadie and Wes standing side by side, with their arms crossed, watching as Amanda and Blake strode through the bookkeeping parlor. Sadie managed a very Amanda-like lack of expression and was the first to look away.

Wes smiled, and it didn't take a genius to figure out he liked seeing Blake's attentions focused elsewhere.

* * * *

If ever she needed a week to fly by like a cheetah on speed, all Sadie had to do was plan a date with Amanda. Friday had come on fast, each passing day bringing her closer to dinner with her oddest, most unapproachable coworker. It seemed even more incomprehensible since Amanda and Blake had begun dating.

The window of opportunity had officially closed. The whole week had been torture.

Sadie had wrestled with guilt for having a crush on Blake and was hurt at being passed over for someone with all the personality of a shrub. Blake was on her mind constantly. His past ran through her head like a film strip, desperately trying to reconcile the deeds with the man. She wished for the freedom to feel him out, get to know him better, and try to understand. She had a feeling that, at the end of the day, Blake was a worthy investment, despite his previous bad judgment.

Should she admit to Amanda she had small feelings for Blake now, before things got serious? Would Amanda still want her to come for dinner if she knew? Had Blake talked about Sadie to Amanda? Made comparisons, assured her he preferred her company?

Her face reddened from the thought. She'd get this obligation over with and then give Blake and Amanda a wide berth from now on. Supposedly, there was some kind of fraternization policy at the firm, but no one had ever really tested it. Even when she'd been involved with Wes, Sadie had gone to great pains to keep it from ever coming to Duncan's attention. Amanda didn't seem to share the concern, and maybe Blake hadn't been informed of the policy. Or, heck, maybe being Iris Avery's daughter meant Amanda could do whatever the hell she wanted.

Sadie gripped the bottle of white wine and knocked a second time. *Come on. Don't tell me I've been pranked.*

Finally, just when Sadie thought she might explode from nerves, the white door opened to reveal Amanda as undone as Sadie had ever dreamed to see her. Her hair fell flat and straight as usual, but she was sans the jangle and cacophony of her costume jewelry, and no loud clothing graced her tall, lithe body. Just an unadorned heather gray sweatshirt and fluffy white socks on her feet. Where were the confused clashes of colors, the jarring, clunky jewelry?

Sadie pointed to the holes in Amanda's light-washed jeans. "We must have the same stylist."

Amanda glanced down and almost grinned, morphing her face into a less robotic impression. She took the wine from Sadie. "I'm glad you didn't dress up. I worried you might."

"Yeah, but I said—"

"I know." She softened the interruption with a flat smile. "But I can't say it's never happened."

Sadie stepped over the threshold and took in the stark quality of Amanda's dwelling. It was as pristine and colorless as Amanda's wardrobe was eclectic and gaudy. "Wow, Amanda. Nice place." She removed her shoes, but even standing on the pure white carpet made her cringe. So white. So perfect. While Amanda closed the door, Sadie approached the only hanging item on the wall. A swipe of gray paint across a white surface inside a double-matted white frame. What was she going for? Asylum chic?

Amanda beckoned her through a hallway, which led to the kitchen.

Sadie was hit with a measure of relief straight away. A far cry from the sterile living room of perfection, the kitchen seemed lived in and used. The colorless scheme flowed through, but lavender dishes, on display in open-faced cabinets, added a muted feminine touch. Fresh hydrangea sat in a fat circular vase with a few inches of water.

Simple. Elegant. A little stuffy, but only because Sadie imagined she could ruin the place with a single spaghetti dinner.

Amanda set to stirring two pans on the stove, then checked inside the oven. "I'm glad you made it. I almost cancelled. It's been a stressful week."

Indeed, it had. "I wouldn't blame you if you had called it off. It's sort of weird, anyway." Sadie didn't know what to do with herself. The large square granite island transitioned into a high bar on one side, so she took a seat on one of the saddle stools. "We hardly know each other."

Amanda pulled a baking sheet from the oven. Some kind of white fish, liberally sprinkled with fresh parsley and spices.

The scent made its way to Sadie. Her stomach grumbled in response. She'd come hungry. In case she didn't like Amanda's cooking, she'd be compelled to eat no matter what. It was smelling like that wasn't going to be a problem.

Using potholders, Amanda slid the pan onto the countertop to cool. "I don't make friends easily. When you offered to help me that weekend, I was extremely grateful, because there wasn't anyone I could really ask. Being an Avery, people have little use for me unless I've got my hands in Mother's pie." She shrugged and turned back to the stovetop. "But then, I thought you might've offered for the sake of spending time with Blake. He's very handsome, isn't he?"

Sadie swallowed. "He's okay."

"Later, I thought maybe you'd keep being nice to me after Duncan announced his resignation. Naturally, everyone will assume I know who's taking his place."

Correctly, I bet. No way did Amanda spend weekends with her mom in Alpine without garnering some idea, but Sadie would die before she'd ask.

For all her ambition, there were lines she wouldn't cross, and bringing the boss's daughter into it was a line, even if a slightly muddy one. "You're head of bookkeeping. I wouldn't ask you to divulge something that isn't your job—or business, if I'm frank—to divulge."

"Agreed. It would be unethical on my part." She pulled a glass serving bowl from a shelf and poured a mound of white, creamy pasta into it from the larger pot. "And Mother wouldn't like it." Amanda set the bowl of steaming pasta next to the fish and added a handful of fresh parsley from a small glazed bowl nearby.

Sadie tried not to moan as the scent of parmesan and garlic wafted her way.

"I had concerns about Blake, too," she continued. "I thought you two were dating."

"Can I help with anything? Would you like me to make plates? Or set the table?" Sadie didn't like where the conversation was headed.

Green beans were drained in a colander in the sink and tossed into a second glass bowl with a dollop of butter and salt and pepper. "Of course not. You're my guest." Amanda pulled two pristine white dinner plates from another shelf and proceeded to compile food on them like they were going to be photographed for the cover of *Food & Wine.*

Which they could've been. They were that pretty.

Amanda straightened after turning a filet just so. "Blake asked me out on Monday." Her straight face expressed an impish happiness. "After assuring me you two weren't involved, of course. Also, you've had ample time to quiz me about Duncan but haven't. Anyone who's kind to me with nothing to gain from it…" She lowered her gaze and grew suddenly shy and more reserved. "Well, suffice it to say, I can use more people like that in my life. We should be friends." She lifted the plates and nodded once, a resolute cap on a declaration that left no room for argument. Or even friendly debate. A distinct layer of pity coated Sadie's recent opinions of Amanda. Usually, she was too busy silently mocking her robotic nature to stop and think about how bad it would suck to be Iris Avery's daughter in a firm where everyone was trying to get ahead.

She followed Amanda into the next room, the formal dining room, where the table was already set with cloth napkins, forks, butter knives, small dessert spoons, wineglasses, and shorter glasses already filled with ice water.

Sweet Jesus. She definitely hadn't dressed for a black tie event.

"Please, have a seat. I'll be right back."

Sadie sat and tried not to touch anything lest she leave a fingerprint smudge on the white—white, white, white, *so much white*—tablecloth.

Amanda returned balancing the bottle of wine Sadie had brought, a bowl of garden salad obviously prepared ahead of time, a decanter of some red oil-based vinaigrette, and two shallow salad plates. She showed no signs of struggle handling her haul. "There's dessert. A chocolate mousse I prepared this morning before work, with raspberries. I don't really enjoy chocolate, but I've seen you eat it. I used some of the raspberries to make the vinaigrette. I hope you like it."

"I can't believe you'd do all this for me." *Especially since I might have a tiny crush on the man you're dating.* Plus, she hadn't done anything to deserve it, besides a self-serving favor.

Amanda set everything on the table and piled salad onto the plates, then opened the wine. "Cooking is how I handle stress. I've had this menu planned for a while. I'm happy to have someone to share it with."

Sadie liberally dressed her salad, fork in the other hand waiting to dig in. She paused and waved it toward the compiled dishes. "You cook like this regularly? Just another plain old weekday dinner for you?" Geez, how was she not thirty pounds overweight and hauling around a second chin?

Amanda took her seat and tasted the wine. "Very good. How lucky you brought a dry white. It pairs well with the fish." She set her wineglass down and reached for her fork. "Not usually pasta. You can see how much the recipe yields."

After that, Sadie didn't ask any more questions. She was starved. She wanted to plow through the meal but ate relative to Amanda's pace. Although, she did have seconds of the cheesy, garlicky pasta. She'd hardly cleared her plate when Amanda spooned dessert into the small bowls. She topped the mousse with fresh raspberries and a dollop of whipped cream she'd made.

A short time later, Sadie licked the back of her spoon, certain she'd bust the button right off her jeans if she tried to stand. She sipped the dregs of her wine and eyeballed the bottle. One more glass ought to do it. Her gaze shifted to Amanda. Sadie had managed to drop a green bean in her lap and smear chocolate all over her pristine napkin, but Amanda was a slow, meticulous eater. Her napkin had only been used to dab unnecessarily at the corners of her mouth. Well, Sadie might've been careful, too, if she'd been wearing white, white, and more white.

She looked around the room. White, white, white. Such an acute difference between this Amanda and the one who showed at work in the festive garb of whatever nation grabbed her attention that morning. "I've had enough wine to finally ask."

Amanda's eyebrows rose slightly. Then she shrugged and went back to her dainty sips of wine and tiny scoops of mousse. "Okay."

Sadie lifted her wineglass to indicate the room. Now that evening had fallen, she noticed the chandelier over the table. Crystal with silver metalwork. Damn thing belonged on a showroom somewhere. "Your home seems a little different." Was there a way to say this without offending her? "From your sense of fashion. Like, the clothes you wear. I expected something a little more…"

"Colorful." Amanda nodded and kept eating. Small bites, slow, measured, robotic. "I've been told I come off as sterile. Unapproachable. The bright colors and the flashy jewelry help me fit in. I learned early on it helps to fit in. I'm not naturally inclined toward big color, so I borrow from coworkers. I wear earrings like Opal does and bold colors like you."

Sadie sputtered. Wine dribbled down her chin. She reached for her napkin to add another blemish to it. "You got part of your style from mine?" She wanted to be flattered but was too offended.

"Sure." Amanda set her spoon down, lifted her wineglass, and leaned back. It was the most relaxed Sadie had seen her. "Your black hair in its simple cut allows you to be playful. Nothing clashes the way it can with pale blond. Take yellow, for example. It washes me out horribly. But you wear these deep, adventurous colors, like fuchsia and royal blue. You like black the way I like white, and it all works so well together. My real problem is I never know when to quit, and I get so frustrated some days. There are times I've closed my eyes, pointed, and wore whatever I landed on."

Sadie sat forward, trying to wrap her head around Amanda's logic. She didn't dress like a blind lady because she didn't have a sense of style—a glance around her apartment said she had some to spare. She did it to fit in, and Sadie didn't have the heart to tell her it only made her stand out. "Amanda, that's... Well, that's crazy. Don't you think it's better to be yourself? Maybe you seem unapproachable because you're hiding behind crazy outfits instead of wearing what makes you comfortable."

Or because she had the demeanor of a sleep-deprived sloth. Sadie couldn't fix that, but she could lend a hand in the fashion department.

Amanda pressed her lips together and seemed to take a second to consider before lifting her gaze to Sadie's. "I don't want to alienate myself from the others."

"Look, Amanda, all you need to do is take your inherent sophisticated flair and sprinkle a dash of color on it. Like the lavender dishes in your white, white kitchen." Sadie drained her glass and pushed it away. "You know what? You're right. We should be friends. And to commemorate our first official day of friendship, we're going back to an old classic."

"Classic? I'm afraid I don't understand."

She stood, slightly off-kilter from her second glass of wine. "Refill that wineglass and point me in the direction of your closet. We're gonna play dress-up."

Chapter 7

November had arrived in style, dumping mounds of snow the day before the mandatory office party, where they all showed up to prove they were festive and full of the autumn spirit. Sadie set a bag of chips next to the impressive spread of real food others had brought. She bit her lip, considered it, then ripped the bag open and dumped the contents into an empty plastic serving bowl.

Look at me, domestic goddess.

She brushed crumbs from her hands, turned away from the table to rejoin the party, and nearly collided with Amanda. "I'm so sorry. Here, let me help." Sadie took the covered dish from Amanda's neatly groomed fingers, unable to resist a whiff. "Oh, man, is that stuffing? I live for stuffing."

Amanda answered in her typical deadpan fashion. "It's not Thanksgiving without stuffing."

Sadie nodded sagely. "Then again, it's not Thanksgiving. Don't you think it's odd to have a party today and then turn around tomorrow and eat all the same stuff with our families?"

"Duncan feels obligated to throw a party for the employees. He's rather sentimental about holidays. Also, he's leaving in the spring. I imagine he'll miss everyone and would like to make a few memories while he can." Amanda smoothed the foil cover on her dish.

Her clothes were different, as they had been lately. Cream colors, light grays, and white, white, and more white. Plus, of course, a touch of color here and there. Bold red shoes or a glittering bracelet. It pleased Sadie tremendously, and she got a wealth of satisfaction every time Amanda snuck her a small grateful smile. This usually came after some complimentary remark on her improved appearance, which had changed drastically since their dinner weeks ago.

The outside changes led to inside changes. Amanda seemed happier and more at ease with herself.

Occasionally, Sadie questioned if they were all changes for the better. She'd noticed Blake looking harassed a time or two, after dates with Amanda. But that was none of her business. She followed her new best friend's gaze across the room, unsurprised it had landed on Blake. "I bet you're right about Duncan. He and Zoey are doing the smart thing, waiting for winter to pass."

Amanda nodded absently. "Hmm. Plus, Mother's glad to have such generous notice. It's given her time to go over her options."

Sadie's gut twisted. She was painstakingly careful not to bring up the promotion around Amanda. Somehow, they'd formed a weird, nebulous, yet genuine friendship. Sadie had no clue how it had happened. Blake had dropped out of her life like a plastic bag in a windstorm, to be replaced by his girlfriend. Kennedy, on the other hand, had formed quite the bond with Blake.

New lines were being drawn in the office, and Sadie didn't know how she felt about any of it. Outside of her career, which she had mapped out down to her fortieth birthday, she wasn't much of a planner. She went with the flow, and this was where the great river of life had taken her.

Blake wasn't meant to be. She'd accepted it, for the most part. It bothered her at times, like when she noticed he wore a forced smile or an unguarded frown. Sometimes, he seemed lonely, and she longed to fix it. But that was Amanda's job.

Unfortunately, the whole forbidden fruit thing made him more appealing. Her crush was snowballing. He looked good in a pair of slacks, but she daydreamed about the Saturday morning he'd been shirtless, scruffy, and wearing loose jeans riding low on his hips.

Heat crept up from her chest and she cleared her throat, pushing away the enticing image. "I guess Blake will be spending the holiday with you at the ranch, huh?" Sadie covered her acute interest in the answer by filling a small plastic cup with warm cider from a Crock-Pot on the far end of the table. Any minute now, everyone else would come streaming by to fill paper plates with too much food.

A golden turkey, still steaming, several varieties of stuffing, cranberry sauce, green bean casserole, yams with marshmallows, and a multitude of pies, pumpkin and apple among them, were crammed together, hot and ready for whenever Duncan gave everyone the okay. First, of course, there had to be mingling, with Styrofoam cups of punch and cider. Then, like every year before, Duncan would insist they each take turns saying what they were grateful for.

It wasn't a bad tradition. When Sadie was chief accountant next year, she'd keep it going. An homage to Duncan.

"No," Amanda said, "I'm flying to Boise to see family."

Sadie's shoulders fell. Geez. Give people a four-day weekend, and they disappeared like doughnuts in the breakroom. Kennedy, Wes, and Nina were all leaving to spend the Thanksgiving holiday with relatives. "Maybe his son can come visit him."

Amanda shook her head. "Seth is spending the holiday in London. Blake called to invite him but was too late. It was sort of crushing to watch Blake's face. Of course, directly after I had to inform him of my plans."

"Oh, wow. Poor guy." Sadie didn't think it was right for anyone to spend the holidays alone. She should know, having spent most of her adult life on her own. "I think I'll go mingle, if you don't mind."

Amanda glanced at her watch. "I'm leaving, actually. Mother's plane takes off in two hours. I'd like to go over what I've packed a final time."

"You're not staying for the party? Why'd you bother to come?"

Amanda gestured toward her dish. "It's my obligation to bring something. The stuffing is cornbread, with apples and sausage. I hope everyone likes it."

Seriously? Sometimes, being friends with Amanda wasn't all that great for Sadie's self-esteem. She glanced at the bowl of mostly broken potato chips and tried not to cringe. "I'm sure everyone will love it. I'll make sure they know you made it."

A flush of pleasure blossomed on Amanda's cheeks, and she smiled as she collected her purse from a nearby chair. "Thank you, Sadie. You're a very good friend."

Sadie watched Amanda disappear into the lobby and chewed the inside of her cheek. *Let's see if you still think that after this weekend.*

Besides, what kind of friend would she be if she let Blake spend the holiday alone? A bad one, if Amanda suspected Sadie of moving in on her territory. Or a great one, if Blake appreciated having company on the holidays.

Sadie found Blake talking with Catalina.

Catalina was pretty amazing, as far as humans in general went. She was a consummate professional at all times and carried herself with an import and grace Sadie envied. She'd taken the Castley account in stride and thanked Sadie for not begrudging her the opportunity to prove herself.

Sadie wedged herself in between the two of them. "Say, Blake, got a sec? Duncan's fidgeting with his tie, which means he's getting hungry. I think we're only waiting on Reba to show up with the glazed ham he ordered from Smith's, but he won't wait much longer."

Blake smiled politely at Catalina, who smoothly moved on to the next cluster of chatting coworkers. He sipped his cider. "How have you been, Sadie?"

"Oh, fine. You know. Making new friends and stuff."

"So I noticed. Wednesday nights are off limits because it's best friend night."

"Don't begrudge me my visitation rights."

"I don't unless it's brownie day. I hate it when you get brownie day. There are never any leftover."

Sadie grinned. Ah, the kicker—she really liked Blake. He made her smile. "Listen, I heard your holiday plans sort of fell through. Amanda just bailed to reorganize her color-coded luggage"—or so Sadie imagined—"and she told me Seth couldn't make it."

Blake shrugged, but the thin line of his mouth gave away his displeasure. "I'm low on the totem pole. Unless I ask months and months in advance, Seth defaults to spending holidays with Jack and Quinn. By the time I thought to ask, he was already telling me Madeline plans to cook for all of them. That's Jack's mother. She's Irish, but since she's married to Quinn's dad, who's obviously American, she gets stuck celebrating all our holidays. It'll be her first time cooking, though. I mean, the whole Thanksgiving setup. I ramble when I'm upset. Sorry."

Sadie didn't mind his chatter but frowned anyway. "Your family background is like something out of a Georgette Heyer novel. Cousins marrying cousins. It's weird, Blake."

A smile threatened in the curve of his lips. He scratched his temple. "As convoluted as it seems, it's all above-board. Douglas and Madeline were dating before Jack and Quinn got it together."

She shook her head. "Still weird."

"Yeah." Blake almost laughed. "I can't wait to see Amanda's face when I attempt to explain it."

Something occurred to Sadie. "Is there a reason Amanda would leave without saying good-bye to you?" She hooked a thumb toward the lobby. "She was here and left without a word. Is that normal?"

"Uh, yeah. I guess. I mean, we spoke yesterday. She told me she had to drop off stuffing, and I'd see her Monday. Not much more to say." He looked away.

Sadie nodded and patted Blake's shoulder. "Well, it's okay. I've decided you're going to spend Thanksgiving with me."

He started to protest.

She held up her hands to stop him. "I don't have family here, and all my friends leave town anytime we get this many free days. I don't do anything major—I definitely don't cook like Amanda. She goes all out for a normal dinner. I'd hate to imagine the spread she'd work up for a holiday. The pile of dishes a meal like that would produce is enough to convince me to keep it simple. Canned cranberry sauce, a turkey sandwich, and some pie from the reduced-price section of the deli. Sparkling wine if I'm in the mood. Oh, but also, there's this silent auction at the Elk's Club on Friday. You can be my plus one. Unless, of course, you've got plans."

He smiled, and Sadie's stomach did that thing again. He'd shaved his face to perfect smoothness that made her itch to run her finger along the square line of his jaw. "You're perfectly aware that I don't. So, sure. Why not. Better than moping in my cabin for four days."

She patted his shoulder. "I bet it'll smell better, too."

He was on the verge of responding when Duncan called him from across the parlor. Reba had finally arrived, and Duncan wanted to give Blake the honor of slicing.

Sadie grinned after him. A date for Thanksgiving, and she didn't even have to cook. Her thoughts turned to the pile of laundry on her sofa. Was Blake worth folding laundry for? She hated laundry, nearly as much as she hated putting copious amounts of effort into preparing food when there were so many shortcuts.

A second later, she turned toward the food table and caught Kennedy's glare from across the room.

* * * *

Sadie's apartment was a rundown unit, part of a community of duplexes. Blake supposed the location made up for what it lacked in fresh paint and even sidewalks, as Flat Creek ran directly behind the complex.

Then he saw the interior. A huge stone fireplace faced the living room front and center, demanding attention the way a big-screen television would. The inside had a cabin-like feel, with warm tones and wood paneling. Sadie had a penchant for fluffy, overstuffed furniture. Two recliners and a light blue sofa crowded around the fireplace, above which Sadie had mounted a small television. Easy to see what her priorities were.

A fire blazed, washing the room, which opened seamlessly into a small kitchen, in the dancing light of the flames. Two rugs, one crisscrossing over the other, were by the door. Sadie's boots were kicked off to one side. Blankets of all sizes, shapes, colors, and materials were either tossed over the arms of the sofas and chairs or folded and stacked nearby on the floor. This was a place he could put his feet up or forget to use a coaster without feeling like he'd committed a cardinal sin. Cozy and warm, Blake was filled with a sudden sense of comfort he'd never once felt walking into Amanda's perfect condo.

Overall, he appreciated the classy elegance of Amanda's home, but he also struggled with making certain he didn't use the incorrect hand towel or forget to remove his shoes. Sadie's house seemed the exact opposite.

Sadie busied herself in the kitchen. She turned and smiled when he stepped inside. "Come on in. I could use your help." She pointed to a bottle and two mismatched wineglasses, one abnormally large, sitting on a butcher block table on the far side of the tiny round dining table with only two chairs—which, unsurprisingly, didn't match. "Fill 'em up."

The kitchen looked like a thrift store display gone wrong. No matching dishes, no design theme, no coordination to speak of. Three hand towels were squeezed together over the oven handle, none the same color. Oven mitts mounted over the stove clashed horribly.

Sadie wasn't much better. She wore plaid pajama pants with holey socks and a tank top. Fresh-faced, same as the day they'd met at the airport. Somehow, the lack of eyeliner made her muted silvery eyes stand out more than ever, like little moons fixed to her face, utterly compelling.

Blake inhaled deeply. "You're the living, breathing opposite of Amanda Avery."

Sadie tossed her head to the side and grinned. "My house dresses like she used to." Her pearly gaze swept from the open collar of his button-up to the polished loafers on his feet. "I should've warned you I don't dress up on holidays. I figure, I dress up more than I dress down, with work. Might as well make the most of a freebie day to ditch the get-up."

"My fault for not asking." He shrugged. "It's habit to dress for an occasion. The last several years, out of some sense of duty, Quinn and Jack made sure they were in L.A. for most holidays. They always tried to say they did it for Seth, because he wanted to see his old friends, but I think they felt sorry for me and wanted to make sure I wasn't alone. They must be really happy to finally be able to stay in London instead of traveling half the globe on my account." He untucked his shirt and held out his arms for inspection. "Better?"

Sadie nodded resolutely. "Loads. We're practically identical now."

Blake laughed and opened the bottle of low-alcohol sparkling grape juice. That was probably for the best.

Though Amanda had the whole blond-haired, green-eyed Quinn thing going on, it was difficult for him to ignore his inclination to find Sadie attractive and alluring. Amanda's grace was often rigid, and Sadie's loose, languid way of moving and speaking put him at ease.

He rolled his shoulders, unsure of when he'd become so tense, and set the modestly filled wineglasses on the table.

Sadie glanced over, cocked an eyebrow, and frowned. "What are you doing?"

"I was going to set the table."

"Remember that time you said I was Amanda's living, breathing opposite? Yeah, we're eating on the sofa. Don't you know there's a game today?" She checked her watch and picked up speed, haphazardly dropping fat slices of tomato on each sandwich and applying the bread topper. She pressed it down and dusted her hands together with a satisfied inspection. "Excellent. Last year, I forgot the tomato *and* I was out of mayo. It was awful. To top it off, we lost to the Seahawks, nineteen to three. Worst Thanksgiving ever. Hands down." She left the sandwiches to set up T.V. trays in front of the sofa. "We can let the fire burn down some if it gets too toasty in here."

"I think it's nice." Blake set a wineglass on each tray, hoping Sadie would choose the weirdly large one. He'd feel ridiculous drinking out of something as wide as his face.

She returned with a sandwich plate in each hand, set them down, and left again, this time returning with a small bowl of cranberry sauce, which she proceeded to spoon onto the plates. "I've got pie for dessert. Pumpkin and day-old reduced-price Dutch apple if you're feeling brave."

She switched on the game and, for the next four hours, Blake forgot to think about anything beyond the score. He even found himself rooting for her team, even though he'd never been much of a sports guy. Her passion was contagious. She shouted and cheered, yelled and cursed at the referees. She clapped and hooted when her team scored and covered her face with her hands when they made a mistake. She had nicknames for the players, depending on their performance. Words like *pecker* were tossed around, and a few Blake was pretty sure she'd made up on the spot.

By the time the game was over, darkness had fallen, Blake's stomach hurt from overeating, and Sadie had come down from her maniacal high after her team won the game.

"I thought we were going to be screwed since so many of our playmakers retired last season." She muttered as she collected their plates. "They were the heart of the team. I was devastated. But we have a few promising rookies." She shrugged at her own assessment and headed for the kitchen.

Blake settled back into the ridiculously comfortable sofa. His shoes were off, in a messy pile near the door. He'd taken off his button-up at some point, and the light gray T-shirt he had on underneath was almost the exact shade of Sadie's eyes. He was about to suggest a movie when it hit him.

He shouldn't be here.

Keeping Sadie off his mind had become a daily battle. He thought about her all the time. What did she make of Amanda's new fashion choices? Had she liked the pecan pie better than the cheesecake Amanda made last week? Wherever his thoughts went, there Sadie popped up to snag his attention. It was too easy to laugh along with her, get caught up in her energy, and let Amanda slip his mind entirely.

The way Quinn had slipped his mind all those years ago.

He didn't know what was the bigger joke—that he thought he could be friends with a woman he was clearly attracted to or that he thought himself capable of monogamy. He stood and grabbed for his shoes, searching the sofa for his shirt.

Sadie returned, her eyebrows drawn in concern. "You all right? Lose something?"

Blake found his shirt, wedged in between the cushions. He yanked it out and laid it over his arm. "I think I should go."

"Sure. Game's over. Are you okay to drive? The wine was pretty weak."

He ignored her and sat again to shove his feet into his loafers.

She let out a small breathy laugh. "I guess it was too much to ask to have a nice, normal Thanksgiving. For whatever it's worth, regardless of whatever put that awful pinched look on your face, I had a good time. And I'm glad you came."

She was killing him. She was so human, compared to Amanda, who was always proper and always said exactly the right words and would never dream of calling his face awful. At least, not to his face. That was a purely Sadie thing to do. He groaned and ran a hand through his hair. "Look at me. I'm repeating old habits. Girlfriend leaves town, and I'm hanging out drinking with another woman, laughing, and forgetting I even have a girlfriend. I'm asking for it."

Sadie dipped her chin and batted her eyelashes. "So, you like me, huh?"

He took a deep breath and made himself look away. Would she ever stop reminding him of Kira? "You're easy to be around. Amanda is more of a challenge." His shoes finally back on his feet where they belonged,

Blake stood and straightened, prepared to leave. "But anything that's worth having is worth fighting for, right?"

"Huh." Sadie licked her lips and crossed her arms. "You see the irony here? You judge me for my ambition, yet I don't believe my desire to become chief accountant is any different from your bulldog approach to earning Amanda's love. Because I'll tell you one thing, Blake, my career isn't a decision I made in a glance, which is exactly how you came to your twisted conclusions about Amanda. And you know what else? I've finally figured it out. She reminds you of Quinn. And I remind you of Kira."

Stunned by her deduction, Blake swallowed and blinked, unsure of how to explain, or if it was even possible. "No, you—I didn't mean—"

"I can tell by the disdainful, disgusted looks you throw my way from time to time. What is it? My height? My hair? My *ambition?*" Sadie turned her shoulders, cocked her head, and twisted her hips like a model on a runway. "Or is it the whole package?"

Blake sputtered. He'd never meant Sadie to know how he compared the two of them. Kira had been so manipulative and cruel, which wasn't like Sadie at all. "Sadie, I'm sorry, I—"

"Go home, Blake. In case it flew over your sloping forehead, you've insulted me twice tonight. For the record, it takes more than a cozy atmosphere to get me into bed. You're so concerned with what you might do, it completely slipped your mind that it takes two, babe. And while your track record sucks mightily, I have a little more class. I'd never fool around with you behind Amanda's back."

He deserved the sharp rebuke and the resulting shame that seared him from the inside out. He opened the door, turning back only to thank her for dinner, but she had a palm out and a look on her face that dared him to speak.

"I already have your ticket for the auction tomorrow night," she said. "Since it's for a local charity, I expect you won't let me waste it. Be ready at six."

* * * *

If Blake ever bought a cabin like Fox Watch, he'd name it Dog House. Because apparently, that was where he lived.

He sat alone at their table and watched Sadie make the rounds. She had on a thick, black sweater dress, with a wide neck that showed off her collarbones and came up to mid-thigh, and furry black boots that laced up the back and had soles like a hiking boot. Fashion and function. She broke up the monotony of head-to-toe black with a thick cobalt blue belt high on her waist, which cast a spotlight on her petite hourglass figure to the point Blake kept having to remind himself to look away.

She seemed to know everyone in the club. From table to table, she shook hands, hugged, laughed, and joked. He'd probably be at her side if he hadn't been such an ass last night.

He moped and tried to figure out exactly where he'd screwed up. Should he have stayed at Sadie's and tempted fate? Ultimately, he'd made a choice and picked Amanda over Sadie. It didn't explain the guilt lapping at his conscience. After all, he was *dating* Amanda. Of course, he owed her his loyalty.

Eventually, Blake forgot to question his motives and got lost in watching the crowd. He felt slightly voyeuristic; it reminded him of the nature shows where camera guys hid behind bushes and captured the secret lives of meerkats or hyenas. Except, these were people, and every personal interaction reminded him he was an outsider.

After a while, Sadie came back to the table, all smiles. She sobered some when their gazes met. "I saw you auctioned on the antique rocking chair. Plan on taking up knitting?"

He didn't dare smile. "Not if things work out with Eric. I'll be busy training him to fetch me a beer from the fridge. But he's been difficult lately." He hadn't given up on his little fox friend, despite Sadie's warnings. It didn't have so much to do with Jack anymore. It'd become a personal challenge. He had to prove something to himself, but damn if he knew what.

She shook her head but seemed amused. "You're a weird guy, Blake. They're about to call the auction winners. You better make another lap around before it's too late. After that, I think we should get out of here. There's somewhere I want to take you."

* * * *

Blake didn't appear too dazzled. "A bar?"

"You could be more impressed." Sadie did her best not to pout. "It's The Silver Dollar. Kind of famous. Come on, let's get a seat and order some hot wings. They have the best hot wings in town."

"We just ate dinner."

This guy really tested her patience. "Consider it dessert. Seriously, what man argues with hot wings?" On an eye roll she hoped he didn't catch, she led them toward the curved bar. The overhead lights glinted brilliantly off the silver dollars embedded in its surface. She signaled the bartender. "Two beers, please. Whatever local brew you've got on tap. And wings."

The bartender nodded and whisked away.

Blake wearily joined her at the barstool to her left.

She cut him off before he could get started on how they shouldn't be drinking together. "Blake, I owe you an apology. So, you're going to let me buy you this beer—like a *friend*—and I'm going to tell you I'm sorry. But first, the beer."

Two thick glasses with beautiful foamy tops were placed in front of them. Sadie sipped and smacked her lips. "Oh, that's good. Snake River's pale ale is tops."

Blake took a tentative drink. "Not bad."

It was as good as an insult, but Sadie hadn't brought Blake here to lecture him on respecting the local award-winning brewery. She took a deep, fortifying gulp. "I'm sorry for flirting with you. It was a crappy thing to do. I hope you know I don't mean anything by it." She paused. "Okay, that's a lie. The truth is I have something of a crush on you. So, yeah, maybe inviting you over wasn't such a grand idea."

It was like she'd slapped him. He jerked, a furious blush sprouted at his collar and raced up his neck to cover his cheeks, and a little beer sloshed over the rim of his glass. His mouth worked, but words didn't emerge.

She patted his shoulder. "It's okay. You don't need to say anything. I'll do the talking. The other day, you asked what was between Wes and me. I told you the truth. As of now, there's nothing. But we have history."

Sadie sighed and looked away. Would she ever get over the embarrassment of her love life? Would anything ever happen to change the pattern, mix things up a bit? She turned back to Blake.

Blake watched her with an unblinking stare.

She had his attention. She took another deep breath and prepared to embarrass herself. "I do this weird thing where I attract men who appear totally normal, but later I discover these life-altering, unbearable flaws. Like drug addictions. One guy I dated for weeks before I realized he lived in his van. Another pretended to have a job but was banging some girl instead. It hasn't happened once or twice, but *every damn time.*" She smacked the bar with her fist with each word. "Without fail. Any man I happen to find attractive, I can safely assume has some freakish problem. Wes was supposed to have been the exception."

Blake took another sip of beer, this time with more gusto. "You and Wes were together. I thought he just had a little thing for you."

"If that idiot has anything, it's an agenda." She gulped her beer and wiped her mouth. Since she wasn't flirting with Blake anymore, she didn't need to concern herself with things like manners. "I got him hired on as a junior accountant for Avery & Thorp, and after that we fell apart. The story that goes around, and the one we intentionally perpetrate, is that he used me to get the job. I believe it, to an extent. But the real story, no one knows. Not even Kennedy or Nina, for all their gossip and gum-flapping."

Blake put a hand over hers, surprising her into looking into his face and realizing how close together they were. Close enough for her to know he hadn't shaved that morning. "You don't have to tell me."

She snorted. "Didn't you have an affair for, like, five years? I trust you can keep a secret."

He pulled his hand away.

Well, it was true, wasn't it? Still, the fingertips of guilt traced her skin.

"I'm about to tell you my dirty little secret, so don't ask me to tiptoe around yours. I was pregnant. I lost the baby shortly before Wes took the job at the firm. Right away, the stress became something else entirely. There's a lot of guilt when you miscarry. Some doctor's think it's some kind of survivor's guilt." She shrugged. It never made much sense to her, no matter what the therapist at the clinic had said. "I couldn't get away from Wes to grieve on my own. We lived together at the time. Then we were working together. I started to pull away. I just needed time, I think, to sort it out in my head. I definitely never intended to lose Wes over it. But then he got weird." She let out a dry laugh. "Because he had to, didn't he? That's how it works."

"Weird how?" Blake's eyebrows were drawn in concern, and one hand covered his mouth in a considering gesture.

Sadie slowly rolled her beer glass between her flattened palms. "Possessive. The more I needed space, the more he tried to cram in next to me. It got pretty bad for a while. He oversaw my e-mails and listened in on confidential office phone calls with clients. I always had to be able to account for my whereabouts. I quit jogging because he questioned the hour I was gone. I guess he thought there had to be a reason I'd pull away from him. And then, I swear, it's awful to say this and I've never admitted it to anyone, but I feel like he suspected I'd done it on purpose. The miscarriage. He never accused me of it, nothing like that. But I think maybe he saw me pulling away from him and assumed I hadn't wanted to have his kid. Anyway, I snapped one day. Couldn't take it anymore. I ended it, moved out, and did my best to explain to Wes what had gone wrong."

Blake nodded and studied his beer, like looking at her just then would be difficult. "That's why he keeps trying to get back with you?"

"I doubt it. I think he has some guilt issues, and he's looking for redemption and forgiveness. Not love. And possibly a leg up. At the end of the day, Wes is every bit as ambitious as I am."

"Oh. Well, I guess dating the chief accountant is the next best thing to *being* the chief accountant."

She gave Blake one of the tiny plates, took one for herself, and heaped the three biggest wings onto her plate. "Anyway, the point is, I'm backing off. I didn't exactly mean to flirt. I wasn't deliberately trying to make anything happen between us yesterday. But it'd be nice, you know? I mean, not us behind Amanda's back. That's not what I…I mean, one day. One sunny day, I'm going to meet a nice guy like you, who's actually a nice guy. I won't always be deceived by a charming personality and dashing good looks. One of these days, I'm bound to peel back that wrapper and find exactly what the packaging advertised."

A dark cloud flitted across Blake's features. "I'm an adulterer. How can you call me a nice guy? I'm exactly like all the other jerks and losers on your list."

"You *were,*" she corrected him. "Last night, you bolted from an innocent situation because you're so determined to be a better man than you were. You'd do anything, even railroad a perfectly normal friendship, for the sake of avoiding past mistakes."

He raised an eyebrow. "Innocent? You have a crush on me."

Sadie propped her chin on her hand. "It's all about intent, Blakey. Like the difference between first-degree murder and manslaughter. I like you, and I can't make myself stop. But I have no intention of sabotaging your relationship with Amanda. Not ever."

He gave her a worried glance over the rim of his glass as he sipped the foamy beer. "Yeah, well, the road to Hell. I'll let you take it from there."

Chapter 8

Blake wistfully recalled Christmas Day.

Seth had made an appearance. Little Maddie had learned how to say uncle. He was Uncle Bake now but couldn't help being a little sad about it. She'd loved the stuffed fox he bought her. He didn't quite have the nerve to call it Eric in front of Quinn, so he'd let Maddie name him. She'd gone with Bear, which they all had a good laugh over.

December had come and gone like a breath, the way time seemed to when there was a lot going on. Reversely, January refused to end. It brought along dismal, gray weather that made Blake long for the cheery white snow of last month, and frigid temperatures. He knew it was bad when the locals proclaimed it too cold to snow. Ice collected on street corners and sidewalks, frozen lumps that wouldn't thaw until early March, according to the lore.

"Are you listening to me?" Amanda's sharp inquiry zapped through Blake's brain fog.

He startled. "I'm sorry. I feel a little spacey today. Must be getting a head cold."

She swiped a carrot stick through a small cup of dressing. "Reba's habit of spreading stories has increased to a troublesome degree. She's become quite close with Nina. I'm not sure why she hasn't been let go. Nina, that is. As Duncan's secretary, she's in a particularly delicate place, with access to sensitive information. It shouldn't be in the hands of someone so keen on gossip."

Stay firm. Blake refused to engage. Not again. Lesson learned.

Amanda ate the carrot slowly, like it might try to bite back. Her gaze hovered on a spot beyond Blake's shoulder. "Kennedy is as much a problem. She's always at the center of the drama and doesn't have the sense to know it doesn't help her professional prospects. She isn't stupid. She must possesses marginal intelligence in order to be an effective secretary. I questioned it when Henry was still here, but I assume you'd have petitioned Duncan for a replacement had you found Kennedy unsatisfactory or slow-witted."

Blake bit into a wing and prayed for patience.

The transition of Amanda's wardrobe had coincided with some less flattering changes in her personality. The more she dressed like herself, the more her identity bubbled up to the surface, taking over her carefully fashioned attitude. She was wary and afraid of alienating her coworkers, while simultaneously wishing to keep her distance. She seemed to have lost the concern as far as Blake went. At least in his company, she spoke her mind freely these days.

Unfortunately, the more she shared, the less Blake liked what she had to say.

Her opinion of Kennedy especially hit a nerve. He felt protective of his secretary. Once she'd finally given up seducing him, she'd become a valued ally and friend. She was better at her job than Amanda would ever realize.

"She's very consumed with office gossip," Amanda continued in her blasé tone. "She tries very hard to engage Pearl and Opal, but luckily, my team is focused on their tasks."

Do not engage. Blake wouldn't be baited into another argument.

Last month, perhaps a week before the Christmas holidays, he'd suggested Opal could stand to be friendlier and more open to Kennedy's attempts to be a part of their group. After all, her desk was stuck in the bookkeeping parlor with the rest of them. Rather than earning Kennedy a friendlier atmosphere at work, he'd merited Amanda's cold shoulder.

The coldest cold shoulder he'd ever had turned his way.

At her angriest, Quinn had always kept an avenue of communication open. Whether because she felt communication was essential in any relationship, even that with an ex-husband, or because Seth compelled her to keep cordial with Blake, she had always answered his call.

Amanda had shut down so completely, Blake hadn't even been able to wish her a Merry Christmas before his flight to L.A. She reminded him less of Quinn all the time, as the edges of her true personality began to fill in the blank spaces.

She blinked at him across the table. She stared and said nothing, which was how she said everything—with lengthy, considering silence.

By now, he'd also learned a fair bit of harsh judgment lived inside those speechless moments. The only person who seemed to have any esteem in Amanda's eyes, outside of her own bookkeeping team, was Sadie.

Just thinking her name had him back in his own headspace. *A nice guy like you.*

He puzzled over the words constantly. How could Sadie think of him as a nice guy after everything he'd told her? The affair with Kira, the ill-advised marriage to Quinn's sister, his absence from Seth's childhood. The list went on. She must've suffered some real crappy relationships if a guy with Blake's résumé seemed like a good bet.

As for her supposed crush, she'd stuck to her proclamation and been on strictly friendly terms with him since their non-date. At the same time, her attraction perplexed him. It ignited a tiny spark of pride. Not because three women in the office had expressed interest—female interest wasn't hard to come by when you were a blond guy with nice eyes and a gorgeous bank account.

Rather, because Sadie's interest was worth something. She was like a beloved queen among their coworkers. People liked her. She laughed at their jokes but wouldn't hesitate to say when it was stupid—usually she had laughed anyway. She answered questions for Catalina, kept a fiery toe-to-toe waltz going with Wes, their every greeting punctured by some kind of outburst, and mended her fences with Kennedy, all while excelling at her job and staying on her usual friendly terms with Duncan, whom she lunched with regularly.

The friendship with her boss was a genuine thing, not a hunt for favor. Invited along once, Blake had been pleased and impressed by the way Sadie seemed to turn it off when she was clocked out. She asked questions about Zoey's pregnancy, what they might name the baby, and how much Duncan was looking forward to life in a big city.

Not a word about the promotion, or Wes.

For a woman like Sadie to like *him*... Well, it did things for the old ego.

Blake polished off his wing and recalled the order he'd shared with her the night of the silent auction. She'd attacked them without consideration for her lipstick or her hair, strands of which ended up coated in hot sauce, in turn smearing across her cheek when she tucked her hair back. He grinned at the memory of her wiping it off with the back of her hand and going in for another wing.

"What're you thinking about over there?" Amanda's tentative smile and bright eyes were the hallmark signs of a woman who expected his answer to have her name stamped on it.

You, darling. But what else could bring such a wistful grin to my face?

Guilt danced in his chest. Eating out with his girlfriend, and all he could think of was another woman. His appetite fled, but he kept his smile in place for Amanda's sake as he pushed his plate away and reached for a napkin. "I was wondering if you were a chocolate or vanilla kind of woman. Valentine's Day is next month."

Liar, liar. Quinn's voice again. *Begin with lies. They're the bedrock of every lasting union. The solid foundation on which love is painstakingly built.*

Love? Blake didn't know about love. Seemed sort of advanced for his skill level.

Amanda's face blossomed into her full smile, which was, Blake readily admitted, quite beautiful. She traced a circle around his wrist with a delicate nail painted a shade darker than her pale flesh. "I like fruit. With vanilla, but only if it's fresh."

A part of him needed her to say chocolate, the darker and more sinful the better. Another part of him also needed her to respect Kennedy as a peer and watch something besides romantic comedies and spaghetti westerns on Netflix. Yet another part of him needed her to be okay with letting him order pizza, just once, and utter an imprecise, imperfect sentence every now and again.

Bizarrely, there were times Blake wouldn't have minded a moment in Kira's presence—a saucy statement, an unpredictable explosion of emotion he never quite knew what to do with, but exhilarated him all the same. Or maybe it was Sadie he thought of—

Amanda's exactly what I asked for. I'm getting what I wanted.

He'd gotten what he'd wanted before, though. It wasn't going after his desires he struggled with—it was desiring the right things. If he craved chocolate, why had he asked for vanilla?

He smiled back at Amanda, giving it his best effort. "I may have to surprise you."

* * * *

Sadie pointed to the middle of the white space on the map, smack in the center of Jackson Lake, white because the map depicted it during the winter months when a majority of it iced over. "That's the spot. Never fails."

Nina and Kennedy squinted at the map, being polite. They couldn't possibly care.

Wes shrugged. "I don't think it's worth the trouble. I'd rather wait till spring."

And then there was Wes, who never bothered with polite.

"Well, it's a good thing I wasn't talking to you, then." From the corner of her eye, Sadie caught Blake falling in behind Amanda as the two of them entered the bookkeeping parlor on their return from lunch. She ignored them and pointed again. "It's either ice fishing or no fishing for months and months, and since I have a pretty big freezer I like to keep well stocked with yummy stuff like river trout, not fishing for months and months simply isn't an option."

"Did you say ice fishing?"

Sadie turned. Blake had approached to glance over her shoulder at the map.

"You ever been?"

Excitement made his hazel eyes glitter. "You do that?" He stuck a finger at the map and looked at her.

"Well, yeah." She waved at Wes. "I was just telling this dum-dum how it's the only fishing you can do this time of year. The season opens in January, and you can fish from sunrise to noon, which isn't long in the winter. Sun doesn't rise till nearly eight. They allow another window in the evening, but I make a better worm than I do an owl. Like, early worm versus night owl, get it? I'm saying I'm not much of a night person—"

"He gets it." Wes had crossed his arms and watched her with an amused tilt to his head and a slight grin only she knew the meaning of. It was the same one she got every time he busted her checking out at a cute guy on the slopes.

She curled her lip at him and stuck out her tongue. Then she looked at Blake to see how much of the exchange he'd been privy to.

His mouth was slightly agape as he stared at her. "Can I go?"

Sadie pursed her lips and narrowed her eyes. She assessed Blake's expression, from the open mouth to the rapidly blinking eyes and eager set to his shoulders.

Amanda's boring him to death. She had an insider's point of view, too, having suffered through weekly "date nights" with Amanda. The woman had no grasp on anything in the realm of *fun.* Luckily for Sadie, she didn't need Amanda for fun. She took care of her own entertainment. But Blake was pretty much at the mercy of Amanda's idea of a good time.

Instead of issuing the invite he so desperately craved, Sadie stroked her chin. "How are things going with Eric?"

No hesitation. "Not great. He's skittish. But he ate the chunk of banana I left on the porch two nights ago. I haven't fed him again, because I don't want to turn him into a pet or anything. I'm just trying to show him I'm a good guy."

Are you a good guy, Blake? Are you really, though?

This guy did weird things to her brain and her heart. There was just something….

Amanda popped up at her other shoulder. "Who's Eric?"

Sadie's heart catapulted into her throat. She forgotten Amanda standing not two feet away.

Blake didn't miss a beat. "A fox who lives near my cabin."

"Oh." Her face hadn't been expressing any particular emotion, but it seemed to relax a smidge. "Sadie, are you coming by for dinner tonight?"

Sadie pasted a grin on her face and hoped Amanda didn't suspect it was forced. She wasn't adverse to good food—*damn* good food, so long as Amanda was cooking—but her back was starting to feel the tension from being stiff so often. Probably because of the stifling atmosphere at Amanda's condo. She refused Sadie's offer to host dinner at her place. To be fair, Sadie might've mentioned frozen meatloaf and canned green beans. The conversation had sort of gone downhill from there.

Sure, she could entertain herself, but Amanda could stand to loosen up and try something new. There were only so many outdated movies on Netflix, right? Winter wasn't an excuse to be idle. Sadie wanted to slap on her snowshoes and walk the bike path along Flat Creek or sled at the bottom of Snow King or head to Teton Village for some night skiing. She wanted to order pizza and wings, put on a horror flick, and scare herself into sleeping with the lights on. Barring all that, she wanted to curl up next to a warm fire. Amanda had her fireplace blocked off because she hated the mess—the sawdust and wood chips, the soot, the smoke, basically all the things Sadie loved about them.

Anything but sit in Amanda's stuffy place and eat yet another five-star meal she spent half the night preparing.

It struck Sadie that Wes was exactly the type of person to appreciate Amanda's down-time habits. A bit of a homebody himself, Wes hated smoky wood fires and had a thing for the same old spaghetti westerns Amanda seemed to have an affinity for. Plus, he was a total food snob. Could it be that easy? All she had to do was dump Wes on Amanda's doorstep and tiptoe away with Blake….

I'm a horrible, horrible friend. She forced herself to look Amanda in the eye. "I'd love to, but I should prepare for ice fishing Saturday. Gotta wrestle my gear out of storage, which will take a good shoveling of snow from around the back patio, and double-check everything. It might be high time to replace my shelter. Maybe next week?"

Blake broke in. "I'm serious. I want to go. Can I?"

At this point, both Amanda and Blake were watching her. Kennedy, Nina, and Wes were on the sidelines taking in the show. Wes had that same smirk on his smarmy face, Nina, a bright, curious gaze as she took it in to report to Reba later. Finally, Kennedy, with her mouth a hard, flat line of disapproval. Each of them waited with bated breath to see if she'd cross the line.

Sadie inhaled deeply and gave her attention to Blake. "I'd love to take you along. If you're going to stick around Jackson Hole, you should learn the basics of ice fishing from someone who knows what they're doing. Anyone else want to join?"

A series of head shakes and muttered declines. Exactly what Sadie expected. None of them wanted to go, and each one of them would have some opinion on why Blake—the one guy genuinely interested—shouldn't either.

Blake's beaming face was like a gem among pebbles. "Wow. I never dreamed I'd go ice fishing. How cool is that?" He directed the last part at Amanda, who looked like her answer might be along the lines of *not very*.

He thanked Sadie again for the invite, and he and Amanda strode away, back to their respective jobs. Exactly what Sadie ought to do. She ignored the three gaping morons and went into her office.

As expected, Kennedy followed and closed the door behind her.

For a moment, Sadie considered warning her. She could feel the righteousness roiling in her belly. If Kennedy didn't tread lightly, she'd get more than she bargained for out of this conversation.

"What are trying to do, Sadie? Play head games with Blake? Or maybe Wes is the target."

Sadie flopped into her chair. Kennedy had her cutest outfit on today. It was Sadie's favorite, at any rate, a corset-style violet top and matching pencil skirt that paired nicely with her blond ringlets and green eyes. Why didn't Wes go after *her*? A woman interested. A woman emotionally available. A woman with killer fashion sense and noble intentions.

"Neither, you jerk. Blake thought ice fishing sounded awesome. Probably because ice fishing is awesome. And why shouldn't I take him? I invited every one of you to come along. Amanda could go if she wanted, but I won't tell Blake he can't because there won't be a chaperone. Screw all of you." She flicked a pen at Kennedy.

Kennedy flinched as the pen struck her in the arm. Her heel even kicked up to the side like she might bat it away with her knee. "Quit that! God, you're so immature. You remind me of a college dude or something. It's all hiking and sports and stupid, uncomfortable hobbies."

"Yeah?" Sadie reclined and poised her fingertips together in a neat steeple. "Well, it seems to work for me. Apparently, dudes like a girl who likes to do 'dude' stuff. And before you fly with that, I grew up doing all this kind of stuff with my mom, for your information. I act like the *woman* my mother raised me to act like, and you can take your jealous ass the hell out of my office if you think I'm going to sit here and let a secretary berate me over my personal affairs."

Sadie hadn't meant to say all that. She really, really hadn't. But she wouldn't take it back, either. In fact, now that the dam had burst, she might as well go all in.

She stood and peered at her best friend. "While we're on the topic, I'm warning you to back off about Wes. You're an idiot if you think all that tension between us stems from a few dates and a misunderstanding. Our relationship ended—" Sadie stopped, unwilling to say the words but knowing she had to or Kennedy would never understand. She briefly closed her eyes and steeled herself. "We miscarried. And we weren't able to come back from it. No, I don't intentionally keep Wes stringing along behind me, Ken. I'd like nothing more than for him to let it go. Let *me* go. As far as Blake is concerned, I understand you two have become friends, but I doubt it extends to you being his keeper."

Kennedy's eyes seemed to solidify and grow bigger at the same time, like water expanding as it froze.

Sadie groaned and came around her desk. "Kennedy, I'm sorry. I didn't mean the whole secretary bit. The part about not letting you rip me a new one over something that's not your business, I did mean. But I didn't mean to be hateful. I'm sorry."

Kennedy blinked and seemed to come to, speaking in a clipped tone. "Sadie Darling Felix."

She cringed at hearing her full name.

"You're a fool. I cannot believe you wouldn't tell me. How could you go through something so awful without telling me?" She raised a hand and curled it into a fist. "Never mind. You're right, I didn't know about your history with Wes, and we'll come back to who's to blame for that later, but I have to tell you, I've spent the last couple of months getting to know Blake. That man is bored to within an inch of his life."

Sadie snorted. "I guessed as much."

Kennedy's eyebrow rose beseechingly. "I'm not jealous, you twit. I'm trying to look out for you. Hear me out. If Blake spends enough time with you that he starts making comparisons and comes to the realization that you're the better pick—which he'll do because you're *Sadie*. Of course, you'd be the one, wouldn't you? You're spunky where Amanda is flat, sparkly where she's dim, and interesting where she's dull. He'll choose you over her."

Sadie rolled her eyes. "You're laying it on kind of thick here, Ken."

"Think about it. Ice fishing versus another crummy old movie. Hot wings and beer versus pretentious fine dining. Oh, don't look at me like that. He's complained more than once about Amanda's stuffy date nights. Tell me what will happen to your friendship with Amanda if Blake falls for you? How will you all work together? Sadie, you're asking for trouble. You're playing with their relationship."

Sadie ran a hand through her hair, which she hated to do because it made the sides puffy. "Why is the concept of friends beyond you?"

Kennedy's jaw tightened. "If you're serious about becoming the chief accountant of this office, you need to take a step back and consider what you're doing. If you're involved with Blake, or in any way cause problems between him and Amanda, you'll lose the respect of everyone who works here. And maybe even your job."

Sadie went to argue but found she couldn't. She nodded slowly. "Okay, I can see where my personal affairs may affect the atmosphere of the office. Then again, you're jumping ahead like a frog on crack. Listen, you remember I told you Amanda reminds Blake of Quinn, the high school sweetheart he screwed over? What I haven't told you is that I remind him of the devil woman he sneaked around with behind her back. Every time he looks at me, he gets a nasty little flashback to the woman who he feels ruined his life. Which isn't really fair, is it? Why does the woman always get the blame in these situations?"

Kennedy rocked her hip to the side and placed a tidy little fist on it. "He doesn't blame Kira. He blames himself for being weak. Not only do you remind him of her in your looks and personality, but you realize you're now in the same position she was, right? Poised to create total mayhem."

"This isn't fair," Sadie snapped. "I'm not trying to seduce Blake. I'm not trying to ruin anything or cause mayhem like some Gotham baddie. Geez, Kennedy, you make it sound like I'm gunning for the guy."

Kennedy's expression turned sympathetic. "I don't think that. But I do think it'd be very easy for Blake's history to repeat itself."

"Funny, that keeps coming up. But what none of you jerks take into account is *my* history. I'm not a slut, even if Blake is."

"Oh, come on, Sadie. That's not what I'm saying."

"Not in so many words." Sadie returned to her chair and turned her attention to her computer monitor in clear dismissal. "But close enough to start pissing me off."

Chapter 9

In the hours before the sun came up, the only color in a gray world glowed from the orange street lamps that lined Broadway. Even as the sky lightened, Blake still couldn't differentiate between the air and the ground—the world was white-washed. Flurries of snow fell sporadically. The thick, stiff coveralls Sadie had loaned him were warm, but not impenetrable. He shivered, then forced himself to stop when he noticed Sadie hardly seemed aware of the frigid temperatures.

Blake felt about as useful as a holey pocket. He was good for shuffling things around at Sadie's command, but beyond that, he had nothing to offer.

From a small storage room off her back patio, they loaded heavy equipment up into the bed of her truck with a metal ramp she used for just such an occasion. An ice sled, she explained, would allow them to haul their gear easily over the frozen surface of Jackson Lake. They loaded a tackle box with ice line, lures, and rods, plus an ice auger, which Sadie told him was the tool used to cut into the thick lake ice. Finally, they added a thermal tent shelter, a tall, round cooler for holding any fish they caught, and a portable heater that ran on propane cylinders.

He wouldn't admit it to Sadie, but the idea of a heater blasting out warm air on a frozen surface seemed like asking for trouble. But he deferred to her experience and didn't make a fool of himself by seeking reassurance.

The truck loaded and the storage room locked up, they climbed into Sadie's truck, and she handed him a small cooler before starting the engine.

"Seems redundant," he quipped.

Sadie grinned as she shifted into drive. "You're welcome to put your sandwich somewhere else."

The drive out to the lake was like something out of a wintery fairy tale. The Tetons rose up from the valley like tyrants looming over their minions—stark, formidable, and terrifying. The sagebrush coated in inches of thick white snow created dips and hollows that made the landscape seem especially foreign, like the surface of an alien planet. The elk were crammed into the refuge, thousands upon thousands, and herds of wild buffalo dotted the hills on either side of the winding highway.

"Wild buffalo. That's unreal."

"I'm always surprised when people are surprised." Sadie paused a beat. "Your poor judgment concerning wild animals, like your fox friend, compels me to warn you buffalo will maul and kill you if you get too close. As will moose. And even elk. Hell, a whitetail deer might have a go if it's got young nearby. Every year, some dumb tourists gets shredded to ribbons because they think Yellowstone is a petting zoo."

Blake raised his hands in defense but kept his gaze trained on the passing landscape. "Knee-high or smaller. I'm stupid, not brave."

Sadie pointed toward the valley opening up in the foreground of the Tetons, showing him where the Snake River wound through the lowest part of the valley, its every twist and turn given away by the evergreens and aspens that grew in thick patches along its banks. "Great fishing in the Snake. When I was a kid, my first stepdad took me fishing east of here, at the other end of town. There's a spot under a bridge with some nice beach-like areas. So, he's got this open-reel, hundred-dollar rod, right? And me, of course, he gave this crappy plastic thing, with thin line that snapped like nothing, and probably cost ten bucks. We're fishing and we're fishing, and he catches the first one, a brown trout a good eight or nine inches long. I wasn't surprised, but I was definitely grumpy. My mom taught me to fish. I knew what I was doing. I hated being treated like I was playing at it when I was every bit as good of an angler as my stepdad, even at that young age. Anyway, a few hours in, he's ready to leave. I'm not. I insist he let me cast a few more times. He grumbles and moans but starts packing our gear slowly, yapping on and on about his great catch, as I keep at it.

"And then, *wham!* Something yanks my line so hard I immediately think I've hooked on to a fallen tree in the water, because it's solid. But then it starts to tug. Fallen trees don't tug. I start working at it. Reel, stop, tug. Let out a little line, then yank it back to set the hook, praying the crappy line doesn't break. It was like some kind of miracle when I reeled in a fourteen-inch rainbow trout. My stepdad was pissed."

Riveted, Blake stared at her profile as she drove, admiring the reminiscent smile playing on her lips at the fond memory. "Does the fish get bigger every time you tell the story?"

Her small fist sprung out and caught his shoulder in a playful attack. "That's my story, and I'm sticking to it."

He laughed and rubbed his shoulder. "You said he was your first stepdad?"

Her jaw fell open, and she turned her smoky eyes to him. "Really? I tell you an amazing story, the crowning achievement of my angling youth, and that's your question?" Her gaze swung back to the road. "Yeah, I had more than one. My mom wasn't the type to settle. You know how guys are. Okay, maybe you don't. Once they have you, they quit trying. The way men say a woman lets herself go. Well, with men, they quit being charming and romantic. They start watching television in their underwear and not caring what they smell like. Mom was a bra-burning mountain girl, with a painfully idealistic image of what constituted love. When they quit making an effort because she was 'won,' she left. They were supposed to chase her on their dashing steeds, move mountains for her, and vow to never lose her again. None of them ever did any of those things. She wanted the fairy tale and never got it."

"What happened to her?"

Sadie kept referring to her mom in past tense. Blake wasn't genius-grade material, but he could do simple math.

Sadie's mouth formed a straight line. "Mountain climbing accident." She pointed to her left, to the severe Tetons. "Climbing to the peak of the Grand Teton. She fell. She survived the fall itself. Broke her back and dozens of other bones. A rescue helicopter found her, and she was lifted to the hospital, where she died shortly after from internal injuries."

Every word hit Blake like a gut-punch as he gazed through Sadie's window at the majestic mountain. His brain wouldn't allow him to attempt imagining the terror of falling from a mountain face like that. "That's—that's awful. I'm so sorry."

She shrugged. "It's a risk she took. It's also why I don't rock-climb," she added sardonically. "Besides, I made it to St. John's hospital in time. I was able to hold her hand and say good-bye, and that's more than a lot of people get."

"I think I'd be angry. I feel the risk wasn't justified. Was it really worth it to her?"

Sadie offered him a quick glance and a small amused smile before focusing on the winding road again as she slowed for a curve. "Hundreds of people climb the Tetons every year, Blake. Besides, I don't hold others' freewill against them. We live for ourselves at the end of the day, and we have to live in a way that jives with our needs. Mom needed to climb mountains. I can't blame her for that."

They'd dropped farther down into the valley to where the trees were, and now a barren forest gorged with snow crowded the highway on both sides. Finally, the trees opened up as they crossed the Jackson Lake Dam. Sadie rounded one final curve and flicked on her turn signal for the parking lot where they'd unload their gear.

He wasn't ready to let it go at that. "Seems rather generous, don't you think? Not holding people accountable for their freewill?" It explained why she thought of him as some kind of good guy. With that kind of mentality, everyone was a good guy.

Sadie flashed him a wry glance. "You misunderstand. Do I hold your freewill against you? Of course not. This is America. Do as you please. Now, ask me if I hold the consequences of how you choose to exercise that will against you."

Blake hiked an eyebrow.

Sadie gave a decisive nod. "Damn right I do."

Gravel crunched under the tires as Sadie maneuvered the truck into position beneath a stand of aspens.

Sadie dropped the gearshift into park, undid her seat belt, and swiveled to face Blake. "Look, I know what you're thinking. You're drawing some kind of correlation between you and my mom, and it's ridiculous. I'm not mad at her because it was her right to go climb mountains. It wasn't your right to be unfaithful to your wife. Now, quit philosophizing, and let's go."

* * * *

Even in the tent with the heater blowing warm air, Blake's extremities were stiff from the bone-deep chill.

Sadie didn't seem to notice. She'd had the physical tasks of hauling the ice sled across the lake while Blake followed, slipping and cursing, with the lunch cooler. She'd used the ice auger to drill out a core of ice to give them access to the water and then put up the tent. Plenty to get her muscles moving and her blood flowing.

Blake stood by, once again the holey pocket of uselessness.

Now, a couple of hours and not a bite later, they were huddled in canvas camping chairs. He was grateful Sadie had thought of something so practical, because it hadn't crossed his mind that he didn't want to park his butt on the ice until she pulled one of the chairs from its mesh bag.

"This is great. I'm having a blast." He sat hunched forward. The words stuttered through his quivering lips.

She grinned, clearly enjoying his discomfort. "Nothing worth having is easy to achieve."

He raised a brow. "So, a normal fish caught off the bank isn't worth having because it would be easy to catch?"

"It's not the destination; it's the journey." Her grin widened.

No doubt about it, she was amused. Well, *he* didn't find freezing his tenders off all that hilarious. "So, it's not the giant fish we're after, it's the freezing our butts off that counts?"

She shook her head and reached for the cooler with their lunches. From it, she retrieved two brown paper sacks and hurled one into Blake's lap. "Here. Set your reel down and eat, grumpy."

He hadn't realized he was ravenous until he pulled out the squished, misshapen sandwich. Peanut butter and jelly. His mouth watered. He ignored the rest of the snacks in the bag and sank his teeth into the soggy sandwich with a moan. "*Ohmgitsgo.*"

Sadie studied him over the rim of her Thermos, yet another thing Blake hadn't had the foresight to bring along. He should've asked for a list of necessities.

He swallowed the wad in his mouth. "It's good."

She smiled. "Thank you. You'll like the cinnamon almonds, too. I made them myself, if you can believe it."

"Not for a second," he replied before taking another massive bite. The sandwich was half gone already.

Sadie's face scrunched up. "Caught me. Got 'em at the grocery store."

Blake successfully hid his amusement. It wouldn't do for Sadie to realize how much he enjoyed her company or how funny he found her or how he was having more fun in the middle of a frozen lake freezing his nuggets off than he'd had in weeks with Amanda.

His good mood snuffed out like a candle. There he went again, comparing the two women.

Fishing rods—short, stocky handheld models designed specifically for fishing within the confines of a thermal tent—were back in hand a short time later, lunches wiped out entirely. A quiet loomed over them that Blake blamed squarely on Sadie. She had a faraway look in her eyes, like she'd become lost in her thoughts. He didn't doubt for a second they had to do with him. Conceit had nothing to do with it; it was the way she kept stealing none-too-subtle glances at him every few minutes, a considering thoughtful gleam behind her ashen gaze.

By the time they were nearing the end of their time window, Blake was tired and disappointed. Not the faintest of tugs on his line all morning, and Sadie's ogling had started to get under his skin.

He finally snapped. "You want to say what's on your mind instead of staring at me like I've turned purple?"

"Fine. You *have* turned purple, by the way, but sure, let's play." Her succinct tone didn't bode well. He braced himself. "You're bored, Blake."

Part of him backed up defensively, while another part of him breathed out heavily in relief. He ran a hand over his face and stared at the side wall of the tent because he couldn't quite bring himself to look Sadie in the eye. "I know."

"You know?" Her surprise convinced him to look at her.

"Why so shocked? You said it."

She shrugged. "I guess I didn't expect you to admit it."

"I probably shouldn't. But, hell, I am bored. At least, I think I am. I don't know. I mean, I convinced myself I was bored with Quinn, too. I'm probably *not* bored, actually, I just have some mental disorder where I tell myself I'm bored to justify seeking out excitement." He stared into the black water through the hole in the ice.

That made a lot of sense, actually.

Sadie broke into his rumination with a *tsk* laden with disdain. It was the first time he'd ever heard her sound annoyed. With him, anyway. "Man, you're *really* hung up on your past. Past wives, past mistakes, past this, past that. What about right now? This minute. This week. This place, this time. Are you going to wait until you're fifty to concern yourself with the present, or wait until it's part of your past, too?"

She'd struck an exposed nerve Blake hadn't realized was there. She'd gone beyond a sensitive spot and stabbed into an open wound.

His first instinct was anger. Sadie didn't know anything about him. She couldn't know how deeply he'd ruined his life and how determined he was not to make the same mistakes. She wanted to believe it had everything to do with women, but there were other things he'd forfeited in his pursuit of a good time.

He calmed himself with a deep breath. She couldn't understand unless he explained. "This isn't just about Amanda. Or Quinn. It goes back to Hunter, my baby with Kira. He came into the world like a bucket of ice water over my head. At that time, my relationship with Seth was beyond repair. It took Quinn threatening my rights to open my eyes to how far away he was. We were virtual strangers. In my heart, Hunter was my redemption. My second chance to do it right. To be a good dad. When I found out he wasn't mine, it killed me." Worse, Kira had ripped him straight out of Blake's life, without ever asking if he'd raise the baby, despite the truth.

He would've done it. He would've raised Hunter as his own had it ever been an option.

Blake ran a hand over his face. The pain had faded, but a new one had sprung up in its place. "Then came Maddie. In a perfect world, one where I didn't screw up everything I touched, she'd be mine. She *should've* been mine. Instead, she's a living, breathing reminder that I don't deserve a redo. Have you ever desperately wanted something you knew you'd never get? I'm forty, rusty at dating, and I'll never get another chance to be a dad. To be a *good* dad, to be a kid's go-to parent. Hell, Seth gets Jack's advice before he asks mine."

He stopped and looked away. He'd never dreamed he'd say any of this out loud. Somehow, it was equally freeing and damning. Hearing the words aloud, he believed them. A tiny bit of the hope he clung to evaporated. He shook his head. "Or maybe I just wanted another shot at having a family of my own, where I have a deeper value than an uncle. So, there you have it. I can't go back in time and be Father of the Year or the World's Greatest Husband, but I can be a better man here and now."

Sadie's eyebrows gathered in puzzlement. "Dating Quinn's doppelganger is some kind of redemption, then? Oh, I get it." The concept seemed to light a fire beneath her, and her sarcasm cut into his vulnerability. "She's Quinn, I'm Kira, and you find yourself at that same crossroads with the same two women. What can you do but the exact opposite of what you did last time, all for some skewed idea of atonement? That's wrong on so many levels; it's inconceivable I have to explain it. Amanda is *not* Quinn. I'm not Kira. You do us both an injustice when you ascribe another woman's traits to our physicality. You're pasting Quinn over Amanda, and it's wrong."

The imagery made Blake queasy. "That's not what I'm doing—"

"It is." Her gray eyes glinted with exasperation. "Look, Blake, I wish the best for you and Amanda. And it's a good thing you don't want to repeat old mistakes. But what you're doing? It's self-punishment. Stop trying to bandage your past before you wreck your future. Your redemption might not come dressed up in Quinn's wrapper."

At that moment, the rod twitched in his hand. Startled, he gripped it with both hands and gaped at Sadie. "I think I have a bite."

A wicked grin burst onto her face, wiping away their conversation like it had never happened. "Reel! Reel!" she squealed, miming with her hands. "Jerk it back once you feel a solid weight on the other end. It'll set the hook so it can't squirm away."

Blake followed Sadie's instructions, exhilarated and suddenly warm to his bones. But, in the back of his mind, behind the excitement and hubbub of reeling in his first rainbow trout, his mind snagged on Sadie's words.

Maybe she was right. Maybe redemption wouldn't appear in the guise of the one he'd wronged. He surreptitiously watched Sadie grapple with the huge fish he'd yanked from the murky depths of the lake.

Maybe redemption came dressed like his mistake.

* * * *

"Do you want to go or not?" Sadie's pout told Blake what answer she expected.

But he had plans for dinner with Amanda after work, and asking if he could be late so he could join Sadie on a shopping trip to a sporting goods store seemed like a touchy thing. "I'm not sure."

She crossed her arms, rolled her eyes, and turned to Kennedy, who leaned against the doorjamb, filing her nails and listening to the conversation like it was a radio program. "You want to go, Ken? I need to re-up my fishing supplies. You can always look at yoga pants or something."

Kennedy offered Sadie a flat stare and an even flatter smile. "Do I look like I do yoga?"

"You look like you could stand to," Sadie offered, with a charming grin.

Blake bit back a laugh. How odd would it be to have a friend so close you could say things like that to one another and survive? "You two have a strange friendship."

Both women looked at him. Their contrasts were many. Sadie was raven-haired, light-eyed, and pale. Kennedy, a golden-curled, emerald-eyed tanning fanatic.

Kennedy spoke first. "Opposites and all that."

"She's wrong," Sadie objected. "Honesty is the root of all happiness."

Kennedy's lips pursed. "There's such a thing as too much honesty."

Sadie cupped her chin in a thoughtful gesture. "I have to disagree."

"Exactly. Opposites. As I said."

All this while they continued to look at Blake and not each other. He couldn't stop himself from grinning. It was like a bad reality television show. They fought. They made up. They hated each other. They loved each other. They fought some more.

"You two should offer marriage counseling." He went back to the ledgers on his desk, puzzling over the latest balance sheet. A small blip, something not adding up in bookkeeping. He'd ask Amanda about it tonight at dinner. "As to your kind invitation, Sadie, I'd better take a raincheck. Maybe this weekend? Amanda's usually down in Alpine—"

He didn't get to finish the sentence.

Every breath, every sound, every thought was banished when Amanda tore into his office. Her arms swung madly at her sides, and her face was set like he'd never seen it—nostrils flared, her bright green eyes wide and hard, chest heaving.

All of it she aimed right at him. "I don't date men who sleep around."

The words hit Blake like a hammer to the face. He involuntarily leaned back and away from her as she loomed over his desk.

She had on a white pantsuit, the upper half a sort of wide-strapped tank top with fat stitches running down either side of the front, and an odd cape-like flap of fabric hanging off her shoulders. It probably looked very chic under normal circumstances, but Blake's brain immediately went into angel of death territory—all she needed were great wings to sprout from her back and actual fire to spark from her eyes. He didn't get a chance to ask a question or defend himself.

Amanda reeled toward Sadie.

To her credit, Sadie only looked confused. Apparently, Amanda didn't strike her as particularly threatening. But then, if Blake had to bet on who'd come out ahead in a rumble, he'd bet every penny he had on Sadie.

Amanda seemed to cool somewhat, as if sensing Sadie wouldn't be cowed by anger. It only made the words that finally emerged from her mouth all the more piercing. "Don't worry yourself over the promotion, Sadie. Your name was eliminated from the pool at the last meeting. Just a friendly FYI." She shot a final nasty glare at Blake and fled his office, little white cape flapping behind her.

He had the sensation of being ripped in two. His body jumped up from his desk, but it took him toward Sadie, not chasing after Amanda, like his brain shouted at him to. Head and heart warred against one another. Following his instinct, Blake stepped toward Sadie.

She stood there near the doorway, her face set in the perfect blankness only shock could inflict. Her eyes stared at nothing, and her mouth hung open slightly, as though she was about to speak. Somehow, Blake knew she wouldn't, though.

Kennedy recovered first and had a hand on Sadie's shoulder, gazing worriedly into her empty expression.

Then, common sense stepped in. Reason cleared its throat and asserted itself. If he didn't go after Amanda, it'd be like waving a giant red flag in front of the entire office. In bold letters, it would read, *I choose Sadie!*

He gave Sadie's arm a perfunctory squeeze as he walked past. Kennedy nodded her understanding.

While Kennedy might approve, Blake couldn't say the same for his conscience.

It railed against him as he rushed toward the lobby, where Amanda had run. His gut told him to go back, his every instinct telling him to make sure Sadie was okay. The blow Amanda had dealt was a devastating one and, at that moment, Blake couldn't say what he was going to do when he finally caught up to Amanda.

In theory, he'd approach her calmly and quietly. He'd ask her to explain what he'd done wrong and how he could fix it. He'd apologize and work to make it right, whatever it was. But in the back of his mind, he didn't think it'd be undeserved if he knocked Amanda down a peg or two. People were entitled to anger but not cruelty.

And what Amanda had done was cruel.

Chapter 10

Sadie sat on the hood of Wes's white Cadillac because she knew it would piss him off. Short of shoving her fist into his face, it was all she had. She might hit him, anyway, given the opportunity. Duncan would understand, especially if Wes gave her a really, really good reason.

Like telling Amanda that Blake and Sadie were making whoopee behind her back.

She didn't have any proof Wes was behind it, but her gut instincts vouched for it. Amanda flying off the handle wasn't some random act of PMS. Nor was the shocking news that Sadie wouldn't be getting the promotion.

Her stomach roiled. She ignored it.

Wes was her concern. Later, she'd deal with her stomach lining as it burned to smoking ruins. Besides, there weren't enough Tums in the world to fix what was wrong. Wine, though, wine might do the trick. Or make things worse, but at this point, it didn't matter. Her future was shot full of holes.

And the dickweed walking toward her now was responsible.

Wes's expression was as black as his name. "Get off my hood before you dent it."

Sadie ran a hand over the smooth white metal like a game show floor model. "It'd be a shame." In her right hand, the one hidden from view, she hefted the big, black metal stapler she'd brought along. Her instrument of torture. "Come clean, or I'm going to make your car look like cottage cheese. A whack here, a whack there." She continued to stroke the hood lovingly with her free hand.

Wes's expression went from whiny and vexed to arrogantly delighted. "The old rumor mill is a useful thing. How can you blame me, Sadie? I learned the trick from you. Fooled the whole office into thinking our relationship ended because I'm a prick who took advantage of you for a career boost. Sorry, but I felt I owed you one."

Her energy, fueled by anger, left her abruptly, like water condensing into air. *Poof.* She slid off the hood. She approached him, tapping the stapler against an open palm. "Did Amanda tell you I'm not getting the promotion?"

Wes's eyebrows snapped together. "I want the job, but I'm not stupid enough to believe Duncan would choose me over you. Amanda said that?"

Sadie sighed. "Yep. Officially, Duncan won't announce anything till spring. At least now I don't have to spend the next couple of months trying for no reason."

Amazingly, something like guilt crossed over Wes's pointed features. He nibbled on his bottom lip. "All I did was suggest to Reba that you and Blake were alone together an awful lot. Reba's a gossip machine. It didn't take but a couple hours for the whisper to find Amanda this morning. By then, it had turned into you and Blake definitely sleeping together behind her back. I only meant to stir up a little drama, Sadie. I'm sorry."

"Why?" She scoured his face for an answer, annoyed with his apology. She wanted a reply she could sink her claws into; she wanted a fight. A bit of her strength returned. The unfairness made her want to crush him. "Jealousy? How much of me do you want, Wes? You want blood, you want tears? You want me to take you back and pretend you didn't turn into a possessive freak after what happened?"

His dark eyes turned stony, and he cocked his head. "Is that what we call it now? A thing that happened?"

The prick of tears behind her eyes forced her to blink rapidly to keep them at bay. "This sucks. I don't want to do this." She made to step past him, but he caught her arm, gently.

"Sadie, I realize you needed space at the time, and I didn't give it to you. But when will you accept that what I craved was the opposite? Neither of us gave the other what they needed. I'm not the bad guy. I don't think there can be a bad guy."

The words smacked of truth, a truth she'd perhaps denied for a long time. She'd turned away from him and given herself over to grief and then healing. It wasn't something she could do with an audience. At the same time, Wes had needed someone to go through it with him. Should she have tried harder? Maybe there'd been some middle ground waiting to be discovered had she been less selfish with her pain.

She swallowed. "It's too late to do anything about it now."

"Says who?" He let go of her arm but stepped in front of her to block her path. "Not long ago, we were going to have a baby." His tone held a touch of surprise, as if it was unbelievable. It sort of was. "We were going to start a family. Tragedy can bring people together or tear them apart, and we let it destroy us when it could've made us stronger. Closer."

Sadie stepped back from him. "But that's *your* way, Wes. I don't share my pain. It's mine."

"Fine." His face relaxed, and he gave her a small, kind smile that she hated, *hated* to see because it brought back a lot of memories she'd made herself forget. "If you can't come to me, I'll come to you. Space is what you need? It's yours. I'll just be there when you need me."

This freaking guy. She squinted at him. "You sabotaged my friendship with Amanda and her relationship with Blake. How can you stand here and speak as if you're truly expecting a second chance? I don't need you. I won't ever need you."

"Because it's not a big deal. It'll blow over. Unless you're really sleeping with Blake." He peered at her.

Wouldn't he love to know. "I'm not. I wouldn't."

"Yeah, well…" Wes arched a finely plucked eyebrow. "He would."

"What the hell do you know, anyway? We aren't tied to our pasts. He's trying so hard to move on, but people like you are exactly the reason he's still beating himself up over a ten-year-old mistake." The words flung toward Wes as though Sadie had no control over them. She jumped to Blake's defense with the slightest provocation.

Wes was the one to take a step back this time. "I think your reaction says more about your relationship with Blake than you realize."

"And I think you're still an idiot who doesn't know when to back off." She turned her back on him, angry with herself for initiating the confrontation. Getting him to take his due credit hadn't undone the damage. It wouldn't take away the suspicion from Amanda or anyone else now that it had taken root.

And it definitely wouldn't get Sadie the job as chief accountant.

* * * *

Sadie wasn't totally surprised to find Blake on her stoop at nearly ten at night. She opened the door for him to enter. "A little late for a visit."

"I got away from Amanda as soon as I could."

Sadie closed the door behind him. "Even I'm tempted to believe we're intimate when you talk like that."

He blushed, as she'd expected. "I wanted to check on you. Are you okay? What Amanda did…" He shook his head and began to pace. "What a crappy thing to do. I wish I could tell you she was being a jerk and hadn't meant it. But I asked Duncan, and he confirmed it." He stopped pacing and gave her a pointed look. "By the way, I also convinced Amanda we're just friends. I can't tell you she isn't suspicious, but she'll come around."

Sadie didn't care about Amanda. In fact, she had a hard time thinking about her at all. The injustice of her "friend" to not bother with Sadie's side of the story before attacking her and crushing her entire world was somewhere in unforgivable territory. "They'll hire Wes. There's no one else."

Blake shrugged. "They might bring in someone from the sister office in Alpine."

Sadie hadn't thought of that. She hadn't thought of much. She'd been so certain of her success and Wes's failure. Still, it was almost too much to hope.

Pity swamped Blake's face. "Sadie, I'm so sorry. I know how much the promotion meant to you."

She nodded and kept her thoughts to herself. Did he really know? Did he know her heart was broken? Did he know how deeply the despair ran? Did he realize the extent of the damage?

Wes remorselessly spread a vicious rumor with numerous and wide-ranging repercussions. Besides destroying relationships, it put her and Blake into the line of fire regarding office regulations, which were against fraternization due to ethical concerns. Imagine what a senior accountant and the company's auditor could pull off if they were to get any ideas during a snuggle-fest.

Her cheeks heated as the image of her and Blake tangled and sweaty popped into her head. She pushed it aside but, for one moment, she let herself imagine how it might feel if the whole world—Amanda, Wes, Kennedy, the firm—faded away, leaving her and Blake with nothing to worry about but each other. She took a deep breath and ruthlessly cut herself off from the reverie.

If Wes had stooped so low in the interest of stirring up a little drama, what might he do with real power? As her boss, he could call private lunch meetings every day, control which accounts she supervised, even assign them according to how often she acted as he pleased, rather than contingent on any experience or skill. He'd govern her, own her, dominate her. He'd have complete control over her, more complete than when he'd been her boyfriend.

The thought terrified her. But what scared her more was what she'd have to do to escape it. "I appreciate your concern. But I think you should go."

"But—"

Her patience skidded straight into its breaking point. "It's a small, small town we live in, Blake. And there's more than your relationship with Amanda to consider if someone were to see you here. Now the rumor is floating around the office, and it won't take long for Duncan to pick up on it. That's if Amanda didn't go straight to Mommy with her broken heart. When we're called in to see Mrs. Avery to defend ourselves against a fraternization write-up, maybe then you'll get it. Hopefully, I'll get my resignation turned in before that happens and they'll let it go. I'll have a harder time getting another job with a mark on my currently unblemished record."

Blake's beautiful hazel eyes looked poised to pop. "You'd quit because you didn't get your way?"

She pushed against his shoulders, firmly, but he didn't budge. Being tiny was frustrating sometimes. "Yes, Blake, you jerk, because that's who the hell I am. Determined. Greedy. *Ambitious.*" The words dripped with as much caustic sarcasm as she could slather them with.

"I don't get it."

"I won't put myself in a position I've already wrestled away from. Regardless of whether it's personal or professional, Wes Black will never rule me again."

Blake seemed to get it then. He studied the floor for a minute before nodding. "One question."

"Shoot." She showed her impatience with crossed arms and a flat glare.

"It's no secret Amanda and I are dating. Why haven't I already been confronted for breaking the policy?"

Because Mama Avery played favorites and would get involved the minute rumors turned nasty. Because Sadie had already gotten away with flouting the policy once before, with Wes. Because fate decreed it. "That's something you can ask Iris Avery."

* * * *

If Blake had learned anything during his time at Avery & Thorp, it was that Sadie was always right.

Always. No sooner had he walked into the lobby on Tuesday morning, the very next day, than Reba handed him a tiny hot-pink sticky note. Iris Avery was waiting upstairs in Duncan's office.

He took his time. In his office, he had a cup of coffee to fortify himself and asked Kennedy if his tie was straight. "Have you and Sadie decided if you love each other or hate each other today?"

Kennedy grinned. "I could ask you the same thing, playboy."

He knew she meant it as teasing, but it was an unpleasant reminder of how close he still was to the man he was trying to escape. "You know Sadie and I aren't involved, right?"

She brushed lint from his shoulder. "Maybe not in the nitty-gritty under-the-sheets way that people assume when they hear how 'close' you two are. But, Blake, I have to be honest with you."

"Please. By all means." In reality, he wished he'd kept his mouth shut. Kennedy was right almost as often as Sadie was.

"You two like each other."

"We're friends. Of course we do."

Her lips pressed together in a frown. "It's more than that. You can pretend with each other all day, but don't expect someone with my deep sense of intuition to fall for it. You like each other, you enjoy one another's company, and I think, had you come into this office without the past clinging to your shoulders like football pads, you'd probably have gravitated toward Sadie from the beginning. You only have your own hang-ups to blame for getting stuck with Amanda."

"Hey, I'm not stuck." Of course he wasn't stuck. How absurd. He liked Amanda just fine.

Kennedy's expression said she didn't care what he thought. "Whatever you say. Maybe my instincts are off. Now, don't be nervous. Iris called me for a meeting one time, but it was only to ask if I felt I deserved the raise I'd petitioned for. I said, 'obviously,' and we went back and forth on the pros and cons for thirty minutes before she caved. She likes a fighter, Blake. But, you know, not *too much* of a fighter. She also doesn't like to be challenged. It's a bit of a tightrope situation, but I bet you'll do great."

Blake walked through the bookkeeping parlor toward the spiral staircase feeling a little less confident than he had ten minutes ago. Next time, maybe he'd skip the pep talk from Kennedy.

Nina's small desk outside Duncan's inner office was vacant, the glossy surface clean of debris and paperwork, as though no one used the space. Duncan was nowhere to be found. Iris Avery sat behind Duncan's large oval glass desk, reclined and surrounded by an air of self-assuredness men and women with power and money wore like an accessory. Blake believed he'd probably had his fair share of it at one time. A few years ago, he'd have never dreamed of being nervous around a woman like Mrs. Avery.

Perhaps the fact that he was dating her daughter and had been accused of cheating was what had his stomach tied in knots.

She certainly looked like Amanda's mother. Her silvery white hair cut stylishly short was brushed back from a square, dominating forehead. Her eyes were the same light jade green behind silver square-framed glasses. She wore a power suit that would've made any businessman on Wall Street look twice, the second time with respect.

"Mrs. Avery," Blake greeted her with his hand outstretched.

For one terrifying moment, he feared the older woman would continue to stare at his proffered hand.

Finally, she sat forward and took it, and they shook over the desk. "Mr. Cobb." She readjusted her glasses as he took his seat. "I appreciate you taking the time to talk with me."

As if there'd been some choice in the matter. "No problem at all, ma'am," he replied good-naturedly instead and forced himself to relax. He didn't necessarily have to feel confident to be able to call on a lifetime of cockiness and arrogance, like muscle-memory for his personality.

He waited for Mrs. Avery to open the conversation, which she did after a full minute of blinking at Blake and turning a fine black pen in her manicured fingers. "Mr. Cobb, it's come to my attention there's something off here in the Jackson office. As you can surely understand, given how new you are to the position, this is cause for worry. We don't want your time here getting off on the wrong foot."

Was he sweating? Blake was certain he was sweating. Big, fat drops would start rolling down his face and soaking the inner seams of his shirt any second. "Yes, ma'am, I understand."

Mrs. Avery leaned back in the chair once more and tapped the fancy pen against the glass in a measured staccato. "If you would, give me a rundown. Be as specific as possible."

Dear God, she wanted *specifics?* Specific as in her daughter reminded Blake of his first wife? Specific as in, yes, he had slept with Amanda, but for reasons he didn't want to look too deeply into, he preferred Sadie's company?

Blake straightened his back but stopped short of loosening his tie and giving away his nervousness. "I, uh, suppose it had to have begun the first time I met Amanda. Kennedy introduced us on my first day. I was immediately taken with her, if you must know."

Mrs. Avery lifted a hand to stop Blake and closed her eyes, her mouth set to a wry smile. "Mr. Cobb," she began, with something uncomfortably close to amusement, "I am well aware of your relationship with Amanda. We will discuss that eventually. However, my main concern is the balance sheet that came across Duncan's desk with numbers that don't add up. The report came from you, so I've come to you for insight into what we think might've happened."

Relief came first. A different kind of anxiety followed. This time, Blake didn't have to worry about guilt but rather a quiet uncertainty that perhaps he'd made a mistake. The report in question was the one he'd meant to ask Amanda about, because the discrepancy seemed to have originated from bookkeeping.

"Ma'am, I'm sure it's a simple math error. A wrong number entered."

Mrs. Avery's wry grin turned to a flat grimace. "I suppose it's easy enough to accidently drop a zero here or there. On the other hand, Henry's last several reports before his retirement indicated a pattern. The reason I hired you, Mr. Cobb, despite your history of personal affairs, is your remarkable track record in a professional capacity. I am not surprised you've entered into a liaison quite against company policy, as you've had little regard for it in the past. My interest was more in seeing if old Henry was as incompetent as his coworkers believed. He quietly reported a few monetary discrepancies to Duncan, and Duncan shared those concerns with me. Now, since you've turned in numbers bearing the same alarming disparity, we know we have a genuine problem on our hands. And you're up to it in your ears, Blake."

The use of his first name seemed both a privilege and a condemnation. "I'm sorry, I have to disagree. Question my ethics as a man any day. I deserve that. But to get myself mixed up in anything like fudging reports, or worse, going so far as embezzling, is not within my character."

"I'm aware. It leaves me wondering if you're blinded by love or merely trying to protect her."

The implication smacked Blake in the face like a wet towel. "You can't be serious."

"Oh?" Mrs. Avery abruptly dropped the pen and sat forward, eyebrows raised as if daring Blake to contradict her further. "You think I'd question my own daughter without good cause? Amanda is in bookkeeping only to avoid accusations of favoritism. But I'll tell you something no one knows—her I.Q. is a hair from genius level. She's damnably smart, which has a lot to do with her social handicaps. Difficulty making friends and fitting in, for example. Personally, I think this is a little sloppy for her. Too obvious. However, if it's not Amanda who's skimming, then it's someone who wants us to think it is." Her expression turned sad and a bit weary. "We have a real problem here."

Blake let out a deep exhale. "I'd say so." And it was his job, as auditor, to get to the bottom of it.

Even if it meant investigating his girlfriend. Blake decided now wasn't the time to play coy. "Is she to be made aware of my investigation?"

Mrs. Avery seemed to consider. "Well, it might cause some undue strain on your relationship, but I do think it's for the best if she knows. She'll understand you have a job to do. And if she's innocent of any wrongdoing, she'll be happy to help in any way she can." Her gaze stopped wandering and drilled into Blake. "As for the company's fraternization policy, it's set in place for a reason. But I'm a fair woman and understand things happen. I consider these circumstances on a case by case basis. For example, no action was brought against Ms. Felix and Mr. Black, for we were aware of their involvement before he joined the firm. They kept it strictly professional, and Henry saw no signs from either one of anything unethical or questionable by any means. They are both valued members of the firm. That said…" She blinked several times. "That said, I think it'd be unwise to continue your association with Ms. Felix so long as you're romantically involved with Amanda. As mentioned, I'm fully aware of your history, Mr. Cobb. I would hate to see it repeat itself in my house."

Blake wanted to die. Mortification burned his skin like fire. It took every ounce of willpower he had to maintain eye contact. "Ma'am. I understand and will take your advice into consideration."

He left the meeting majorly embarrassed and slightly annoyed. Mrs. Avery had no right to dictate who he socialized with outside of work. By the time he'd returned to his office, another obvious notion occurred to him. He had Amanda's mother's blessing and a second chance to make things right with Amanda. So, why had his first thought been of Sadie?

* * * *

Blake wasn't expecting company when Duncan's Mercedes sedan crunched through the snow and parked behind his car.

Eric's ears jerked up, and he froze in his spot less than three feet away from where Blake sat crouched, painfully still, with his arm extended to offer the piece of sirloin to the sly, sly fox.

The car door slammed shut, and Eric bolted.

Still crouched, Blake's head drooped. He stayed there until he heard Duncan's footsteps approach.

"What are you doing?"

Blake stood up straight and rolled his shoulders. He'd been in that same position for the last half hour, and all twenty of his digits were numb from the cold. It was the closest he'd come to feeding Eric right out of his hands. He tossed the chunk of meat on the ground for him to find later. "I'm trying to make friends with a wild fox."

Duncan nodded in an approving way. "Most guys buy a Corvette when they hit their forties. I like your style, Blake."

Blake noticed the six pack in his hand. "Why don't you come in and crack me open one of those?"

Inside, Duncan sat at the small dining table and immediately twisted the caps off two bottles. "How'd you enjoy your chat with Iris this morning?"

Blake crossed to the sink, washed his hands, and toweled them dry before joining Duncan and taking a heavy swig of beer, so cold it made his eyes water. "She thinks Amanda's embezzling small amounts, in the low thousands, through bookkeeping, or someone is making it seem as though she is. Did you know she has a genius I.Q.?"

Duncan nodded wearily. "Yep." He smacked his lips after a heavy chug. "She's definitely too smart. I'm erring on the side of a frame job."

Blake shook his head. "That's a complicated thing to pull off in a firm this size. Avery & Thorp is tiny. It won't take much digging to find out where the money's going."

"What's important is we keep it quiet. I know, Mrs. Avery knows, you know, and Amanda will know. No one else has any idea we've stumbled onto anything. It needs to stay that way." His look said Blake had been officially warned—if he opened his mouth to anyone, there'd be consequences.

"I'm an auditor," Blake reminded him. "I investigate discrepancies. I find the money. You don't have to remind me how to do my job."

"Fair enough." Duncan seemed satisfied with that. After a short pause, while Blake waited for him to reveal the real reason behind this little visit, his boss finally took a deep breath and gave Blake a keen look. "But I'll remind you, Sadie isn't on the need-to-know list."

Blake sat forward and rubbed his eyes with his fists. "You want me to do this all over again? Going through it with Mrs. Avery was the most awkward and embarrassing moment of my entire career. I can't imagine there's a whole lot left to say on the matter."

Duncan ignored him. He was, after all, the boss. "I have to ask, Blake. Are you sure you're not interested in the Chief Accounting position? You're the most qualified person around for miles."

Duncan's pleading light brown eyes made Blake uncomfortable. He almost looked sad, as though the alternative, if Blake rejected him, was too terrible to contemplate. And since it apparently wasn't Sadie, perhaps that was the case.

Blake considered it seriously in the interest of giving Duncan a wholehearted answer. Did he want the job? In his heart of hearts, no. Good grief, no. Not even a little. And say he took it anyway, what would Sadie think? All the time she spent suspecting he wanted the job, for him to take it after convincing her he didn't, seemed like a surefire way to lose her trust forever.

Which mattered because?

Not going there.

Blake shook his head. "Sorry. Not interested."

Duncan nodded slowly, accepting but disappointed.

Blake went for broke. "Congrats to Wes, I suppose?"

Sitting up a little straighter, Duncan's eyebrows gathered quizzically. "The pool is shrinking, admittedly, but I still can't say for sure."

"I don't understand how Sadie isn't the automatic choice." He rested his elbows on the table. "Her reaction is pretty severe, like it's the end of her career or something. She's talking about turning in her resignation." He paused and waited for a tell from Duncan. For all he knew, she'd already done it, but Duncan remained passive as he took occasional sips, so Blake continued. "I understand a five-year plan, but setbacks are part of the climb. You have to adjust for them. She's so levelheaded, so career-minded. I can't understand why she'd take it so hard."

Duncan studied the bottle between his palms. "Wesley Black is a controlling, manipulative sociopath. He's so genial and easy to talk to, you'd never guess it. There're little things you wouldn't look at twice if you weren't paying attention. As quiet as he and Sadie kept their relationship, everyone knew when it went down in flames. Of course, it eventually grew into the rivalry we all know and love today. Sadie's mission is to crush Wes professionally, while Wes formed a unique friendship with Reba soon after she started last year. He sets something in motion, perhaps the casual mention of a private matter, and Reba has it all over the office by lunch. When it comes back to him, he somehow manages to act the innocent lamb, while taking credit with the same breath. Sadie's personal affairs have been the rumor mill's bread and butter since their split. It's his way of controlling her—or attempting to, I should say. Sadie isn't the cowering type. She rails and fights every time Wes gets in her way and lets the rumors fly." Duncan smiled with more than a hint of pride. It faded abruptly, replaced with a miserable frown. "But if he's her boss?" He emitted a frustrated grunt and pushed himself back in the chair. "I don't know who the hell Iris is going to give my job to. She's keeping her own council on the matter. The same names are in the hat, but it's a game of musical chairs, with Sadie officially out of the running."

"Yeah, the whole office got the memo on that." Blake did a poor job of keeping the bitterness from his tone. Amanda's heartlessness still bothered him.

Duncan gave a small shake of his head. "This is strictly off the record, Blake. You never heard these words pass my lips. I'll deny them with my dying breath. But this is the truth—Amanda Avery is a petty, unkind woman." His eyebrows drew together again. "But her mother isn't. And that's why I'm confused why Iris would consider Wes and not Sadie."

Blake wasn't totally convinced about Mrs. Avery. "Especially if you've shared your opinion of Wes with her."

"Oh, I have." Duncan drained the last of his beer before cracking open a second. "I wonder if Amanda's the reason Sadie isn't in the running. I say Iris is an upstanding woman, but when it comes to her daughter, who can say? Would she refuse to hire Sadie based on Amanda's dislike, despite qualifications?"

Blake considered Mrs. Avery—blunt, formidable. "She wants me to investigate her own daughter for embezzling. You think she'd question Amanda's ethics but hold her opinion of who should run the Jackson office in the highest esteem? I don't doubt for a second it made Amanda's day to find out Sadie wouldn't be getting your job, Duncan, but your theory misses the mark. I think," Blake added quickly and respectfully. Easy to forget he was talking to his boss in the cabin's casual setting.

Duncan didn't seem to notice as he raised his eyebrows and tipped his longneck toward Blake. "Well, I've got one more theory for you, bud. You might consider looking outside the firm for friends and lovers in the future. You're ankle-deep in the whole mess."

Blake swigged the last of his beer. "Now there's a hypothesis I can get on board with."

Chapter 11

Blake's car rolled to a stop behind Sadie's truck as she tossed the last horse blanket on top of the loaded tack.

Sadie's shoulders fell dejectedly as she watched him climb out of the vehicle. Why did he keep doing this? Sunday morning, his girlfriend was probably at church with her family, and he went straight to the woman everyone and their uncle thought he was boinking in his downtime.

"You're gonna have to move your car. I'm on my way out."

He was uncomfortably attractive in a pair of faded jeans. He looked nice in slacks, but something about rumpled Sunday morning hair and loose denim had Sadie entertaining visions of climbing into his lap and asking how he liked his pancakes. She didn't even know how to make pancakes.

He settled his hands into his pockets. "Can I help?"

She'd hefted the final saddle and was sliding it into the truck bed. She grunted from the effort, glad to have an excuse for the sweat gathering at her temples, despite the chill winter air. "I've got it."

He sighed. "Can I ride along?"

Sadie shoved her hair back from her face and whirled on him. "What do you want, Blake?"

He peered at her.

Sadie caught on to something irregular in his narrowed hazel gaze. "You have something on your mind. This isn't a social call."

He shook his head. "I need to talk to someone. Someone smart."

"Firm full of people with four-year degrees, yet so few meet the criteria."

The nervous tic in his jaw didn't escape her. Nor did the slightly protruding vein in his forehead or the tight lines around his mouth. Whatever he had stuck in his craw, it was doing a number on his face.

"Fine. Move your car and you can ride with me to Triple L Ranch. I'm delivering this horse tack for my neighbor. His truck broke down this morning."

Things had changed between them since Amanda's outburst. Blake spent less time socializing around the office, which had normally included casual conversations with Sadie, and more time with his head up Amanda's rear end, trying to prove his loyalty. Not only to Amanda, but the rest of the firm. Everyone had their eyes on him, waiting for the slightest hint the rumor was true. Meanwhile, Sadie worked harder than ever, putting in longer hours and running herself ragged so she wouldn't have time to think. Basically, she'd been royally screwed out of everything she had her eye on.

Including Blake.

They rode down Broadway until Sadie made the turn onto Highway 22. After another five minutes of silence as she drove over the Snake River and into the little town of Wilson, Sadie snapped and cast him an annoyed glance. "Spit it out already, would you? You're making me nervous over there, chewing your own face off."

Blake abruptly looked toward her and quit nibbling the inside of his cheek. "Sorry. Nervous habit."

She shrugged and gave her attention to the road. The speed limit had dropped, and she hit the brakes late, giving them both a nice little jolt as good as any cup of coffee. "Better than smoking, I guess. You said you wanted to talk, so talk. I can listen and operate heavy machinery at the same time."

He sighed. "I don't know where to start. There's a personal problem and a professional concern. What would you like to hear first?"

She didn't want to go anywhere near the personal problem. Best to get it out of the way and end the conversation on a professional note. "Hit me with the good stuff. Your personal issue, which I'm gonna go out on the highest limb ever and say has something to do with Amanda and the meeting you had with Iris Avery last Tuesday."

"And you," he added quietly.

Sadie's mouth went dry. *Not good, not good, not good.* "What about me?"

"Specifically, that I should stop being your friend as long as I'm dating Amanda."

A hot rush of indignant anger pounded in Sadie's ears. She gripped the steering wheel like she might choke it. "Oh, I see. You and Amanda can flout company policy, no biggie. That's one thing. It's Iris's company. She can do whatever she wants. But it's audacious as hell to say who you can and can't be friends with." She stopped and bit her lip to shut herself up.

Maybe Blake didn't want to be her friend. Maybe he'd come to break up with her for good, cement the vague sense of loss she'd been immersed in.

Blake slapped his thigh. "Thank you. That's how I see it. I feel pressured to work it out with Amanda, but it's got an unsavory selling-my-soul feel to it." He stopped to clear his throat. "The whole freewill thing, ya know."

Sadie licked her lips. Mrs. Avery saw her as some kind of threat, then? *Is there hope?*

She shut down the thought before anything dangerous could sink its little claws into her heart. What kind of person was she, anyway? Amanda was her friend. Or had been, at any rate. They hadn't spoken since Amanda's cruel tantrum. Although, Sadie imagined there'd be more unpleasantness in the future if Blake didn't stop coming around.

"We've covered the awkward personal aspect." She sneaked a peek at his profile. He looked worried. "Mind if we move on to your professional concerns? If this has anything to do with the promotion, I wish you wouldn't. I don't want to talk about it. I've accepted it. I've even decided I won't quit. I didn't come this far in my career only to let some oily haired control freak ruin it. I'm tough. I can handle anything he throws at me."

Keep saying it. Say it until you believe it, Sadie. Thatta girl. She turned left onto North Fall Creek Road.

A frustrated groan came from Blake's side of the cab. "Taking a step down was supposed to simplify my life." A moment of silence passed before another little *oh well* sigh escaped him. "I'm glad you're sticking it out."

She dared another peek in his direction. He looked back at her with a warmth in his pretty, pretty eyeballs that set her pulse skittering. Especially knowing it wouldn't take much for them to go from warm to hot. She whipped her eyes back to the road and determined she'd keep them there. She couldn't take any more tender exchanges like that one. None of this was fair.

"So," she prompted. "What's the deal?"

"Money. Someone is skimming. It's Amanda or it's someone who wants it to look like Amanda. Mrs. Avery wants me to investigate her daughter."

The news hit Sadie like a karate chop to the wind pipe. She took the next opportunity to pull off onto a rocky patch of gravel next to the highway. She set the parking brake and twisted to stare at Blake. "Someone is embezzling out of *our* office? Are you sure?"

Who? Who in their right mind would try something so brazen in such a small firm?

Blake rubbed a hand over his face, worry etched into every line. "I'll lose my job for telling you. Everyone is under investigation at this point."

"Then why are you here?"

"Because you're the one person I'd bet my job doesn't have anything to do with it."

His faith in her honesty undid a few of the frail bindings holding her heart in check. She wanted to take his face in her hands and see what that charming mouth of his could do, see what passion did to those hazel eyes.

She swallowed hard. "Do you suspect anyone?"

He stared out the windshield like the answer lay straight ahead. "Wes and Reba work as a team. He's the source of most of the rumors that go flying around the office, and whether she's aware of it or not, Reba's the vehicle. That sort of chumminess raises a red flag. Then again, access to certain files is a factor. That puts Kennedy and every member of the bookkeeping team in an interesting position, as well as both file clerks. Most embezzlement cases aren't the work of a single individual, but a team. Hell, Amanda is still a suspect. Iris suggests I should make her aware of the investigation, trusting she'll understand I have a job to do."

Sadie quirked a brow. "Suggestion with air quotation marks?"

Blake nodded. "Pretty much. What she thinks I should do is what I'm expected to do." He looked at her.

His eyes were worried, but there was still the warmth, still the kindness, still the *something*. Did Amanda see it, too? Or was it just for Sadie? She'd almost die to know. What if Blake was waiting for something from her? He couldn't possibly know how she felt. What would happen if he did?

"What do you think, Sadie?" He leaned forward and bit his lip slightly in an expression of gentle coaxing with a hint of desperation. "You've got something I don't, and that's exposure. You've worked with these people for years."

Sadie set aside the sexual awakening Blake was eliciting, mentally dousing herself in ice water as she closed her eyes and considered her coworkers. She'd worked beside them daily, had for years. Wouldn't she have known if one of them were shady as all get out? Worse, a thief?

Amanda was off-the-rails crazy. But that didn't make her guilty. Besides, the amount being embezzled couldn't be much, or the trail would be a lot easier to follow. Blake could've pinned the guilty party in a single afternoon at the books.

Nina and Kennedy were above reproach. Call her biased or loyal, Sadie knew the two of them intimately. She'd have known if something were off.

Pearl and Opal were infamously tight. They could pull it off, but not without Amanda catching on. If they were in on it, Amanda was certainly involved.

Xavier and Trish were part-time and had the lowest level of access granted to any employee.

She had to put Catalina in the same category as herself. One of the most ambitious players at the firm, Sadie didn't see her risking it for the monetary pay-off.

Wes and Reba—

Like a lightning strike. "Wes!" Sadie gave Blake a wide-eyed stare. "It has to be Wes. Wes and Reba. Why keep their friendship low-key the way they do if not to avoid drawing attention? It makes sense."

She slumped at Blake's noncommittal noise.

"I don't know. This goes back to Henry's time. Someone beyond smart has been getting away with this for a long time. Wes strikes me as a here-and-now person. He seems more concerned with you than with money."

"I disagree, but it's nice to know you don't think him clever enough."

Blake smiled at her with endearing camaraderie. Like they were in it together, them against the world. "Not nearly."

Once again, Sadie's insides unraveled, leaving her raw and vulnerable. She covered her face. "Blake, you're killing me." It was as much a plea as an admonishment. Despite how her face burned, she made herself meet his gaze.

He watched her.

"Look…" She swallowed. *Just say it. Be done with it.* "I like you. Okay? We talked about my little crush, and I know I said I'd let it go. But you're not helping when you smile at me like that. It's not fair. You're with Amanda, and every time I get a rush from being with you, or a blush crawls over my skin because you smiled or said something vaguely flirtatious, I don't even feel guilty. I mean, I do, when I remember to, but mostly I just think how unfair. And the truth is, my crush is growing legs. It's going places I didn't give it permission to go, getting stronger and scarier."

She shouldn't have said anything.

Heat, raw and utterly unmistakable, gleamed from Blake's gaze as it traveled down to her mouth and back up to meet her eyes. Acknowledgment, desire, acceptance—all of it bloomed across his face like a lily spreading wide for the sun.

They stared at each other. Despite the ice and snow outside, the cab of her truck was growing warm enough to make her sweat beneath the collar of her jacket.

Without warning, Blake blinked twice, in rapid succession, and reared back from her like she'd burned him. He closed his eyes, mouth shut in a tight line. "Every time. Every *damn* time." He opened his eyes. The coals had gone cold. "It's not fair. I don't mean—I just… I like you, too, Sadie." He finished with a shrug and the quintessential neck rub men the world over seemed to have down pat. "You're right, though. This has to stop." He shook his head and settled back into his seat.

She didn't recall saying anything about making it stop. But now she had her answer and could move on. Confronted with her feelings, Blake stayed true to Amanda; the admirable, honorable thing to do. Even so, it hardened Sadie against him, in her heart of hearts. Ultimately, it spelled rejection. The worst part, however, was that Amanda wasn't *the one*. And they both knew it.

There didn't seem to be anything left to say.

Sadie checked her mirrors before creeping back onto the winding highway. She distracted herself with thoughts of Wes and Reba and breaking up their little operation. Blake didn't need to believe her. She'd prove it on her own.

* * * *

Wes lazily trawled Sadie's office like he was thinking of buying the place. Running a finger across her plant shelf and inspecting it for dust. Staring dispassionately at photos of her mother and various earned certificates framed and displayed on the built-ins on the far wall. "You can always apply to be my secretary."

Sadie ignored him as best she could under the circumstances. She wanted to accuse him of theft, throw some proof in his face, and see him escorted from the building. She needed the proof first. Digging any up had proved a fruitless effort so far. Even Nina, second only to Reba in her gossiping status, didn't have any secret tidbits on Wes. Certainly not any that would help Sadie's case.

It didn't help her hands were tied. Helping Blake in any obvious capacity was out of the question. Not only did he want to investigate other potential suspects, but she couldn't give away that he'd confided in her.

"What the hell do you want, Wes? If you have something to say, wait and ambush me in the parking lot, like I did to you." She brushed lint from her black blazer with the royal blue trim. She'd needed to feel powerful today, but it wasn't working.

"Or we could have lunch together and discuss our future. Our *professional* future," he added, with a slight bow and a smirk.

Again with the games. "Screw you. I know about you and Reba. I think you should get the hell out of my office. Or maybe we should have lunch." She injected the perfect note of dumb innocence into her tone. "In Duncan's office, maybe." She'd hoped to catch a glint of fear in his dark eyes.

To her great surprise, he smiled. A wide, feral thing that showed off his canines, and a great deal of his true personality. He settled his hands neatly into his slacks. He had the nerve to look down on her with something close to pity.

As angry as it made her, it also made her nerves sing. This was Wes at his nastiest, and prior experience told her he had something up his dirty, thieving sleeve.

"I'll take it." So smooth. So sure of himself. "Because I'm not the only one with a little secret." He paused, tilted his chin and narrowed his eyes in a mockery of deep thought. "How was your Sunday morning joyride with Blake? I meant to ask. Probably not nearly as fun as last week's late-night visit. A Monday night, no less. Kinky."

She itched to slap him.

But Wes held the cards that mattered—the ability to spread a rumor like wildfire. Unlike before, when he had nothing but supposition, these were supportable claims.

Blake had been at her place last Monday night. She'd made him leave, but there'd be no proving what happened behind closed doors. Any more than she and Blake could prove they'd done nothing more than deliver horse tack yesterday.

Wes appeared to sense her defeated gloom. He didn't dig in with another bloodthirsty grin. The very image of humility, he smiled kindly. "I hate to pester you, but I wanted to ask again what your plans for lunch were."

Sadie almost bowed to the game. But if Wes was the culprit behind the embezzlement scheme, she wouldn't have to put up with him for much longer. "Suck it, Wes. My plans are to eat alone, because I find my own company immeasurably more enjoyable than yours."

His eyes became hard, little stones, but his smile didn't waver. "I wish you the best in your impending job hunt. I've decided you'd make a poor secretary, after all. Can't take direction."

Chapter 12

March was supposed to be a month of spring. Flowers ought to have begun blooming and the weather become more mild and friendly. Someone hadn't given Wyoming the memo. Snow still fell, dumping by the gallons. Blake grew weary of piling on nine layers of clothing just to check his mail. He'd never been much of a beachgoer, but he'd eat a tire for a chance to wear flip-flops outside for a day.

He'd spent weeks investigating accounts at the office—all while maintaining secrecy, even from Amanda, despite Mrs. Avery's wishes. He wanted an opportunity to look deeper into bookkeeping without feeling led. Amanda would have her own ideas and suggestions, inevitably coloring his.

When he'd finally decided to bring her into the fold, after reaching yet another dead end, he wished he hadn't. She hadn't shed light on his problem, only another shadow. As heartily as Sadie had pointed the finger at Wes, Amanda adamantly insisted Sadie was the obvious offender.

He desperately needed a break from Amanda. Friday night had taken its sweet time showing up, and the minutes seemed to crawl until the weekend came and Amanda disappeared to Alpine for two whole days.

No fancy dinners at perfect place setting and exact manners. No cheesy Western movies. No stilted, robotic conversations about things like color scheme and horses, which were but a few samples of Amanda's idea of enlightened conversation.

Curled up on the opposite end of the sofa, she cast Blake another hard stare. "Sadie was smart to attempt to take advantage of me by pretending to be my friend. She made sure I didn't look twice at her."

Blake checked a weary sigh. "I keep telling you Sadie is your friend. Now you know the rumors were false, and what you did to her uncalled for, there's no reason to keep hating her. There's nothing between the two of us."

The lie settled in his stomach like soured milk. Well, *partial* lie. An emotional connection sizzled between them, one he hadn't asked for, but strictly speaking, they'd never been physical. And he wouldn't admit to any of the fantasies he'd dreamed up if his very life hung in the balance.

"Anyway, Sadie isn't responsible. She has too much invested in her career to do something this stupid."

Amanda's chin hiked defensively. "That's hardly enough to exonerate her."

Blake managed to keep his eyes from rolling in his head until they could stare at his brain and ask if it was hearing what he was hearing. "There are other people in the office to consider." He hoped to guide Amanda's efforts toward more useful ideas. It was some kind of torture for someone he respected to be bad-mouthed while he sat by idly, offering but the vaguest of defenses for her character. "Wes has the same access as Sadie. Nina and Kennedy both could've managed it, given their respective proximity. Plus, I'm not convinced it's one person working alone. Even Reba could be behind it. She's friends with everyone. All she'd need is an accomplice willing to fudge a few digits here and there. Where the money comes from doesn't concern me so much as where it's ending up."

"Wes and Sadie both have far more access than Nina." Amanda said the secretary's name with equal parts amusement and disdain, like it was laughable to consider her. "She doesn't go into Duncan's inner office unless he's there, but both senior accountants keep a key to his office and files. In fact, the morning I met Wes in Duncan's office, I was rather upset because Nina was gone. She'd gone out for a break, since Duncan was at a luncheon with potential new clients, which left zero accountability for who came and went."

Blake narrowed his eyes. "Is Wes smart enough? Whoever's behind this, they know what they're doing, and they know their way around the system. Last week, I overheard Wes asking Kennedy a technical question. Unless the two of them are working together, I don't think it's Wes." No matter how bad Sadie wanted it to be.

Amanda nodded once, slowly, her stare riveted on the television set. "Someone smart. Wes drives an expensive car, which is a fairly blatant display of where he spends his paychecks. It's far more likely the perpetrator would drive something less showy to keep from attracting the wrong sort of attention."

You mean like Sadie's old Ford pickup truck?

Blake missed his cabin. He wanted to sit outside in the cool, dark air and see if his little fox friend would come out for a little leftover fajita meat from Blake's lunch. The spices might turn him off. Maybe if he rinsed it. Then it occurred to him Eric might actually be *Erica* and take the meat back to her den to feed her kits. He should definitely rinse it. Did foxes have kits this time of year? He gathered they didn't hibernate. But probably spring, like most other woodland creatures, would be the time for babies.

How adorable would a baby fox have to be?

Blake's mind wandered until Amanda snapped her fingers next to his ear. He startled and stared at her. "I'm sorry. Lost in my thoughts." He didn't like it, her knack for physically controlling him. Snapping was as bad as whistling. Damn if she didn't remind him of—

He looked into Amanda's eyes, staring blankly at him in return as though devoid of internal machinations, and it finally happened.

Blake mentally pulled apart the two women. Amanda's essence had meshed with her appearance, and Blake finally saw *her.*

She blinked. "What are you thinking about over there, all moody and quiet?"

He took a final stab at unearthing something relatable and likeable from her. "Actually, I was thinking of the fox that lives near my cabin. Which is where the name Fox Watch came from. I've almost got him eating from my hand. I was thinking he'd like my leftovers from lunch today." He smiled in anticipation of her reaction. Because foxes were cute, no matter who you were. Except, he was wrong, and Amanda didn't break into bubbly excitement.

Sparks ignited behind her jade eyes. Her nostrils flared. "It's difficult for me to fathom how your brain went from discussing the very serious allegations against Sadie as an embezzler, to the fox that lives near your ugly little cabin. I think personal feelings have compromised your judgment."

Blake's fuse burned down a fraction. "And I think a bookkeeper doesn't tell an auditor how to do his job. Sadie's accounts will be investigated along with everyone else's. But you're right about one thing; I don't think she did it. She's too focused on her career to be willing to jeopardize it for financial gain. I've been doing this long enough to know there's something to be said for motive, and Sadie simply doesn't have it."

It was like he'd hit a hidden red trigger button he hadn't known existed. Except, he *had* known, because he'd seen the same manic, spastic expression on Amanda's face when she'd stormed his office two weeks ago and blasted Sadie into pieces.

His fuse burned lower still. And as it burned down, something else built up—anger, frustration with trying to do the right thing, and failing. He couldn't put a name to the force gathering in his chest, but he was nearing the end of his rope with Kira.

Kira.

A mountain crumbled inside him.

He hadn't been working up to an explosion—only a painfully obvious conclusion that had been dancing before his eyes—hell, his heart—for weeks and weeks. He'd been too stupid and stubborn to see it. Or maybe he'd seen it and looked the other way, because if he was tired, tired, *tired* of anything, it was making mistakes.

Amanda was Kira. Amanda was controlling and thoughtless. Amanda had no empathy. Petty and unkind, which were all things he'd say were the total opposite of Quinn. In fact, Quinn would despise her.

His whole life seemed to revolve around screwing up. Every major event in his life came preceded by some terrible decision he'd made. And he was probably about to do it again.

"Amanda, I think we should break up." He didn't wait for her reply but stood. "I'm sorry. Everything about this was wrong. From start to finish. You deserve better than someone who wishes you were someone else." He actually believed that. He stalked toward the door and grabbed for his coat.

He glanced back once before stepping over the threshold and wished he hadn't.

Amanda Avery, the girl who couldn't emote, had a pair of tears running down her otherwise expressionless face.

* * * *

Monday morning rolled around, and Blake found a million and one excuses to spend most of the day in his office, avoiding Amanda, who shot him nasty looks every time they were within eyesight of one another, and Sadie, who had his insides knotted like a pretzel. Did the right words exist to explain how he'd gone home with Amanda on Friday but was in love with Sadie on Monday? Luckily, he had paperwork galore to distract him. Personnel files were stacked neatly on his desk, awaiting his attention.

At ten after five, he braved the bookkeeping parlor, peeking out his doorway. Amanda was nowhere in sight. Nor was Sadie.

Kennedy glanced over from her desk. "You're safe, Blake. Amanda's gone home for the day. Left early, which is most unlike her." She stapled together a stack of papers. "You two having problems?"

If only she knew. Blake pressed his lips together. It'd get around eventually. "I sort of broke up with her over the weekend."

He'd expected surprise at the very least, but his secretary only sighed and shook her head sadly. "It was Sadie all along, wasn't it? One day, I won't hate her for being the pretty one."

Blake scratched his ear. "It's uncanny how you do that."

She gave a little one-shouldered nonchalant shrug. "I'm not privy to any special information. The lines are there for everyone to see. Try reading between them sometime, Blake. You and Sadie have been caught like charged ions since you met. The air snaps and crackles. It's infuriating, to be honest. When's it my turn for a hot office romance? Wes is totally off the market now that I know the truth about why they broke up. Clearly, you're unavailable." She combined the statement with an eye roll that made it seem like it was all Blake's fault.

"Um… I'm sorry. I guess?" He shuffled closer to her desk. "Listen, maybe you can help me out. I think I'm in love with Sadie—"

Her hand shot out, and her golden eyebrows snapped together. "Whoa, buddy. *Ahem*, I mean, Mr. Cobb, sir. What's this you *think* business? What's really going on in that handsome head of yours?"

Duncan had magically popped up at Blake's side from thin air. "Did someone say handsome? Talking about me behind my back, huh?"

The joke fell flat as Blake took in a deep breath, but Kennedy's mouth fired like a shotgun before he could assure Duncan it was nothing, nothing at all, and make his escape to find Sadie and tell her everything.

"Actually, I was talking about Blake." She relaxed into her chair, balancing the stapler between her palms. "He thinks he's in love with Sadie. From the wild look in his eyes and his nervous shuffling, I'm guessing he's going to say something to her. Which he's free to do, since he dumped Amanda this weekend."

Duncan stared at the floor, hands in his pockets, and seemed to deeply consider the matter. Finally, he smiled jovially at Blake. "Why don't you let me buy you a beer, Blake?" He turned to Kennedy and winked. "I owe you one."

As though in a daze, Blake followed Duncan through the town square to The Silver Dollar Bar. He was quickly learning it was a local favorite as well as a tourist attraction. Settled at the famous bar for the third time with the third coworker to bring him here, he was vaguely tempted to count the silver dollars himself.

He sipped his local brew and tried to curb the anxiety racing through his system. It pulsed through his veins and pounded in his temples. With each minute that ticked by, he grew more certain he had to tell Sadie. He had to tell her everything, right now.

Duncan sighed deeply. "So. You're in love with Sadie now?"

Blake nodded. "Probably since she showed up at the airport in a dirty ball cap and mud-crusted hiking boots and smoothly put me in my place. But I've never done this before. I'm not sure how it's supposed to go."

"Done what?"

"You know." Blake gestured aimlessly, unsure of how to explain himself. "Storm the castle. Get the girl."

Duncan pushed his drink aside. "You're a mess, man. A real mess." He dropped his hands on the bar, like they weighed a ton, and looked at Blake with weary exasperation. "How do you go from Amanda to Sadie in the space of a few days? Have you thought about what Mrs. Avery said to you? You're fooling around with your career, buddy."

"Don't worry about Mrs. Avery." Blake had that aspect figured out. "Instead, why don't you help me work out how I explain myself to Sadie? Look, I know it's crazy, but I got in my own way. I tried too hard and made a mistake, which is something I have to do before I can get things right, apparently. But now I see what I refused to look at. You were right about Amanda, and I was blind to it."

"If I was right about her, why don't you trust I'm right about everything else? Tell me, Blake, why do you *have* to be in love with someone? You're saying it has to be Sadie, because it wasn't Amanda. What's if it's neither? And I'm not saying this as your boss. I'm out of here soon, and this will end up being someone else's problem."

Blake took a careful sip. He still had to drive to Sadie's after this. "I don't, but I am. I'm telling you this is nothing like Amanda. Visually, Sadie made me want to run for the hills the second we met. I made the mistake of seeing with my eyes instead of looking with my heart. But now I *see*. And Sadie's basically perfect, isn't she?"

"Hey." Duncan's hands shot up defensively. "Don't come at a married man with a question like that."

"Sadie is fun. She's honest and kind and hardworking. She can take care of herself. She's a great friend, someone you can rely on. She's everything you'd want in a partner."

Duncan's pitying expression made Blake doubt himself like nothing else could have. "Blake, I can't help you, man. I want to, but you're flying off the edge here. Stop and think this through. Call a lifeline. Someone who knows you and can help you figure out what you should do next. Because I get a sense of you rushing headlong into a brick wall. The impact is going to hurt, and the reverberations will be felt far and wide."

Blake considered Duncan's advice as he dropped a twenty onto the bar and saluted. "Chances are I won't change my mind before I pull into Sadie's driveway."

Duncan shook his head. "Whatever happens, just remember I live for the words, 'I told you so.'"

* * * *

Sadie peeked through the curtains and groaned at Blake's form standing in the shadow cast by the eaves. Her body defied her mind as her pulse picked up speed.

She flipped on the porch light and swung the door open. "Didn't we decide this had to stop? Really, we have to stop meeting like this. You know, all clandestine and deliberate." She crossed her arms and rested her hip against the doorjamb, barring him entry.

She'd had enough of the head games, the teasing, the hinting, the little looks that meant everything and nothing. It all led to Blake headed home with Amanda on his arm, so what did they matter? What did *any* of it matter?

"You should go, Blake."

He had the old deer-in-the-headlights expression. "But… I love you." His gaze dropped.

The floor could've come out from under her. "I'm sorry, *what?* When did you figure this out?" That wasn't the question she should've asked. She stood erect and massaged her temples to keep her brain from leaking out. "Blake, what are you doing?"

He rubbed his neck and seemed to want to stare at everything but her. "I had it wrong. Amanda isn't anything like Quinn."

"And you think I am?"

He nodded. Barely. Just the slightest nod, but enough to shoot her temper straight to red.

God, she wanted to punch him. She stepped forward and settled for a hard jab at his chest. "What is your malfunction? Amanda is not Quinn. I am not Quinn. No one but *Quinn* can be Quinn!" Her voice rose on its own accord. The shortsightedness, the ignorance… More than anything, the insult that she should only be worthy as long as she existed in the outline of another woman sketched by Blake's skewed memory. "You need a therapist, okay? There's something off about a man who wants to remake every woman he meets into someone else."

"It's not that!" Blake's hair stood on end as he ran his hands through it like a man in desperate need of a rope, but Sadie would give up accounting for waitressing before she'd throw him one. "It's—I only mean there are certain traits, that's all. Things you have in common. Things I admire."

"You don't love someone because of their traits," Sadie snapped. "We are more than the whole of our parts. I add up to more than my idiosyncrasies, more than the mere characteristics of my personality. I'm a human being with faults and fears. I make mistakes. I can be ugly, Blake. As ugly as Amanda, and far uglier than Quinn. So, no, you don't love me. You don't even *know* me." She went to slam the door in his face.

His hand shot out, catching it and holding it. "Sadie, please." Hardly a whisper.

Why was he doing this? With one hand, he offered her everything she wanted. With the other, he shaped it into something meaningless and lamentable.

"Please," he said again. His expression begged her. His eyes squeezed shut and popped open again, and a whole world of bewilderment and grief opened up to her.

He seemed so lost. She wanted to help him find his way, but not like this—not as the second-place runner-up for Quinn's stand-in.

Blake cast his gaze on the ground like it hurt to look at her. "Sadie, it's not supposed to go like this, and I don't know what I'm supposed to do. Damn it." He grabbed at his hair and pushed off from the porch. He halted in the small patch of grass that was her yard, hands on hips, head hanging, hair wild. "I don't understand. For Quinn and Emily, it happened all so perfectly. They met someone, they fought it, they realized the error of their ways, and then… And then, that was it. They found their soulmates and lived happily ever after." He shook his head and regarded her again. This time his expression was guarded. "I know how I feel about you. I know that you're what I've been looking for. Whether you like the sound of it or not, the qualities I appreciate are those you share with my ex-wife, yes. That doesn't mean it's not about you, though. I don't want you to be Quinn, but I also can't help wanting you for the same reasons I still want her."

Sadie couldn't believe her ears. "*Still?* Do you hear yourself?"

"No! I didn't mean—"

"I've got it bad for you, Blake. *You.*" She took a long stride to stand in front of him and drive it home. "Not someone like you, not a suitable substitute, not someone who happens to remind me of you. I'm not settling for someone similar to you, or someone who has the same sense of humor, or the right clothes, or an interchangeable personality, or who laughs at the right jokes or cries on cue. I deserve better than that." She clenched her jaw and ground out the last words through a sieve of iron, because it pissed her off that she needed to say them. "I am Sadie Darling Felix, and I am worth a thousand Quinns. And any man who thinks he's going to waltz into my home and tell me I'm good *enough* doesn't deserve me."

It was as though she'd slapped him. His face opened up as light dawned, eyes wide, mouth agape. He blinked stupidly. "You're right. You aren't Quinn."

Sadie didn't need this. Wes, Blake, Duncan—they'd all let her down, and she was tired of giving them the power to do the job. "Screw you, Blake. Leave and take that chauvinistic, unrealistic, degrading fantasy of some other poor woman squashing herself into the mold of your ex-wife with you."

This time when she slammed the door, it crashed against the frame without any resistance. She fell against it. Her breaths came harsh and heavy, weighed by the realization that Blake was just another psychopath, after all. So, why did it hurt to turn him away? She clenched her fists to keep her hands from shaking. One bone. She'd throw him *one* bone, but if he screwed this up, she was done.

She closed her eyes and bit her lip. Turning around, she pulled the door open a few inches and peeked out at Blake.

Motionless, he stood where she'd left him.

She licked her lips and spoke quietly into the shadows. "This is it, okay? The only lifeline you're gonna get, so listen carefully. You're not in love with me, but you aren't in love with Quinn, either. You idolize her. You idolize your marriage before your affair, because it's the last time you can remember feeling good about yourself or feeling whole. Before you became cheating slime. But you can't move forward by going back. Quinn is the past. I can be your future, but not like this."

She pressed the door closed. The click of the metal latch sliding home seemed to her like a ref's whistle blaring into the quiet.

Round one.

Chapter 13

Sadie crouched next to the filing cabinet and did her best to ignore the beads of sweat forming at her hairline and dripping down onto her temple, sluicing through layers of her makeup. By the time she crept out of here, she'd look like a melting candle.

Why did Wes keep his office at such a stifling temperature? She understood it was mid-March in Wyoming, but eighty-five degrees was a tad excessive.

Quietly, Sadie pulled open the bottom drawer of the filing cabinet. It glided toward her silently. She flicked through the folders, a veritable neon rainbow of colors. Old paper files wouldn't likely lead anywhere, because mostly everything had been digitized years ago. But Wes's portal password might be scribbled down anywhere. Sadie had hers tucked away in at least three different locations, given how often it changed and how difficult the random mix of letters and numbers could be to memorize.

Blake might've helped her, but Sadie wanted to take a gander herself. She knew Wes's style and might catch on to something Blake wouldn't. After all, there was a lot to be learned about a man when you'd shared his bed.

Blake certainly didn't have *that* distinction.

And it had to be Wes. No doubt in Sadie's mind, Wes was behind the missing money. His expensive car and severe case of self-deluded, egocentric entitlement all made sense now. He strutted around like the next big cheese because he believed he was getting away with stealing right under their noses.

She couldn't wait to rub his face in the evidence, see the terror and surprise expand his beady eyeballs until they exploded from his sneering face, and watch as Duncan—

"What are you doing on the floor?"

Sadie jerked and whacked her shoulder against the cabinet with a thud. The resonant shock of Amanda's voice made her skin feel like it was going to peel off. When her breath returned, she swallowed and addressed Amanda without looking up. She shuffled through the files as though she had the right. "Searching for an old file I misplaced. It might've been one I gave over to Wes." She sniffed and straightened, kicking the drawer shut with her boot. She tugged her cardigan down. "It's not here. Might be in archives."

Amanda's face hadn't changed a bit, no matter what emotional hardships she'd suffered the last several weeks. No new lines around her eyes. Her placid features gave away nothing. She clutched a glaring orange folder to her chest like a shield. "You shouldn't be in here."

Unbidden, last night came to Sadie. Her face warmed. How could she have faced Amanda if she'd given in to Blake last night? It seemed like every point on the compass led to a brick wall. No matter where she turned, potential pain, either for herself or someone she cared about, whether it was Blake, Amanda, or her own heart, stared at her. And she did care about Amanda, despite everything.

Sadie tucked a sweat-soaked strand of hair that had stuck to her forehead behind her ear. "You're right. I'll go."

She tried to step past Amanda.

Amanda stepped once to the left, barring the way. Her green eyes were pale and creepy in the dim room. "You think he's guilty, don't you? Blake told you about the missing money, and you'd like it to be Wes."

Sadie swallowed past the lump in her throat, threatening to choke her. If Mrs. Avery's daughter pointed the finger at Sadie, it'd be enough to make her a person of interest. Blake wouldn't have a choice; he'd pull every file Sadie had touched in the last year. He wouldn't find anything, but the investigation would go down in her personnel record for all time.

It was enough to paint a brilliant red slash over years of impeccable professionalism.

"I don't want it to be anyone, actually," she parried. A little early for a verbal spar, but she'd taken the risk breaking into Wes's office. Now she had to outsmart the bridge troll to escape to safety.

Except, Amanda wasn't really a bridge troll, only a deeply misunderstood woman.

Sadie gave up on making a run for it. "You know, I lied to you, Amanda. And I owe you an apology. Because I do like Blake."

It floored her when Amanda's brow gathered in pained puzzlement. She almost looked like a normal person when she moved the muscles in her face. "You're involved with him?"

"No." Sadie shook her head in adamant denial. "No, no, no. I would never, ever do that to someone I consider a friend. I probably wouldn't do it to an enemy. That's not the kind of woman I am. You spent enough time with me to know if I were. I wouldn't eat at your table, then spend the night with your man." It disgusted her to even think about it. "When I say I lied to you, I only mean that I sort of had a thing for Blake, back in the beginning. But you were so happy he'd asked you out, I dialed back instead of telling you the truth. He didn't want me, anyway, and you both seemed happy. I've had a bit of a..."

Was there a grown-up way to say crush? Was there any way to explain it that didn't make her look like a desperate, lovelorn spinster drooling after Blake all these months?

"...a crush, I guess." She'd have to read a dictionary at some point. Expand the old vocab. "I'm only bringing it up because I feel I owe you more, I guess. I don't want to flail my arms and beat feet every time you enter a room. I've liked Blake for a long time, ever since you began dating. But I've never pursued an intimate relationship with him. Likewise, Blake never attempted one with me," she added, wanting to be clear. "Besides, he sort of told Kennedy point-blank he didn't want to date me. But we did have fun together. And he does have this very sad underdog thing going on that I can't help but want to support, despite his history, which just screams red flag—"

"What are you talking about?" Amanda's face had dropped the pained expression, leaving only confusion in her wide green eyes. Her head tilted slightly, and her blond curtain of hair draped over one shoulder like a fine woven scarf. Sadie could kind of see her appeal. If a man were into that kind of thing.

She hesitated to dive into Blake's past, but he owed Amanda full disclosure. Besides, she had to have heard at least some of the details in all the time they'd been dating. She did her best to inject the perfect note of nonchalance into her voice. "I only mean the thing with his third wife being his first wife's sister, and his second wife being the mistress from his first wife. It took me a while to wrap my head around it. I actually drew a diagram."

She broke off. Amanda's eyes had grown in circumference.

Please, Blake, tell me you told her. Tell me you didn't hide this from her...

Sadie didn't know what to do but keep going and try to dig her way out. "Anyway, it's like he was trying to fix the whole mess with that last marriage but didn't have the first clue of how to go about it. I get the sense he's going through something similar here. He's trying to atone, but not in the right way. I can't help but root for the guy, you know. Years later, he's still got himself strapped to a gurney."

Five years, precisely, which didn't sound as impressive as say, ten, so Sadie didn't enumerate.

"Anyway," she plowed on in the wake of Amanda's gaping silence, "no one else seems to be clinging to the past. His first wife is married with a toddler, the mistress disappeared with the guy who was the real dad of their baby together, and his third wife fell for a beach bum in Hawaii. So, really, who cares?"

It was like the plot for a long-running soap opera had spewed from her mouth. No one would ever believe she'd actually been trying to help Blake, not make him sound like a cautionary tale from the Deep South.

She ran a hand through her hair and let out a puff of air. "I've screwed this up. Amanda, I'm an idiot. I shouldn't have said anything. All I meant to get across was Blake's a reformed moron douchebag who's trying way too hard to repair something no one can even remember was broken. More to the point, you're my friend. *Were* my friend, but I'm down to still be friends if you can believe I never meant to cause any upset between you and Blake. His recent change of heart notwithstanding," she added with an eye roll, because *silly, silly* Blake seemed to think he was in love with her. "I'd choose your friendship over Blake if it came to that. He's confused right now, that's all. Seems to think I'm his ex-wife incarnate."

Amanda's expression went stony, then considering. "He went to you?"

Sadie rubbed her eyes carefully, conscious of the mascara she didn't want smeared all over her face. "Yes. It's like I said, though. He's hung up on this idea of redemption, but I'm not what he thinks I am. I'm not his salvation. Neither are you. We're just women, you know? Neither one of us can cleanse him of his guilt or undo his mistakes."

Amanda opened her mouth to reply when Wes strode through the door and froze.

"What are you two doing in my office?" His dark gaze swung from Sadie to Amanda and back.

Sadie's nerves couldn't take much more. Between dumping Blake's past into Amanda's unsuspecting lap like a bowl of wet noodles and Wes busting them in his office, she couldn't do anything but wait for Amanda to drop her like a hot rock.

The moment suspended in time like stretched putty.

Amanda's gaze drilled so hard into Sadie she could almost feel the scrutiny hit the back of her skull, and Wes's eyebrows, thin and over-plucked as ever, formed a deep, suspicious V.

Finally, Amanda looked at Wes. "I borrowed your office to have a private moment with Sadie."

Sadie almost wilted with relief. *Oh, Amanda. Bless your strange, strange heart.*

"Yeah?" Wes set his hands on his hips in a cocky fashion. "What's wrong with having a private moment in Sadie's office?"

"You were late turning in your budget report this morning." Amanda didn't skip a beat. "I asked her to accompany me to retrieve it from your desk." At that, she delicately tapped a sheet sitting on Wes's desk. Sure enough, his budget report, lacking only a signature. "If you wouldn't mind?"

That did the trick. Wes came around his desk, took a fine pen from his breast pocket, and signed the report with a flourish, looking only a tad sheepish as he handed it to Amanda. "I apologize. I had some errands to run this morning. They took longer than I expected."

Straight-faced, Amanda took the report like it was money he owed her, tucking it possessively into the folder in her hand. "No harm, no foul. Actually…" She turned to Sadie then. "If you wouldn't mind, I'd like to talk to Wes." Her gaze darted to the door and back. "Alone."

If Sadie could take anything, it was a hint. She saluted, a dumb little motion that probably gave her away a thousand times over. "Gotcha. See you later then."

She didn't need an excuse to walk away from Wes's office as quickly as her heeled boots allowed. But she couldn't help sneaking one final glance at Amanda and Wes as the door closed on their private conversation.

What could a megalomaniac and a bridge troll have to talk about?

* * * *

Blake stared at the text message on his phone.

Part of him was shocked he'd said anything at all, and the rest of him didn't understand why he hadn't done it sooner. Sooner as in five years ago.

I forgave you when I met Jack.

The sentiment was nice, but Quinn's message still hit him like a punch to the gut. In the years since Jack had entered their family, Blake and Quinn had done their best to remain friendly and cordial for Seth's sake. Blake had manned up and become the kind of father Seth needed, because if he hadn't, Jack would have.

But no one ever discussed the affair. In small ways throughout the next several years, they'd become something of friends, but Blake never brought up Kira or Hunter and never asked Quinn if she forgave him for ruining their lives. Then again, he hadn't so much ruined her life as set her free to find Jack.

Why couldn't it work the same way for him? Last night, he finally broke down and asked Quinn in the most passive manner possible—with a cowardly text message—if she'd forgiven him and did she believe he was a different man than the one who'd snuck into supply closets with another woman at the office.

Her first message: *I'd be proud to call you my husband today, Blake. Jack read that over my shoulder and frowned deeply, but he gets it. You aren't the same person you were. Please, for all our sakes, get over it and forgive yourself.*

He'd smiled, reading that. He'd spent a lot of time daydreaming of his old life. Quinn at his side, entertaining clients from the office with talk of her writing process. He hadn't been proud of her then, only glad she had some value in impressing his high-flying clients who were all Clementine Hazel fans. Quinn had been a decorative piece, pretty to look at and useful at times.

He'd been crazy about her for most of his life, but one day she faded into the background like gray wallpaper. He found himself not caring about the things she talked about or how she might feel. And that was before Kira came along.

Okay, so maybe his old life hadn't been all that great. It included an affair, a nonexistent relationship with his son, and a wall between him and his wife that kept him from seeing her completely. Sometimes, he found it easy to blame Quinn. She was smart and self-reliant, elegant and the coolest customer around, as smooth and poised as the loveliest swan. Kira had been exciting. Fun and intriguing. He never knew what she'd say next or where she'd want to go. She was a lot like—

An image of Sadie popped into his mind.

Damn it. Blake dropped his head on the desk, letting it fall heavily. He deserved the resounding smack of pain. He squeezed his eyes shut. How in the hell could Sadie still remind him of Kira? How could she have the best qualities of two polar-opposite women?

And how could he fall for someone so perplexing when he'd come all this way to get away from complication?

He lifted his head at the quiet knock on his door.

Kennedy poked her head inside. She didn't react to his position, head hovering close to his desk, or what had to be a big round red mark on his forehead. It still tingled from whacking against the desk. "Nina's ready for her meeting with you."

Blake sat up and straightened his tie. "Lovely. Send her in, please."

Kennedy nodded and disappeared.

Nina entered seconds later, closing the door behind her and shuffling over to take a seat opposite Blake.

He checked his notes and dove right in. "Good morning, Nina. I just have a quick question for you."

"Of course, hon. You go on and ask anything you need to."

Right. He thought carefully on how to phrase the questions so he'd garner more information than he gave away. "Amanda mentioned being in Duncan's office a while back. This would've been shortly after I was hired. You weren't at your desk at the time. Something about going out for coffee?"

Nina nodded seriously. "That's right. The coffeemaker upstairs went kaput, and Duncan was out. I knew he'd want a cup when he returned, so out I went to get him some from Pearl Street Bagels just down the road here. Have you been yet? They're fabulous. I could take you some time." She laughed and covered her heart with her hand. "Oh, but what am I thinking? You've got better offers than that, I bet."

Then she winked.

Blake longed to whack his head onto his desk again. Instead, he smiled benignly. "That'll be all, Nina. Thanks."

"You sure?" True concern scrunched her features. "Nothing went missing, did it? Mr. Perry's got some nice things upstairs. Antiques and such."

Blake gave her a reassuring smile. "Of course not. We're just trying to pin down some missing paperwork." In a manner of speaking.

She left and Blake rubbed the nape of his neck.

So far, he'd confirmed Duncan's office had been left unattended for a short time, meaning potential access to any number of company portals. The money could've bounced around from account to account and, in such small increments, it'd never get noticed. He had Amanda at the scene, and Amanda put Wes there. Blake needed something to give and break the case, because the paper trail had seemingly dead-ended.

Unfortunately, it stopped in exactly the right place to implicate Amanda. The more the evidence pointed to her, the more certain Blake became that it was intentional. Then again, the money never lied. And it definitely didn't disappear without a trace. Yet, no withdrawals matching the missing funds were in any of the balance sheets or reports he'd gone over so far.

By the time Wes arrived for his turn at questioning late in the afternoon, Blake had a headache blooming in his left temple, and the numbers on the numerous printouts he doggedly perused had blurred into a mass of sticks and squiggles, no longer holding meaning.

Wes wore an amused smirk.

Did he know why he'd been asked to Blake's office? Perhaps the time had come for laying out the cards. Blake didn't have the time or, frankly, the inclination to get prior approval from Duncan or Mrs. Avery.

He sat forward and clasped his hands together, studying Wes over the ridge of his interlaced fingers. "I don't find much funny about embezzlement, personally." He shrugged. "But if it amuses you, I'd like to hear more."

The asinine smile fell away. Wes's throat bobbed with a great nervous swallow. "I-I thought this was about Sadie." He leaned toward Blake, suddenly nervous and unsure. "You're saying someone is stealing from Avery & Thorp? That's..." His eyes widened, and he glanced beyond Blake at the far wall. "That's absurd. There's not a single person I would point the finger at." He blinked rapidly and met Blake's gaze once again.

Blake nodded solemnly. "That's part of the problem. No one seems to have a personal financial motive, and the paper trails dead-ends in a... Well, we'll call it an unlikely location, more apt to be a red herring than a true indication of who's responsible. For some reason, Amanda's being targeted as the culprit." Blake watched Wes carefully for his reaction.

He squinted in concentration, then snapped his fingers and sat back as though he'd managed to figure it all out in three seconds of passing consideration. "Sadie," he said simply.

Blake didn't laugh, but he did sigh. "I doubt it."

"Why? Because you're into her?" Wes's eyes were like pools of tar.

Blake didn't know how Sadie could've stood a relationship with this guy, when mere eye contact elicited an *ew* from Blake's inner voice. "It's not for you to question the audit director, Mr. Black."

Wes blinked and backed down, glancing sheepishly at Blake's desk.

Nothing like pulling rank to remind a mere accountant where he sat on the totem pole. "I understand you were in Mr. Perry's office during a time when he was not. Nina was also not at her desk. May I ask what you were doing?"

Again, Wes swallowed nervously. "It's not what it looks like. I wasn't alone—"

"I'm aware Amanda entered the office behind you. And what it looks like doesn't concern me nearly as much as what it actually was." He stared at Wes, openly waiting for an explanation.

Wes licked his lips. "Fine. I was looking for clues, okay? It was right after Duncan announced his resignation and the Castley account was assigned to Catalina. This was maybe a week or two later. I didn't exactly mark it in my planner. Everyone was off to lunch, and I took a peek while Duncan was out to see if he'd made some note of possible candidates. I only wanted to know if I'd made the list."

Blake cocked an eyebrow. "Find anything useful?" He was playing hardball, but he had a sinking feeling in his gut Wes was telling the truth.

Wes inhaled deeply, stood, and pulled his wallet from the back pocket of his slacks. From it, he withdrew a tiny folded yellow note. He handed it over to Blake and sat again.

Three names, copied in Wes's looping style of writing.

"Congratulations," Blake offered, dropping the tiny note on his desk as though it meant nothing. Which it didn't. It had no bearing on the missing money. "You must've been thrilled."

"I owe you a certain level of respect, but don't patronize me, Mr. Cobb. You aren't happy for me. I'm sure you feel Sadie was more deserving than me." He looked somewhat put-out that he didn't have Blake's vote.

Time for a slight change in subject. "You said you thought this meeting had to do with Sadie. Elaborate on that." A personal matter, Blake didn't have the power to force Wes to explain a thing. However, the old adage went to walk into a room like you owned it—the same could be said for discussions. Blake assumed the information was his due.

Wes swallowed again. A lot of nerves for a guy Blake presumed innocent. He might need to reassess. "She may have mentioned to you that I said something about how I've seen you visiting her outside of work. At all sorts of odd hours."

Blake drummed his fingers lazily across his desk. "You're following her?"

A hint of shame crept into Wes's features. "I recently moved into the same apartment complex. I haven't told anyone. You'll have noticed they're not the nicest in town. Anyway, my living room view is of the parking lot. Sadie's car." He raised his gaze to meet Blake's squarely. "And yours, every time you drop by."

Blake smiled cordially. "That'll be all, Wes."

Wes offered Blake a wry, flat stare as he stood. He looked like he might throw one last comment over his shoulder as he walked out, but Amanda stormed in a second before he reached the door.

Her wild eyes were alight with an inner fire Blake had seen a time or two now. He braced for impact.

Fists clenched tightly at her sides, her rigid jaw hardly moved when she spoke. "A word, Mr. Cobb." Today, she wore a silvery body-hugging dress that stopped a fraction above her ankles, with a deep slit cut up the back, allowing her to walk. The casual T-shirt-style neck and sleeves kept it from looking like a ball gown, but it still gave the impression of unnatural height, and the heavy collection of bangles on her thin arms gave a touch of sophisticated power and dominance.

Like Quinn, she could own a room with her sense of style. Unlike Quinn, she didn't hide her anger behind a poised, stony glare that gave little away. No, Amanda's anger manifested as a warhorse she then mounted and rode to meet the enemy.

Wes's face had frozen in unveiled anticipation, black eyes darting between Blake and Amanda, eyebrows raised.

Blake pointed toward the door. "Good talk, Wes. I'll let you know if I need any further information from you."

Wes left, and Blake took the few seconds of distraction to contemplate his odds of survival in the next sixty seconds. Judging by the plumes shooting from Amanda's ears and her flared nostrils, they weren't looking too great. He should've updated his will last year when Quinn suggested it.

* * * *

Sadie wouldn't lie to herself and pretend she hadn't expected Blake's stiff, overly formal visit to her office. She'd actually been on her way to explain and apologize when Kennedy had informed her he was doing regulation auditing interviews. She doubted Kennedy knew what was really going on and didn't tempt fate by enlightening her. She'd already screwed up, letting Amanda figure out Blake had told her about the embezzlement scheme.

Another item on the list of perfectly legitimate reasons he had to glare at her stonily as he entered and closed the door behind himself. He didn't sit when she indicated a chair. He stood, hands clasped behind his back, those gorgeous hazel eyes pinned on her.

His ire enticed a low heat to sweep through her belly. She licked her lips. She couldn't tell him to stop regarding her like a displeased sovereign lord because it was turning her on.

Could she? She scooted up her to desk and eyed him head-on. "I'm sorry."

That seemed to do the trick, at least momentarily, as the fierce expression faded. "What?"

"I said I'm sorry. What, you've never heard an apology before?"

She guessed not, given the last few women in his life. From what she'd heard of Quinn, the woman had her pride. Probably wasn't easy to wrangle humility out of someone beloved by the whole country—Sadie included. She had a few Clementine Hazel novels sitting on her bookshelf at home. As for Kira, she didn't sound like the kind of person who was ever actually remorseful enough to apologize, the kind of person with a hazy excuse for everything.

Blake's green and brown gaze scrutinized her deeper than they ever had, raking over her face like they were trying to find something. They were so vividly bright, the kind of hazel that made her want to contemplate the actual numerical ratio of jade to gold.

The connection hit Sadie. "She named herself after your eyes. Clementine Hazel."

He tilted his head, as though surprised with the turn in conversation. "Seth's, actually. When he was tiny, they were as green as hers. Her first attempts at a writing career were under the name Clementine Green."

Sadie frowned. "Doesn't quite have the same ring, does it?"

Blake glanced at the floor and back at Sadie. "You had no right to tell Amanda about my past with Quinn. Or Kira. Or Emily," he added pointedly, driving home each name like a nail.

She closed her eyes and let her head hang. "I know. I know and I'm so sorry, Blake. You'll never, ever believe me, but I thought I was helping. I stupidly assumed you'd told her. I only intended to explain that I think you're a good person trying to make up for bad decisions you made a long time ago. You're just…" She looked at him, trying to figure out how to say it right this time. "You're a good man, Blake. Your heart's where it's supposed to be, and I wish you could see that that's enough."

He took a few strides forward. His stance had relaxed, his hands no longer bound tightly behind his back but set loosely in the pockets of his slacks. He glanced at her from beneath enviable long lashes. "If you're wondering why I think I'm in love with you, you're welcome to repeat everything you just said."

The warmth of long-buried feelings and the heat of bone-deep attraction had her feeling like she'd stepped into a sauna. She couldn't seem to see past Blake's mouth, her thumb itching to tug his bottom lip to hers, especially with words like *love* slipping from between them so casually sincere. Sadie groaned and shook her head. "Gah, you're stupidly good-looking. It pisses me off. I can't tell whether I'm feeling emotions, or just a physical reaction to your perfect jawline."

He laughed and cast a shy glance at the floor. "It can't be both?"

"Stop smiling," she demanded, unamused. "You're making it worse."

His smile widened. Then he did the thing men do where they open their mouths and ruin everything. "Amanda caught you going through Wes's office." His raised eyebrows invited an explanation.

Abashed, Sadie took a deep breath. "You're clearly not looking into him as a suspect. What harm is there in me poking around?"

His face grew solemn, the smile but a remnant. This was Blake the audit director. "A good deal of harm can come from a vigilante approach. If I were interested in you as the embezzler, I'd have to consider you planted any evidence I happened to find. You have motive, and now you've had opportunity. I don't believe it, but Mrs. Avery's not interested in my gut feelings. It's even more difficult to take you seriously since you and Wes are pointing the finger at each other."

Her hand shot up. "Hold on, hold on. I thought this was all hush-hush."

Blake shrugged. "I made an executive decision." The lines of his face seemed to morph into granite as his gaze hardened. "Sadie, my personal feelings aside, I'm warning you. Do not impede my investigation. You'll make yourself look guilty and, by my favoritism, you'll implicate me as well. I wouldn't put it past Mrs. Avery to believe I'd shield you if I thought you were responsible."

The suggestion stunned her. "You wouldn't do that."

The granite softened, but his steady stare became more intense, like a fire burned behind his green-gold irises. "Truthfully? I don't know what I wouldn't do for you, Sadie."

Chapter 14

Sadie stood, wineglass held aloft like a queen's scepter, and addressed her subjects. "No judgment, no harassment, no rude remarks, and the first person to call me a home-wrecker gets the boot." She glared expectantly from Kennedy to Nina. "Are we clear?"

They glanced at one another before looking back at Sadie and nodding, Kennedy's obviously perfunctory agreement accompanied by an eye roll.

May they roll right out of your face. Sadie smirked as she took her seat. "Now, I need help."

Kennedy nodded enthusiastically at this, stopping only to sip her wine. "Bet your ass you do."

Irritated, Sadie snapped back at her. "Oh, shut it. I'm so tired of your crappy judgmental attitude. Blake likes me. Get the hell over it already."

Nina sat forward, the hand not holding a wineglass held up in a placating gesture. "Come on, girls. This is our relaxation night. If you're going to argue, I'm going home."

Sadie inhaled and exhaled, counting as she did so. "I am only asking for my *friends*"—she glared at Kennedy—"to give me some advice. I'm sorry I wasn't honest about my feelings for Blake. He was all up Amanda's butt, and your disapproval—yeah, I'm looking at you, Ken—was like a floor trap just waiting for me to take the next step. Besides, if I'd told you, it wouldn't have mattered, because until recently, he refused to acknowledge his feelings."

"Feelings," Kennedy interjected pointedly, "he only grew because you insisted on forcing yourself into his life. All those outings, all that time spent together. Don't deny you were hoping, Sadie. You want help? Have the stones to be honest."

"Fine!" She threw her hands up. Wine sloshed over the rim and onto her wrist. She ignored it. "Fine, fine, fine. Yes, okay? Yes, I dared to hope.

I dared to hope this really nice, funny, hot guy would like me. And now it seems he does, only he doesn't."

Nina and Kennedy wore identical confused expressions. Gathered brows, tilted heads, the whole shebang.

She knew how they felt. Disheartened, Sadie cooled down. "His entire relationship with Amanda was based on her likeness to Quinn. Physically, they're strikingly similar. I saw a photo in Blake's cabin, Quinn with Jack and her little girl, Maddie. It's eerie how much they look alike. Same hair, same eyes. Poised and sophisticated, blah, blah, blah. Blake was so determined he was getting a second shot at the marriage he ruined years ago, he looked past every single flaw Amanda has. Meanwhile, all this time, he's liked me. Sorry, Kennedy, I know how that bruises your damn ego. Anyway, I'm the new Quinn. If I sound bitter when I say that, it's because I am."

Nina shook her head sadly. "That's so wrong I don't know where to start."

"Therapy?" Kennedy suggested.

"He's finally decided to acknowledge this thing between us," Sadie continued, "but I'm afraid he's only in love with the traits I share with Quinn. What about the rest of me? What about my fears and my passions? My desires and how I like it in bed? That's not stuff I'm going to have in common with Quinn, and if I get into something with Blake, and he…" She sighed and shook her head. "I don't deserve to go through what Amanda went through, where Blake suddenly realizes I'm my own person and ditches me for the next Quinn twin to cross his path."

Nina frowned sympathetically and reached across to pat Sadie's knee. "Hon, that's ridiculous. Blake's been hanging around you for months now. Surely, he knows you're as different from his ex-wife as you are similar?"

"Yeah," Kennedy added, "and wasn't it your differences that kept him away to begin with?"

"I'm all for giving us a shot, but he whipped right past me, straight into the deep end." She licked her lips and blinked back moisture. What the hell was this? Frustration, maybe. "It'll never be easy for me. Every guy, every time. Maybe Blake doesn't have some secret destructive habit or freakish fetish, but he's definitely damaged goods."

Kennedy inhaled in the way that told Sadie one of her big speeches was coming.

Sadie shot a hand up to stop her and closed her eyes. "No, Ken, I don't need you to rail into me, okay? Obviously, in your eyes, I don't deserve Blake for whatever reason, but I don't need the abuse."

Kennedy cleared her throat and leaned forward to set her wineglass on the coffee table. "Actually, Sadie, I was going to reprimand you for something else. I'll do my best to be nice about it, but hear me out. All these guys—the dude in his van, the man with ankle monitor, the one with the drug problems—they all had reasons to be ashamed. I can't imagine it would've been easy to come clean to you, a gorgeous, sleek, put-together accountant with her life all in order. With each one of them, as soon as you found out their dirty secrets, you bolted. Not one of them had enough of your heart to make you stick around. How do you know they weren't trying? The guy on the ankle monitor was sober, right?"

"Not by choice," Sadie responded drily, tossing back a large swallow of wine.

Kennedy kept it coming. "The dude living in his van might've been saving up for an apartment. The guy with a drug problem could've seen you as a positive influence to help him change his life around. But you take one look at these mighty flaws, and you're done."

Sadie shot up and marched toward the sink. She tossed the remainder of her wine down the drain and rinsed her glass. If she drank any more, it'd be too easy to launch herself at Kennedy and strangle her. "Awesome. It's *my* fault they were all losers. Somehow, I'm not surprised you see it that way." She turned around, arms braced on either side against the counter. "But you know what? They hid things from me and lied about it. They came to me broken, and it's not asking too much to want someone whole for once. I didn't owe any of them a second chance."

Kennedy rolled her eyes again, this time flavored with a longsuffering groan. "Gah, you're so freaking sensitive! I'm not saying it was your fault. I'm saying you obviously didn't love them, genius. If you had, you wouldn't have walked away. You'd have stayed and helped them work through their demons. Blake has a demon, too. Its name is Quinn. And you can either walk away from Blake because he's damaged or help him excise the crap out of it."

Sadie glared at Kennedy and chewed her bottom lip until it hurt. That was one way to look at the situation. At least, she liked the idea of comparing the flawless, superlative Quinn to a demon.

"You think I love him?" she asked Kennedy quietly.

Nina regarded them with wide eyes, glancing from one to the other, like watching a tennis match.

Kennedy shrugged and relaxed into the sofa. "Probably, Sadie. You've mooned after him for months. You've heard his worst, and you're still here, right? Still caring what he thinks, concerned he loves you for reasons that have nothing to do with you. If you don't love him, you at least care about him, and that's close enough to consider if the relationship is worth pursuing, right?" She sipped her wine almost nonchalantly.

Sadie recognized a vague apology, the merest suggestion of acceptance, in Kennedy's spiel. "Kennedy, you're a real pain in the ass to be friends with, you know it?"

Her best friend grinned. "I'm worth it, though."

Nina held her glass up for a toast. "Since you brought the wine, I won't argue. Now, since that's finally over, anyone else interested in discussing the investigation?"

Sadie filled a plastic cup with water from the faucet and rejoined her friends.

It hadn't taken long for word to spread once Blake had spilled the beans to Wes about the investigation. Friday afternoon, the office had been a veritable beehive of activity, everyone moving from group to group in a fevered gossip-fueled frenzy.

Nina leaned forward and lowered her voice as though they were still at work and might be overheard. "The shouting coming from Duncan's office was like nothing I've ever heard in all my time at Avery & Thorp. I'll tell you what. I've never seen Mr. Perry so red in the face. Blake, though, to his credit, hardly blinked. He explained himself so quietly, I couldn't catch a word of it through the door. Your name came up plenty, though, Sadie. As did Wes's."

The embezzled funds didn't concern Sadie, but Blake getting in trouble for showing favoritism toward her during an investigation made her ten shades of uneasy. "Mrs. Avery had intended to keep it quiet," she explained. "But for some reason, Blake let it fly to Wes."

Kennedy narrowed her eyes and pondered the floor. "I have a hard time believing it's not a simple bookkeeping mistake. There's no one I can imagine stealing from the firm. We're all dedicated to our jobs. As for Amanda, the likely suspect, according to the gossip zooming about the office, tell me her motive, because I couldn't find it with a magnifying glass and a map."

Nina shook her head. "I certainly don't envy Blake the task of finding out."

Sadie cleared her throat. "Enough about that, then. Who else is wringing their hands over Wednesday's announcement?"

Duncan told them all Friday morning to expect Mrs. Avery, as well as the elusive and not oft-seen Mr. Thorp, Wednesday afternoon to announce the next chief accountant.

The question drew sympathetic looks from her friends.

Sadie waved them off and wished she hadn't dumped her wine. "I'm past it, guys. Really, it's fine. I've had time to adjust. I'm not going to walk away from my career to avoid Wes. I'll keep doing what I'm doing, which is working hard and sticking to my five-year plan. Besides, it's not like the Jackson branch is all Avery & Thorp have to offer. I'd accept a transfer if the opportunity came up. It's cheaper to live in Alpine, anyway."

Not that she'd be happy about the move. The action was in Jackson, but for her career, there was little she wouldn't consider.

Oh, no, there I go sounding like Kira again. Me and my awful ambition.

Kennedy sighed. "At this point, I don't care. I'm on okay terms with Wes. He'll be so busy trying to fill Duncan's shoes, I doubt he'll have much time for being a tyrant."

"Well, to show my professional aptitude in the face of adversity and disappointment, I've purchased a lovely bottle of cabernet sauvignon for the lucky victor," Sadie disclosed haughtily. "Whoever he may be."

Kennedy swirled the wine in her glass and grinned. "Wes hates red wine."

Sadie smiled back. "I know."

* * * *

Blake couldn't be happier to see the backside of Pearl Harris, and not because of the view. Since Amanda had stormed his office to accuse him of lying about his three wives and numerous affairs, and he'd stupidly corrected her—just the one affair, thank you very much—he'd become the sworn enemy of Amanda and her horde of bookkeeping cronies.

Neither Opal nor Pearl interested him as suspects. Their authorization came directly from Amanda, and they were both devoted to her. If they managed access, they wouldn't allow the trail to lead back to her. They'd have set someone else up for the fall. However, in the interest of fairness and keeping anyone from guessing which way his thoughts were leaning, he insisted on each employee visiting his office at least once for a benchmark interview.

Someone smart was behind this. And Blake had two people left to interview, both plenty intelligent if in different understandings of the word.

As Kennedy smartly entered his office and took a seat with a defiant lift to her chin and a steady gleam in her eyes, he didn't doubt for a second her street smarts were above par.

"Kennedy." He smiled warmly. "Just protocol. No need for the 'tude."

She relaxed a smidge. "If you say so."

Blake checked his notes. "First, what's your highest clearance for accounts?"

She looked like she might argue but went along, answering gamely. "A level below yours, Mr. Cobb. I can move files from the main company holding to your personal inbox and print balance sheets but have no access to account details, and transaction sheets in my window are locked."

Meaning she couldn't change figures like the senior accountants were able to.

"There was a small window of time a few months back, early to mid-November, when Duncan's office was left unattended." He handed her a timetable he'd printed out, with the movements of a few other key employees for reference. "It was shortly after Duncan announced his resignation. Anything stand out to you during that time? You probably notice quite a bit from your view in the bookkeeping parlor."

Kennedy took her time studying Blake's carefully considered timetable.

No one seemed to be able to pin down the exact day this had all occurred. Duncan had no lunch meetings scheduled, and Nina hadn't made a note of the broken coffeepot in her daily planner. Amanda always stayed in the office for lunch. The only shining detail was that Wes had stayed for the lunch hour, a rare occurrence.

Finally, Kennedy glanced at him with a small nod. "I do recall the day Wes stayed for lunch. I thought it was odd, because not only did he stay, but he didn't eat. He skipped lunch altogether and hasn't done it before or since. And yes, I was here that day, because we were still working through Henry's old mess." Her back straightened. "I worked quite a few lunches those first six weeks."

Blake had to smile. "I know you did, Kennedy. Remind me to buy you a beer sometime."

That seemed to pacify her. Her shoulders relaxed. "That's all I can tell you, really. If Wes went upstairs, I didn't catch him at it. Nina came and went, with a stack of manila file folders, getting copies made next door, since the copier kept acting up. Now"—she held up a lone finger—"Amanda did go up, but that's standard procedure, since the hardcopy employee files are kept upstairs, and Mrs. Avery requires a physical copy of all payroll activities for auditing purposes. Government auditing," she amended. "You know, IRS and tax stuff."

"Sure." Blake nodded. He made a note.

Catalina was his next visitor. It struck him he'd managed to completely ignore and avoid, without trying, the most attractive woman in the office. She looked like she'd been dipped in a vat of caramel. Her skin was honey-colored and flawless, with the apples of her cheeks resting high on sharply defined bones, and lips plumped perfectly and painted a dusky shade of mauve, brilliant and eloquent against her glowing skin. Her eyes were bright and golden, marked hazel by only the faintest specks of dark hunter green.

The very standard of beauty.

And yet, Blake preferred Sadie. He'd been a leg man most of his life, but there was something to be said for standing next to a short woman, who had to tilt her head back adorably to look up and meet his gaze. With the passage of winter, he'd discovered her eyes were the exact same shade as the dark snow that got plowed to the sides of the roads, darkened by dirt and road gravel. Not the most poetic description, but the shadowy gray matched her eyes near exactly.

Her hair, despite its similarity to Kira's, seemed playful instead of severe, because of the strands she perpetually tucked behind her ears. She had a fullness to her face and a mean, lean body from her interesting and varied activities outside work. How would he ever keep up with her? Last week, she'd mentioned ice skating and rock climbing. His first thought had been to finagle himself an invitation to join her. He wanted to do it all. He didn't want to miss a thing.

Catalina adjusted her blazer, and Blake focused on the matter at hand.

"This'll only take a moment," he assured her.

She smiled politely. "Shoot."

Ten minutes later, Blake settled back into his chair and chewed on the end of his pen. Finally, a picture had begun to form. He hadn't been looking in the right direction. All he could do now was hope he was wrong as he redirected his efforts toward a most unlikely suspect.

* * * *

The bookkeeping parlor pulsed with the frantic energy of every employee in the office crammed into the space. Most stood, while others, like Opal and Pearl, sat comfortably at their own desks.

Kennedy's desk had been commandeered by Mrs. Avery, who leaned against one side, and Duncan, who stood in front of it to address them all. Mr. Thorp was a thin, looming figure in the back. He had a gaunt face stuck in an expression of distaste. Kennedy had gone over to stand by Sadie, who watched the proceedings from the doorway of her office with something between a scowl and a smirk.

Mrs. Avery studied them all openly, including Blake, while they pretended they didn't notice her scrutiny.

Blake had offered her a friendly handshake when she first arrived. It had shifted the power somewhat. Mrs. Avery must've imagined he'd be nervous after what had transpired with Amanda. But the more time

Blake had to think on it, the more he resented the involvement in his personal affairs.

Duncan didn't need to clear his throat and smile disarmingly to get everyone's attention; he had it in spades, as most were too afraid to stare at Mrs. Avery or dare look too long at the imposing visage of Mr. Thorp.

"Hello, everyone," Duncan said. "Thank you for arriving a few minutes early for our announcement. I'd like to take this opportunity to thank you all. I couldn't have asked for a better team of people to work with day in and day out. You made my job a joy and a challenge." He nodded and laughed at someone's sarcastic remark. "The best kind of challenge, I assure you. Mrs. Avery is going to announce who'll be stepping up to take on the position as chief accountant for the Jackson office, whom we've informed beforehand. As you all know, my last day is a few short weeks away."

Blake quickly glanced at Wes, whose eyebrows had furrowed in confusion, and had to smile. Blake had guessed correctly, after all.

The third name on the list.

"We'll also be announcing a few other staffing changes you can expect in the weeks ahead," Duncan added, before thanking them all again and stepping off to the side.

Everyone clapped politely, even Sadie. She winked at Blake, and he turned back to catch Mrs. Avery glaring at him. He refused to let his smile fade.

Mrs. Avery's inherent power seemed to freeze the whole room, as though no one dared breathe until she offered them a jaunty little wave and a smile meant to put them at ease. It worked. Blake caught a few relieved smiles. Wes still seemed deep in puzzled thought.

"Many thanks," Mrs. Avery began in her clear, concise voice, "for making this such a difficult decision."

A sprinkling of hesitant laughter.

"It's the mark of an outstanding staff when there's no easy answer to filling such a critical role in our company. It's wonderful to have so many excellent, trustworthy candidates, and a pleasure to get to know some of you better throughout the course of the process. I hope you'll all join me in welcoming Catalina Trujillo into the upper folds. Darling?"

She held out a hand, and Catalina, beaming and blinding in her happiness, stepped forward to shake it with fervor. The office broke out in pleasantly surprised applause.

Blake spied Sadie grinning, the delight at not having to work for Wes beating out envy or shock at having a junior accountant swoop in and steal the promotion. Wes cursed.

Just wait, pal. It gets better.

Faces were more open, less strained. It wasn't a stretch to imagine the tension between Sadie and Wes had imprinted itself on to the atmosphere of the office the past several months, and now it was over.

Mrs. Avery cleared her throat, and the room grew silent once more. "I have one more announcement to make. A few other changes are coming to Avery & Thorp. Wesley Black and Amanda Avery will both transfer to Alpine, trading with staff members in that office whom we believe will make a stronger team here at our Jackson branch. The two of you may find me in Duncan's office for details."

Eyes popped out of heads all around. Sadie gasped, hand over mouth, and her gaze darted to Wes, who appeared more puzzled than ever, and perhaps slightly panicky. Amanda's head hung and her shoulders drooped. Blake guessed she'd known about the surprise announcement. He grinned. So had he.

As the crowd broke apart at the meeting's conclusion, Blake silently followed Sadie as she attempted to escape into the sanctuary of her office. Kennedy winked as he passed by, and he caught up in time to catch the door with his foot. He peeked inside as Sadie lowered herself behind her desk.

"Don't just stand there," she told him shortly. "Come in and shut the door. The babbling out there is giving me a headache."

He did so and stayed standing as she shuffled distractedly through a colorful few files on her desk. "I thought you'd be happier about Wes's transfer."

"I am," she agreed tiredly. "But I'm bummed I lost out to Catalina. A *junior* accountant, of all things."

Should he explain? He decided Sadie could handle it. "You and Wes, your little rivalry... It's been noticed. To the point, in fact, that both Duncan and Mrs. Avery felt you were both too preoccupied by one another. You have to admit, you've been somewhat caught up in your personal life lately. We all have, actually. All but for Catalina. Duncan gave her the Castley account you and Wes wanted so badly as an audition of sorts. She's been taking classes, working late, and actively pursuing new clients in her time off instead of fishing and collecting firewood." He smiled at Sadie. "Not that I'd wish it any other way."

She smiled back. A little sadly but accepting. "Yeah, I can't really regret that stuff, either." She paused, reached into one of the deep drawers of her desk, and retrieved a bottle of red wine. "The funny thing is, I bought this cabernet sauvignon for our new chief accountant, knowing Wes only drinks white wine. Coincidentally, it's Catalina's favorite, a useless tidbit of information I gleaned over years of office small talk. In a story, they'd call that foreshadowing." She plunked the bottle onto her desk. "How does Wes feel about his transfer?"

"Unhappy, I'm sure," Blake answered with a frown. "But there's a pretty hefty penalty for bullying. It was transfer or step down to Catalina's now-vacant position of junior accountant."

Her nebulous gaze slammed into his. "What are you talking about?"

"I'm talking about Wes's sudden knowledge of your comings and goings. As well as his threat to tell everyone I'd been visiting you."

Her fine eyebrows formed a smooth, black V. "How could you possibly know about that?"

"When I interviewed Reba last week, I may have insinuated I knew more than I did about her relationship with Wes. Out of fear she'd been fingered as our thief, she spilled her guts. I learned Wes threatened you with some vicious rumors recently. I might've ignored it, because my concern is the missing money, but then she went on, quite disgustedly I'll add, to say he'd actually attempted to use the leverage to score a date with you. He'll be attending a sexual harassment seminar in the spring."

Sadie scratched her head. "I still don't know what he really wants from me."

Blake had an idea. "Same thing I wanted from Quinn, probably. Another chance to get it right. The only difference between Wes and myself is I took no for an answer. It's looking like it was probably the right thing to do, after all."

"Oh, there's much more than that setting you and Wes apart," she assured him with feeling.

"I appreciate you saying so." He headed for the door. "We'll catch up more later, Sadie. I have to go arrange a meeting with Mrs. Avery for the three of us." He grabbed the doorknob and turned back to catch her mouth drop open from surprise. "Oh, and to tell Duncan who our thief is."

Chapter 15

"I don't know if I should do this." Sadie wrung her hands and peered out the passenger window of Kennedy's old Subaru.

Her friend groaned. "You dragged me out of bed for moral support, which you've never needed in all the years I've known you. Just go in there, say whatever the hell it is you need to say so you can look at yourself in the mirror tomorrow, and let's go get a breakfast burrito already. I'm starving."

"You're always starving. And anyway, it's ten to nine. They'll quit making breakfast burritos before we're done here."

"You're short because you didn't eat enough as a child," Kennedy sniffed. "Also, you're wrong. They make breakfast burritos until ten."

"I'm short because my mother liked little men."

"I don't know what I'm supposed to say to that. But if you don't go inside, we're leaving."

"She might not even be home." It bolstered Sadie's spirits to think her knock might go unanswered. "The parking is in the rear. For all I know, she's in Alpine."

"It's Thursday." Kennedy's voice betrayed her waning patience. "We have the morning off, Sadie, not the whole dang day. Now, quit stalling. Besides, didn't Duncan tell you she'd be home packing?"

Sadie was torn between laughing and flinching. "He did. But I like to think he's wrong sometimes."

Kennedy gripped the wheel and closed her eyes. "Three, two—"

Sadie flung herself from the car. "Fine. I'm going." She slammed the door shut and flipped Kennedy the bird as she walked up to Amanda's door.

She didn't want to be here. Not even a little. But at the same time, a feeling of guilt had settled into her bones. She felt responsible for everything that had changed, including Amanda's transfer. Since she'd left work early yesterday, before Sadie could pin her down and try to apologize one last time, she had no choice but to ask Duncan for the time off to track her down before she left town.

Sadie bit her lip, pain spurring her into action, and banged her fist on the door. She remembered the doorbell at the last second.

Amanda's face flushed a light pink when she swung the door open and stared out at Sadie. She frowned.

"Sorry," Sadie mumbled.

Amanda's face relaxed but only by a slight degree. "What do you want?"

"One last shot at telling you I'm sorry." Sadie refused to wring her hands or slouch her shoulders. She stood tall, with a proud lift to her chin. "I know how it must look, with Blake suddenly deciding he's into me. I just need you to know nothing ever happened between us. Still hasn't, actually. I can't explain what clicked in Blake's brain that made him—"

"A dirty, cheating liar?" Amanda snapped. She had on a pair of white denim leggings and a ribbed gray tank top. The hand not holding open the door fisted on her hip. "What's more surprising is that he didn't settle for another affair."

Sadie borrowed a response from Kennedy and gave Amanda an impassioned eye roll. "I'm getting pretty tired of people saying that with total disregard for my morals. Never mind Blake, what about me? You think I'd do that?"

"No." Amanda's cavalier expression became something more compassionate. "I think he understood you weren't the type, but it's irrelevant. Understand, Sadie, he made his choice, and I'm glad for it. I don't believe people change. I dodged a bullet."

She almost laughed. "Of course people change. We change all the time. Consequences shape us, teach us who we are, who we're compelled to be. Blake's past is…" Unsettling? Unfortunate? Disparaging? Confusing? "Well, it's his past."

"You're not worried?" Amanda's gaze narrowed. "I believe once a cheater, always a cheater. What if he worked for another firm and met someone else who makes him think of the other woman he loves so much?"

Sadie's stomach turned over, but she quelled the unease with the thought of Blake's long-suffering remorse. "I don't know, Amanda," she admitted. She had hopes for Blake. More importantly, she believed in him. "I can't compare to Quinn, but I don't want to. Either Blake will figure out I'm immeasurable, or he'll continue to measure me using the wrong tool, and it won't work out."

That about summed up the bud of their relationship at this point. With the right care, it would blossom. Or it would get eaten by something big and hungry, like his ex-wife's ghost.

Shrewdly, Amanda studied her. "I hope you're right, Sadie. You were a good friend to me. I suppose I can't hold you at fault for Blake's issues. Besides, it's not sour grapes when I say I'm glad it ended before I found out about his past. Had I known from the start, I would've never gotten involved. You could've had him all along."

I did, actually. Where it counted. Wiser thought than said. "Yeah, well, whether we get together or not is yet to be seen. I'm not interested in trying to fill another woman's shoes. I've got my own pair, and they fit just fine."

"I admire you." Amanda stated it with an air of finality. "When I get settled into my new apartment in Alpine, I'll have you down for the weekend. You can help me plant the huckleberries Mother's letting me transfer from the ranch. They won't bear fruit until August, but I make a decent jam. Also, I should apologize for suspecting you of stealing from the firm. I knew it wasn't you, but I wanted it to be."

Sadie grinned at her candor. Well, well. She and Blake weren't in the clear—they had a meeting with Duncan and Mrs. Avery tomorrow—but at least she had managed to repair her odd, unforeseen friendship with Amanda, and that counted for quite a bit.

Her elation lasted until Wes came up behind Amanda and slid a hand around her waist.

Sadie stared at it, not able to make sense of what her eyes were telling her brain.

Wes followed her gaze and smirked. "Weird, right? You think you know someone, work alongside them for years, and one day you look up and realize you've never really seen them before."

Amanda turned her head and smiled at him.

Sadie tried to reign in her skyrocketing brows and ground-scraping jaw. "Th-that's great." A boyfriend swap. Fantastic. Maybe Blake could show up and make it a real party. "I guess I'll, uh, go then." She hooked a thumb toward the driveway and took a step back. "Kennedy's waiting in the car."

Wes stepped over the threshold and spoke to Amanda over his shoulder. "I'll walk Sadie to the curb."

"Okay. See you, Sadie. Thank you for coming by. It means a lot that you want to repair our friendship, despite everything."

"Of course." Sadie smiled. A weak thing, but she did her best. "See you around."

Amanda waved her fingers and closed the door, leaving Sadie and Wes alone on the small front porch.

He peered at her from under dark lashes. His eyebrows had grown in a little. Actually, they needed a good plucking, but she wouldn't be the one to tell him. He was Amanda's problem now. "Why do you seem so surprised to see us together?"

"I guess the two of you never occurred to me." She narrowed her eyes, recalling a small moment. "Although, you sort of did once but in a tongue-in-cheek way I never put much stock into. It does make a profound sort of sense. Is this a recent development?"

"Are you asking if I got with Amanda behind Blake's back?"

She'd been thinking more along the lines of the missing money. Had Amanda and Wes been working together all this time? "I guess I'd be curious to know if that was the case," she said instead. Blake seemed to have the embezzlement handled. Sadie wouldn't stick her nose into it again. Besides, it wasn't as though Wes would spill all his secrets if Sadie said please.

For the first time in a very long time, Wes's smile came close to the genuine article. His real smile; not the nasty, sneering one, or the cocky one, or the one he wore when he was silently judging her and wanted her to know it.

She peered at him. "I haven't seen that smile in ages."

He toed an imaginary spot on the concrete that was as smooth and flawless as the rest of Amanda's dwelling. Sheepishly, he met Sadie's gaze. "I offered to help her pack since we're both making the move down to Alpine. We were stacking dishes into a box and something between us clicked into place." He shook his head. "Unlike anything that's ever happened to me. It was like I'd never noticed her before." One eyebrow rose sardonically. "I was too busy staring at you."

Sadie hooked her thumb into the loops of her holey jeans and chewed her lip. Was it possible to find a touch of closure right here and now? Walk away from Wes with a garbled chapter of her life closed at a satisfactory end?

"Wes... Tell me, why were you so keen to get back with me? I'm not trying to poke or prod or make this uncomfortable, but it seems we're on the cusp of an understanding."

He took a moment, studying the ground beyond the porch. "I guess if I want a clean attempt with Amanda, I should break free from the old crap weighing me down." He inhaled and looked at Sadie. "I do blame you."

It was like a slap to the face. Sadie reeled emotionally and physically, taking a step back from Wes and his penetrating gaze. She hadn't imagined he still had the power to hurt her, but her heart seemed to crack open in her chest. "How could you think I'd hurt my own baby to escape you?"

"I don't want to blame you." In his face, an apology dawned like an old wound reopened. "I wanted another chance with you, because I was certain I'd eventually let go of those old feelings if we were together again. If *we* healed, I'd heal. And if you still loved me, I couldn't possibly keep blaming you. I'm sorry, Sadie. I wish I didn't feel like this. It's hard to love someone you feel deep in your heart has betrayed you."

Sadie's breath caught on her explanation. "I lost the same thing you did. And I carried the guilt like an anchor around my neck for a long time."

He nodded, looking miserable. "I know. I made it easy, shoveling all the blame your way. But I can't help how I feel, Sadie. I still can't escape the idea that you were happy to have an excuse to end our relationship."

"Well, that sucks. I don't know if this counts much for closure, but thank you for being honest with me, at least."

"Have a nice life, Sadie."

She turned her back. She didn't know or care if he waved or watched her go. Shakily, she trudged through the freshly falling snow and climbed back into the Subaru's passenger seat.

Kennedy leaned over and gripped her knee. "Are you all right?"

Sadie blinked. Her eyes were dry and stinging. "Closure isn't the magically cleansing event I always imagined. More like cauterizing a wound with whiskey and fire."

Kennedy patted her leg and checked over her shoulder for traffic. "You have to get a grip on reality, my friend. No one ever said all endings were happy. In fact, most of them suck righteously."

Sadie nodded and was surprised to find the sentiment a soothing one. "Yeah, I guess you're probably right."

"You know what else I'm right about?"

Sadie grinned. She didn't even have to guess. "Breakfast burritos are served till ten. Yeah, I know. I was stalling for time."

* * * *

Sadie's personal dealings with Iris Avery were few and far between. There'd been her hiring interview, which had gone smoothly. Later, there had been an inquiry into a missing file, which Sadie had been called upon to answer for. They'd found it, quite accidently moved to the wrong client's portfolio, and Sadie faced no permanent action on her record for the slip up.

This meeting was something else entirely.

She understood from the get-go she'd be doing more listening than talking. Her presence seemed to be more of a formality than a necessity, and she'd have given anything to bow out. If for nothing else, to escape Duncan's disappointed glances and Mrs. Avery's open, searching regard, which she made no effort to hide or soften.

This is how lab rats feel.

Sadie's throat was dry, but she didn't want to call attention to herself by moving to get a small paper cup from the dispenser not three feet away from her chair. They were all seated at the big oval table in the upstairs conference room. Sadie settled in for the long haul, her back straight, hands folded demurely on top of the table.

Blake stood and spoke cordially to Mrs. Avery with an easy smile. "You'll forgive me if I address my personal concerns before getting down to the business at hand."

Where in the hell did this guy get his confidence? Then Sadie recalled he'd *been* Mrs. Avery not long ago. Once a partner, always a partner.

He straightened his tie. "I apologize if I've offended you in my dealings with Amanda. Unfortunately, I didn't feel the relationship was working out."

Mrs. Avery rolled her shoulders and managed to appear bored. "Amanda may have struggled with your decision at first, but you'll be pleased to hear she's moved on." It didn't take an expert on body language to tell how unhappy the news made Mrs. Avery. She must already know of Amanda's new relationship with Wes. She didn't appear to like it one bit. She sat forward and glared at Blake. "I'll go out on a limb and assume you'd like to continue your blasé disregard for company policy in the interest of pursuing a romantic relationship with Ms. Felix. Is this correct?"

Sadie's internal organs cartwheeled. She almost came to her feet to protest. What about *her* permission? What the hell did a bunch of suits think they were doing, deciding her fate?

Then again, if she *did* want to travel that particular path, it would certainly help to not have to hide it from coworkers and bosses.

Blake's only sign of nerves was the quick glance he cast at her, which managed to say plenty in lieu of words. *Trust me.* He smiled at Mrs. Avery. "We're not asking permission."

Sadie's mouth fell open at the same time as Duncan's. They glanced nervously at one another, but neither dared interrupt as Blake continued.

"I'm afraid I'd take it rather personally if you objected. Surely, you're aware of the many breaches of policy within the Jackson branch. Wes

Black and Reba Garcia were involved for quite some time recently, as were Wes and Sadie at one point, a fact which you knew upon his hire. I assume you're already making the same allowances at the Alpine office, given how Amanda and Wes show no signs of keeping their new acquaintance quietly under wraps." He stopped and laughed quietly. "Wes's name just keeps popping up, doesn't it? The company's ladies' man."

Sadie's cheeks warmed. She wanted to smack Blake. She also wanted to hug him, kiss him, and take him somewhere, like the backseat of her pickup. She couldn't believe he'd go to bat for her. For them.

Blake seemed to have run out of things to say. He unbuttoned his blazer and sat next to Sadie, an amused grin alight on his face, eyes dancing with silent laughter.

It was a long time before anything happened. Water gurgled in the dispenser in the corner. Heated air whispered through the floor vents. Duncan's shoes scraped softly against the carpet as he shifted uncomfortably. Sadie noticed how he blended into the deep brown walls with his russet-colored dress shirt and beige tie.

Mrs. Avery had reclined into her chair to nibble on her pen.

As for Blake, he didn't appear to be waiting. He'd given Sadie's knee a single, encouraging squeeze before reclining in much the same manner as Mrs. Avery, not flinching or bowing from her scrutiny.

Sadie felt like the only person aware of the tension in the room.

Finally, after what seemed an eternity, Mrs. Avery sighed and tapped her pen against the table. "Well, Blake, you've certainly given me much to consider. I've made up my mind, but it wouldn't be prudent of me to continue without asking if you're sure."

Sadie looked from one to the other. Sure? What did Blake need to be sure of? Of *her?* What kind of question was that?

Spurred by the scent of an insult flying right over head, Sadie spoke up for the first time. "I'm sorry I have to ask, but can someone fill me in on why this is such a weighty decision? I'm starting to take offense over here."

Mrs. Avery raised her eyebrows at Blake. "By all means, do the math for her."

It was a rude joke to make about an accountant, but Sadie made allowances. At this point, she just wanted an explanation.

He turned to Sadie, his smile gone. "Conflict of interest. I'm the audit director. The gatekeeper for every account held by this office—and for every accountant who manages them. In order for us to be involved personally, I'll have to resign."

Sadie's mouth fell open at the same time she berated herself for not figuring it out sooner. She'd been so wrapped up in herself, in what she might have to sacrifice, she'd given little thought to what Blake might be willing to give up. "You can't quit your job to date me. It's the most ridiculous thing I've ever heard in my life. I don't even know why we're having this conversation. Isn't there a thief running willy-nilly around Avery & Thorp as we speak? Priorities, people."

Amusement and unspoken words swam in Blake's gaze. "I'm not asking for your permission any more than I'm asking for Mrs. Avery's."

Sadie looked away. She'd get lost in there one day.

Mrs. Avery didn't appear overly amused by Blake's blunt speech. "It comes down to the matter of what to do with you, Mr. Cobb. Do I let you walk away from the firm, thus ridding myself of the problem altogether?"

"You could," Blake agreed, swinging his gaze to look at her. "But you won't want to once I hand you your embezzler, along with a map to your missing money."

With a resigned sigh, Mrs. Avery admitted defeat, leaving Sadie stunned by how masterfully Blake had negotiated the meeting. "Welcome to Avery & Thorp, Mr. Cobb," she said, with a wry glare. "I hope you enjoy your new role here as senior accountant. As for our replacement audit director, I'm tasking you with bringing Kennedy Hale up to speed. You claim she's ripe for the job. I expect you to help her prove it."

Sadie covered her mouth with her hands and stared at Blake like she'd never seen him before. Who *was* this guy? "Does Kennedy know?"

Blake's smile couldn't contain his pride, though there was evidence he was trying to fight it. "Not yet. You can tell her if you like."

"No, of course not." Sadie grabbed his arm, wanting to squeeze him. "You tell her. You're the one who deserves to be standing next to her when she unleashes her ungodly squeal of happiness. It's going to hurt. Your ears will bleed, and your skin will shrivel, but that's the price for helping some people."

Duncan broke in, exasperated. "Can you two at least wait until the meeting's over to start mooning at one another?"

"Sorry." Sadie straightened immediately, not daring to even peek at Mrs. Avery.

Duncan bowed his head. "Now, Blake, I think you've danced around it long enough. You asked me for time on Wednesday afternoon, and I gave you forty-eight hours. Time's up. We need a name, and we need proof."

Blake's hand slid into the briefcase at his feet and resurfaced gripping an aquamarine file folder. "It's all here." He pushed it across the table.

A heavy silence followed as Mrs. Avery went through each page of the file, handing them to Duncan for further scrutiny afterward.

Duncan shook his head at the third page and pinned Blake with a desperate look that caught Sadie off guard. "I can't believe it."

Blake shrugged. "I can. Call me jaded."

Duncan cast a pained glance at Sadie that troubled her. It couldn't be Wes, after all, or Blake wouldn't have let Mrs. Avery transfer him. It couldn't be Catalina, could it? Although, if Sadie had to *hope* it was anyone, who would blame her, really. After all, she'd still love to see herself behind Duncan's desk. But she had to be honest with herself. It was someone close to her, or Duncan wouldn't be giving her such a pitiful look as he slid a page toward her.

Sadie took a deep breath and scanned everything—places highlighted where the math didn't add up, unrecognizable account numbers, and finally a name. She dropped the page and glared sharply at Blake. "Nina? You're blaming Nina for this?"

He indicated the file. "There's evidence, Sadie. I'm sorry."

"But she couldn't have—"

"Access to Duncan's files? Access to the bookkeeping hardcopies, which made casting Amanda into question quite easy to do by rewriting the totals, then making clean copies to wipe out the evidence of tampering?"

Sadie couldn't believe it. Her friend. Nina had spent time in her home, laughed, and commiserated with her. "How did you figure it out? I mean, the trail's here." She picked up the page once more, her hands shaking. She took in the numbers, how they all added up, and stared at Blake. "But this isn't something you'd have accidently stumbled on to. How did you know to look into Nina's activities?"

"The day Amanda caught Wes rifling through Duncan's desk when he was out, Nina told me she left to pick up coffee because the coffeemaker broke, which is why she hadn't been here to catch Wes in the act—"

"Or prevent it altogether," Duncan added darkly, his face down, still studying page after page of Blake's report. His face was flushed a dull red, and his jaw locked in place like it'd been sown shut.

Blake continued, "I questioned Kennedy about that day, hoping she'd remember if anyone else managed to sneak upstairs. She mentioned Nina coming back to the office and heading upstairs. Only, she didn't have coffee. Kennedy remembers seeing Nina return with a stack of files from making copies next door. Manila files," he added, looking at each of them in turn. "Plain old manila file folders, the likes of which I haven't seen in this office since my first day on the job."

Sadie's breath caught. Reba's bright, flashy folders and sticky notes of every imaginable color. Of course. "They were Nina's personal copies. Weren't they? Copies she didn't want getting mixed up with the others."

"Or stored on the copier's memory." Blake shrugged sadly. "The copier acts up from time to time, so that's easy enough to believe, but when two office appliances create one convenient circumstance too many, it's a reason to look closer. I cross-referenced files that had red-flagged Amanda and worked back from there. Each one corresponds to a movement in Nina's second bank account. It actually belongs to her deceased mother. Instead of closing the account, she continues to use it as a means to launder the money stolen from the firm."

Again, Sadie was floored. "How could you possibly know that?"

"I asked for forty-eight hours so the sheriff's office would have time to issue warrants, which were granted immediately. The account's been frozen. Nina will have likely discovered it by now."

Duncan rubbed his forehead and began to pace. "We let her go to lunch. What do we do? Confront her when she gets back?"

Blake stood and re-buttoned his blazer. "This is no longer a private matter, Duncan." He nodded toward Mrs. Avery, who'd finished scanning the pages and watched Blake with mingled pride and wariness. "The sheriff will take her into custody at her home. I arranged it in the interest of her privacy. What you decide to tell your staff here is up to you, Mrs. Avery, but I didn't think you'd appreciate a public display of one of your most trusted employees being carted from the office in cuffs. It wouldn't look good to clients walking in the front door, I assure you."

It took five more minutes for Sadie and Blake to escape the conference room. Sadie flopped into her desk chair, sad, disheartened, and exhausted from the morning's revelations. Blake perched on the edge of her desk and pulled his tie loose.

"That was awful," she moaned in a small voice.

"Yeah." He looked at her pityingly. "I'm sorry. I wanted to tell you first, but my loyalty has to be to the firm. I hope you understand."

Sadie nodded. She did, actually, and she admired Blake for his professionalism. If only he'd always sported such dashing notions of fidelity.

He stood up straight. "Listen, I need to take care of a few things. You and I, we're not done. Not by a long shot. But when I come to you, it'll be with a clear conscious and a free heart. Expect me for Sunday dinner."

A clear conscious and a free heart.

Sadie's skin tingled at the promise implied, driven home by the fiercely hopeful contemplation written on Blake's face, like a hastily scrawled love note, quick and passionate. He had a hand on the door already, her prince dashing away to slay one last dragon before he'd dare take the princess. God forbid he let it rest; it might come back and steal his happy ending one day.

When had she become such a romantic?

She didn't argue with him. It wouldn't do any good, judging by the determined set to his shoulders. Instead, she settled for a small nettling. A little something to remind him what he'd traded Amanda in for, in case he'd forgotten. "Just don't show up expecting to need a fork. I hear there's a sale on those little frozen potato things at Smith's."

He cast her a parting grin over his shoulder. "No worries. I have deft fingers."

She was glad he left before her vivid imagination grasped on to the image of his deft fingers and what other use she might have for them besides potato bites.

Chapter 16

"What can you possibly have to say to me, Blake?"

He leaned back comfortably, his hands tucked loosely into his jean pockets as he contemplated Amanda. "Only an apology."

Amanda rested her hip against the doorjamb, crossed her arms, and peered at him with eyes that weren't quite as intriguing now that he knew what lurked behind them. Or rather, what didn't. "I've been getting quite a few of those lately," she remarked offhandedly.

Blake guessed Sadie would've come to see Amanda. Her courage to face a person she felt she'd wronged was part of the reason Blake was here doing the same—putting himself at the mercy of yet another woman he'd screwed over, albeit unintentionally.

"You deserve them. I never meant—"

"Oh, please." Amanda rolled her eyes. "Spare me. This apology is for your own sake. You carry around guilt like an accessory, Blake. I'm not sure you'll know who you are without it."

The rare insight unnerved him. "You can hold it against me if you want, I guess. However, I am sorry I didn't tell you about my marriages. You never asked. Just like I never asked about anyone from your past. I assumed we'd get there eventually. That's how most relationships work."

"Like you'd know," she deadpanned. "What does it say about you that Sadie knew what your girlfriend didn't?"

"Sadie picked and prodded until I told her just so she'd zip it." He wanted to smile at the fact now. He'd had her right there and hadn't realized it. "You know, she and I are friends at the heart of this thing. She's easy to talk to. She's fun, curious, and determined when she's after something. Not a bad friend to have."

The corner of Amanda's mouth quirked up and she glanced past Blake. "No. She's not. Friendly, helpful, loyal." Her gaze binged back to Blake, and her tone hardened. "Honest."

He understood it for a warning and figured he deserved it. He'd been honest with Sadie so far. Painfully and embarrassingly so. He planned to keep it up indefinitely.

"I suppose if I'm still going to be friends with Sadie, I'll have to eventually get used to hanging around you, as well?"

Blake shrugged. "Not necessarily." He couldn't imagine doing couples stuff like double dates and movie nights with Wes and Amanda. "I think you and Sadie do well enough on your own."

Amanda smiled thinly. "I don't forgive you, Blake. But I do wish you and Sadie the best. At least until you meet another pretty blond who reminds you of your first love." She backed into the house and went to close the door.

Blake waved and offered her a flat smile. "Actually, Amanda, thanks to you, I'll never again look twice at a woman who looks too good to be true. You're not the first woman I pursued on such simpleminded criteria. But you're definitely the last."

* * * *

Sadie almost couldn't bring herself to speak.

Duncan and Kennedy seemed plagued by the same grief. Nina had been a trusted friend, a personal confidant. Sadie had relied on her for advice and counsel, trusted her with secrets, even let her use the big wineglass occasionally. Countless nights, Nina had curled up on Sadie's sofa to talk about work and bemoan Wes. Side by side, right there with Sadie and Kennedy, meanwhile betraying them all.

They'd been let in on the contents of Nina's statement, the local police department having passed it on to Duncan for the formal internal inquiry, which Blake would spearhead in his final capacity as audit director.

Sadie sipped her iced tea. Beer seemed like a bad idea at the moment. It'd be easy to overdo it just to kill the awkward buzzing in her head and the anguish in her heart. "How could she?"

It came out as little more than a desperate whisper. It wasn't a random statement, a berating, but an honest question that burned her up inside.

Kennedy stirred the olive in her martini. "Money's like a drug for some people. In her statement, Nina claimed she 'borrowed' to pay off the debt she inherited from her mom, but she could've paid it back if she'd wanted. Instead, she discovered how easy it was to manipulate the paper trail from her position. Why stop? It's not like she had the prospect of a promotion to work toward. She was the top-dog secretary. Nowhere left to go."

"The stealing isn't what I'm talking about," Sadie clarified. "I want to know how you sit at someone's table, drink someone's wine, smile at their jokes, love them, and be there for them, all while carrying around this huge, hurtful secret. Ken, she was our friend."

She didn't like it, but Sadie couldn't help Blake's affair from popping into her mind. Had he spent his day with Kira, only to go home to his wife, hold her, and whisper his love in her ear? How many lies must he have told? Emotions faked, stories made up.

Kennedy shook her head in her doleful, judgmental way. "You're taking it personally, Sade. Nina didn't steal from you. Or me. She stole from Avery & Thorp."

"I don't care." Sadie refused to make a single excuse for Nina. "She might as well have reached her hand straight into my purse and snatched my wallet. That's what it feels like."

Duncan broke in for the first time. He slumped over the bar and stared at nothing. Of all of them, he had it the worst. He'd trusted Nina implicitly, would've vouched for her to the ends of the earth. "Our commitment to the firm is what makes it so easy to take personally. I liked Nina. I respected her. I felt truly lucky to have her. I'm more disappointed than anyone with what she's done. But her actions don't define her. Sometimes, good people make crappy decisions. That's all there is to it."

Sadie shook her head. "I disagree."

"Oh?" Duncan's eyebrows rose. "I guess that means Blake is taking a pay cut for no reason."

"Don't make this about Blake."

"If you'll make excuses for a guy you've known less than a year, you ought to extend the same understanding to one of your best friends. Nina stole money from Avery & Thorp for half the amount of time Blake spent being unfaithful to his wife. At what point does one merit your forgiveness, Sadie?"

She drummed her fingers on the bar as Kennedy and Duncan watched and waited for her answer. "I guess," she began slowly, trying to come to terms with the point Duncan made, "the difference would come down to remorse. And time. Blake has had years to change. Nina was a thief up until the moment she was caught this morning. Maybe in time, Duncan. But not yet. I can't forgive her yet."

Duncan left a short time later, his full beer untouched on the bar.

Kennedy sighed and tugged on one of her golden curls. "Seems like we're coming up on one of those curves in life, you know? Everything's about to change. Can you feel it, too?"

Sadie nodded. "Nina, Wes, and Amanda all gone from the office. We'll have a new boss and new coworkers." She glanced at Kennedy and winked. "A new audit director."

Kennedy's proud smile blossomed, and Sadie was happy to see it. "I owe Blake one. Speaking of your new flame, don't listen to Duncan. Blake is a good guy, his *personal* résumé notwithstanding. I'm glad you're going to give him a chance."

"I think you were right, Ken. About the other guys. The losers and idiots I kept falling for. Maybe they did see a relationship with me as some kind of new start. At least, this time, I won't be waylaid by Blake's big, dirty secret. And I think I've got the stones to stick it out." She rubbed her chin thoughtfully. "Wow, it sure feels weird to agree with you on something. No wonder I never do it."

Kennedy pressed her lips together and studied the long fingernails of one hand. "I guess I should apologize for being a jealous snot all the time. If it weren't for me, Blake might've been spared that awkward time he had with Amanda. Then again, he probably needed to figure her out for himself. Anyway"—she flapped her hand as if shooing away a fly—"I'll work on my issues. I have severe middle-child syndrome. I always feel underappreciated, left out, or overlooked."

Sadie snorted. "It's impossible to overlook you. You're wearing lime green eyeliner."

Kennedy batted her lashes. "It makes my eyes pop."

"Because they're trying to escape your face."

That earned Sadie a punch to the arm. "This is why we can't be friends."

"Wrong." Sadie punched her back. "This is why we're *best* friends."

* * * *

Blake considered insecurity a predominately female trait.

Women spent hours to make their hair just right, caked makeup onto their faces to hide the tiniest of imperfections, tortured themselves in heels to seem taller, and wore push-up bras to make their breasts seem bigger. They never accepted that what they had was adequate. It puzzled him whenever he stopped to wonder about it. He did so more often in his time with Kira, for she had cared far more about that kind of stuff than Quinn ever had.

In contrast, Blake—and most men he knew, with few exceptions—wore what shoes were the most comfortable, chose suits according to their fit, and underwear hardly registered as a concern so long as he remembered to wear them. The only thing he smeared on his face had an SPF label, and he'd never wasted a minute of his time stressing over the particularly deep wrinkle that had formed between his eyebrows as soon as he turned thirty-five.

He sat on the front stoop at Fox Watch, vainly attempting to count stars between the thick boughs of evergreens overhead, pretending not to notice Eric sniffing beyond the tree line, and marveled at his shot confidence.

This is how women must feel all the time. Like nothing is good enough.

Blake wanted to change everything about himself. He wanted to be wiser, kinder, and worthy of respect and trust. He wanted to be loved. If it were as easy as throwing on a pair of stilettos and combing his hair just the right way, well, hand over the four-inch heels and Aqua Net, ladies.

He chuckled to himself but stopped abruptly as Eric's nose crept from behind the closest tree trunk.

Small, black, and busy as it tested the air with quick, jerky sniffs. Finally, the little fox's head emerged, and he raised his snout.

Blake held on to the small piece of smoked chicken from his solo dinner. Tonight, Eric would have to brave the porch if he wanted the goods. It was probably some dumb caveman mentality still lingering in the ancient lobes of Blake's male brain, but a part of him felt like getting Eric to approach him—take food from the palm of his hand—would be the equivalent of strapping on a push-up bra. He'd strut around Fox Watch feeling like a million dollar bill.

That was the kind of confidence he needed to approach Sadie with tomorrow. In less than twenty-four hours, he'd have to explain himself, and she wouldn't like most of what he had to say.

But Blake was going to be honest, even if it meant shooting himself in the foot. He refused to make the same mistakes he made with Quinn and Emily. Had he been honest with Quinn about his waning interest in their relationship, maybe they could've gone to counseling or something. Maybe Kira would've never happened. And had he told Emily he felt obligated to return her love, love he didn't truly feel, they might've avoided their disaster of a marriage altogether.

Eric sniffed the air, the ground, and himself.

Blake smiled, afraid to laugh and frighten him away. He held the chicken in his open hand, hovering next to his bent knees. *Come on, little buddy. Uckle Bake wants to be your friend, not make slippers out of you. Come on.*

To Blake's astonishment and delight, Eric strolled out into the open, nose to the ground. He paused, glanced up, and stared at Blake with the curiosity of a cat. In reality, he was more like a small dog. Maybe foxes were nature's melding of the two species. Cat and dog, as one.

Blake didn't dare move. In the dark, with a pale moon beaming through a gape in the eaves overhead, he could make out Eric's form and most of the details as he inched closer, one small wary step at a time. Blake had imagined his yellow eyes would glow in the dark, but they were difficult to see, fringed by thick, black lashes, covering them like an awning.

And then it happened. As though Eric had simply made the decision and acted without questioning it, he loped forward, sniffed Blake's hand, and greedily snatched the chicken. He ran with it, stopping a foot away to check if Blake had pursued him.

Besides the grin stretching his face, Blake hadn't budged an inch.

The fox studied him curiously for a second before turning his back and devouring the lump of chicken.

A gasp from his right drew Blake's attention.

Eric's, too. The little fox froze, then darted into the trees as Sadie approached, her mouth covered with her hands.

"Oh, my God!" The excited whisper was akin to a shout trumpeting into the quiet woods, spearing through the bubble of calm. "I wouldn't have believed you if I hadn't seen it with my own eyes. You did it. You fed Eric!"

Blake stood to greet her. "Where's your truck?"

She hooked a thumb over her shoulder. "Down the road a little bit. I parked at your neighbor's. I didn't want to chance it with the recent snow. My truck tires are looking a little shoddy."

He made out the wool cap on her head, the ends of her hair curling out on the sides from being tucked behind her ears. In a thick pea coat and heavy wool scarf wrapped multiple times around her neck, she looked cozy. A pang of longing for simple affection made his heart contract. He wanted to wrap his arms around her and bury his face in the crook of her neck, take in her scent, and feel the scratch of wool against his cheek.

Instead, he tucked his hands into his pockets. Even after enticing a wild animal to eat from the palm of his hand, he still wasn't ready for Sadie. He'd have to do more than sit still and appear nonthreatening for weeks on end to earn her trust.

He offered her a lame, limp smile. "I was just preparing myself for tomorrow."

She came close enough for him to see her smile. "What's to prepare for? It's only dinner."

If she wanted to come at this lightheartedly, she was going to be disappointed. Blake couldn't fake levity when everything was on the line. His future, his happiness—his redemption. "I need time to get my thoughts in order," he answered, solemn in response to her teasing.

Her smile faltered and she reached for his arm. "Blake, this isn't a make-it or break-it situation. We have all the time in the world to figure each other out. All I need from you is a shot at being myself before you decide you only want Quinn. Maybe I can change your mind." She shrugged and looked over his shoulder, not meeting his gaze. "Maybe not. We'll try, and if it doesn't work, no harm, no foul."

He almost laughed as he gathered her to him. "You're so wrong. It's kind of cute."

She struggled and stepped back from him, a hard set to her jaw. "Don't call me cute. Short doesn't mean cute, and there's not a damn thing cute about what I said."

"Sure there is. I think it's cute you believe I'll settle for trying when I'm determined to succeed. Sadie, I meant it when I said I'm in love with you. I have some things to say, and some of it is probably going to piss you off. Or make you doubt me. Or ruin everything before it even begins, but if that's the cost of candor, so be it."

"Oh, Blake."

He had no trouble making out her sad gaze in the semidarkness. And if he had, her tone would've clued him in.

"You're gonna screw up everything, aren't you?" she asked. "At some point, I'm going to have to conclude it's intentional. You purposely go through life destroying every chance at happiness you get. Maybe you do need a therapist."

Little arrows shot into his chest; each one a tiny zinger. "Maybe," he agreed, clearing his throat. "Let's go inside."

"Let's not. You can turn on the porch light if you want, but I'm sitting down right here. That way, I can leave without the awkward exit. With my luck, the doorknob will jam, or the hinges will stick from the cold. I'll be huffing and angry and yanking on a door that won't open. You'll laugh, and I'll throw something at your head. It snowballs from there."

"If that's what you want, that's what we'll do." He turned away so she wouldn't catch the grin threatening to sprout and trekked to the front door to reach inside the cabin and flick on the pale yellow bulb mounted to the eave over the porch.

A flash of the reflective eyes of a fox surprised him. Eric was still prowling around, curious and hopeful.

Sadie sat on the porch near where Blake had been earlier.

His nerves hummed as he joined her.

"Well," she said into the quiet, "get on with it, Blake. Jab away at this nice shiny new thing we have. Poke holes to your heart's content." Her head was turned away from him.

Steeling himself, he said the words he hated before they ever passed his lips. "You are like Quinn."

Sadie's shoulders went rigid, but he made no other response.

He was glad he couldn't see her face. "You're impeccably loyal. You're not afraid to stand up to a bully like Wes. You work hard. You're funny. All of these things you have in common with Quinn, and each one is a trait I admire. But…" He put a hand on her shoulder and gently encouraged her to look at him.

She did, with a guarded expression and pinched mouth.

"But," he said again, tracing her jaw with his index finger and idly studying her mouth, which was most unlike Quinn's in a very good way, "you're also like Kira."

Sadie's eyes blazed furiously.

Blake charged onward. "You're spontaneous and interesting and fun. I never know what you'll want to do next. You make me imagine a world with infinite possibilities. Once, you asked me what I did for fun. The answer is, whatever you ask me to do, Sadie. I want to go. I want to ice skate and fish on a frozen lake and chop my own firewood with a chainsaw named Lambert."

At this, something that might've been a smile in wait lurked behind her keen, smoky gaze. It was like clouds parting for a thin beam of sunlight. It made him hopeful.

He dared a smile. "Finally—"

She briefly closed her eyes. "If you compare me to one more woman, I'm out of here."

"Finally," he repeated, "You're like neither of them. You have an oomph and drive that Quinn lacks and a compassion and graciousness that somehow peacefully coexists with your ambition, forever setting you apart from people like Kira, who was a manipulator and a user. And Quinn, she bored me." His hands went up defensively, despite no one around to take offense. Maybe he just couldn't believe he'd said the words out loud. "She's boring," he said again, this time more confidently, more certain in his honesty. "Maybe not to Jack, who has personality to spare, but to someone like me, who apparently needs to be entertained and dragged out of my comfort zone. So much of what went wrong in my past is my own fault. I'm not blaming Quinn or making excuses, but that's the truth of the matter. I was bored. I would've stayed bored. The last piece of the puzzle comes down to one fundamental difference—one thing that definitively sets you apart."

Sadie's expression softened into an inscrutable mask. Probably hiding her emotions in case he said something irrevocably stupid and truly ruined everything.

He wanted to tell her to breathe. To trust him. He tucked his finger under her chin and ran his thumb over the smooth skin of her jaw, his gaze torn between her captivating eyes and her seductive mouth. "You're Sadie Darling Felix, and you are worth a million Quinns."

He dropped his hand and took a deep breath. Time for the final act.

From his pocket, he withdrew the ring he'd kept in the canister on his desk, showing it up in the light for Sadie to see. "I've kept this. My first wedding band. The one Quinn gave me." Without further pontificating, he hurled it into the dark woods.

Sadie watched it fly, her head following the arc it made as it left his hand and landed with a soft thud several yards away. She looked at him with wide eyes. "Was that hard for you?"

Blake shrugged one shoulder. "Impossible until I met you."

With a tremulous smile, she scoured his face and blinked away moisture gathering at the corner of her eyes. "You're saying you don't want Quinn anymore? You're sure? I get the big symbolic gesture, but if there's any doubt—"

"I'm sure." He squeezed her hand. "After all this time, I finally broke down and asked her if she'd ever forgiven me."

"Did she?"

"A long time ago, but that's irrelevant. Because I realized something. Her forgiveness didn't mean anything to me. She suggested I forgive myself, but even that isn't what matters. The only opinion that counts is yours. If you believe in me, then I can believe in myself."

Sadie scooted closer and tilted her face to his. "So, you don't want Quinn? Or someone *like* her? It's just you seem sort of hung up on the whole blond thing—"

Blake grinned. For an answer, he lowered his mouth to hers.

Sadie responded instantly, her mouth opening for him, her hands coming up to grip his shoulders and encircle his neck.

When they came up for air, he shook his head. "I'm sorry, what were we talking about? I forgot."

Sadie's grin made his pulse skip. Provocative, feline energy radiated from her heated gaze. "Nothing that matters."

Epilogue
Six months later

Blake squeezed Sadie's knee. "Don't be nervous."

His intentions were sweet, but he had no idea Sadie's churning stomach had nothing to do with meeting Quinn and company. She smiled weakly. "Honey, I realize an airport isn't the best place in the world for traumatizing conversations, but there's something I need to tell you."

His hazel eyes grew concerned, and his brow creased as he turned toward her. "What is it? Are you all right? You look a little pale."

The hard plastic seats made facing him uncomfortable, but she wouldn't survive this trip with Blake assuming her weakened state had anything to do with his ex-wife. Sadie had her pride, after all.

She tucked a wayward lock of hair behind her ear. "You remember that talk we had? A few months ago. The one that turned kind of awkward?"

Blake briefly closed his eyes. When they opened, they couldn't quite meet hers. "Sadie, forget I ever said anything, okay? I feel stupid every time I think about it."

"You shouldn't."

He gave her a flat smile. "I didn't mean to pressure you or make it seem like a deal-breaker. I'd just had that extra glass of wine, and we started talking about the future. Yeah, I want a family with you. I want kids. But I have no idea what I was thinking, bringing it up a whopping three months into our relationship." He shook his head as if trying to dislodge the memory. Then, he glanced at her with a small grin. "I'm lucky I didn't scare you off for good."

Sadie took a shallow breath. "I'm very hard to get rid of. Takes more than discussing our future to put the fear in me." The secret she had was doing a fine job, though. But at least she could put one thing to rest—Blake hadn't changed his mind.

His expression turned earnest, and his gaze searched her face. "Sadie, I mean it. Your reaction made me regret ever putting the idea out there. I know the gleam of panic in a person's eyes when I see it."

"I know, I know," she conceded. "I was caught off guard. That's all. I've focused my life on a single professional goal. A part of me never considered that starting a family might alter that trajectory. In fact, the whole idea was this distant, hazy thing. But now you're in my life, and you're big and solid. Hazy ideas are taking on sharp edges. It's scary."

Regret blossomed in Blake's hazel eyes seconds before he dropped his gaze. "I'm sorry. Let's make a deal. How about we go one day at a time?" He looked up, hope replacing the regret.

Despite her discomfort, Sadie leaned over the space between them and planted a quick kiss on his lips. "I've never been the kind of girl who flies by the seat of her pants. I like plans. I wanted to wait until this trip was over to come clean—" Her stomach protested, and the faint beginnings of nausea hit the back of her throat. "But I'm going to need you," she confessed miserably, cradling her belly. "I went off my pills two months ago."

Blake stared at her, frozen.

Doubt exploded inside her. She blinked back sudden unexpected tears. "I just—you talked about how you wished you'd have been a better dad to Seth and how it killed you when you lost Hunter and how you wanted another chance but you think you're too old, and I thought I was doing this really beautiful thing for us. But now I'm pregnant, and I think I might've made a terrible mistake. What if you were just shooting the breeze and don't really want another kid? But you do, right? You said...."

Her panic escalated. Everything she'd kept tightly held inside for weeks broke free. She wept soundlessly, taking big, measured breaths so she wouldn't hurl.

Blake's blank expression killed her.

Finally, he blinked a few times, and his eyes refocused. He pointed at her stomach, where she still rested a hand. "You're pregnant? I talked about a wanting a baby, and you...*made* one?"

She closed her eyes, sniffed, and wiped away the tears slipping down to her chin. "I know, it was stupid. I'm stupid. Everything is stupid. I'm going to be sick." She stiffened at his hand gently sliding around her shoulders.

"Hey. Look at me."

Sadie squeezed her eyes shut and rubbed them furiously before daring to meet Blake's gaze.

His radiant grin had a manic quality. "I can't believe this. You're giving me a *baby*? I can't tell you what this means to me." His gaze filled with wonder as he stared at her stomach, then back up to meet her gaze. "Thank you."

She covered her mouth as another set of tears plopped over the rim of her eyes. "I can't seem to stop crying. And eating. God, I eat constantly."

Blake laughed, his eyes growing misty. "How far?"

"About six weeks. I'm at the barfy, emotional part."

"Great!" He gathered her hands into his. His eyes hadn't left her face. "I loved you already, but now it's like—" His hands mimed something bursting, and he made little explosion noises. "I've never been this happy. Not ever. My heart's going to beat out of chest and fall onto the floor."

Sadie swallowed. Her heart felt heavy with affection for him, and her stomach heavy with something else. "I love you, too, Blake, but you're gonna make me puke."

"Fair enough." He kissed her softly on the cheek. "Let's talk names. I've always liked Seraphina for a girl and Oliver for a boy. Oh, maybe it'll be twins."

She grimaced. "I'm serious. I'm terribly nauseous."

"Wouldn't that be great? Seraphina and Oliver Cobb. Or we could choose rhyming ones. Chad and Thad. Casey and Lacy. Kelly and Shelly. I bet they'd hate that," he concluded thoughtfully. The unmistakable gleam of glee shone from his gaze. He snapped his fingers. "Got it. Reuben and Steuben. Billy and Lilly? No? Okay, Gilda and Tilda."

"My God, you're loving this, aren't you?"

His grin was outright devilish. "So much. How do you feel about Vinnie and Minnie?"

"That's it. Out of my way." She covered her mouth and ran for the nearest bathroom.

* * * *

The first thing Sadie noticed was how ridiculously good-looking everyone was.

Emily—that would be Quinn's big sister and Blake's third wife—assured her that she was a newcomer to the "pretty club" herself. Since picking up surfing from her beach-loving husband, Boston—a fine specimen in his own right, with sun-kissed tresses and big blue eyes—Emily had swapped pale skin and a corporate wardrobe for a golden tan and cut-offs, plus a trimmer figure thanks to her new active lifestyle.

Seth was coming into adulthood in style. He had Emily's thick brown hair and Blake's incredible hazel eyes. Maddie, Quinn's daughter with

Jack, had the chicest, sleekest blond bob in southern California, and Jack's remarkable turquoise gaze.

Sadie wouldn't admit it in a million years, but Jack put all the men to shame on nearly every level. With his buoyant personality, obvious adoration for Quinn, friendliness, and quick wit, he stole the limelight everywhere he went. He looked every bit the movie star he was quickly becoming, as his roles in America increased. Unfortunately, he didn't seem to have an off switch. Overall, she preferred Blake's quiet watchfulness at her side and looked forward to tame evenings full of bad television and unhealthy snacks.

And then, of course, there was Quinn, whose regal aura was the perfect foible for Jack's incessant energy, and made her the dignified center of the family, whether any of them realized it or not. Sadie had dreaded meeting them all, but none more than Quinn. She feared being cast back into her looming shadow of perfection. She'd seen pictures and knew Amanda had been but a pale, pale imitation of the original.

Sadie hadn't counted on falling in love with her, too.

Quinn and Jack had decided to kick off their summer in L.A. with a family party, which neatly served the dual purpose of catching up with their college student son and introducing Sadie to the family.

Somehow, Sadie ended up alone in the kitchen with Quinn, while together they prepared the salad for dinner. Jack was the chef of the group, so everyone else got relegated to prep cook status.

After the fifth glance Quinn snuck, Sadie finally found her backbone. "What is it?" She hadn't meant to snap, but Quinn's height didn't help the whole intolerably intimidating thing she had going on. It made it much, much worse. Sometimes, being short sucked.

Quinn smiled and went back to tearing romaine leaves. "Nothing. You just have that glow."

Sadie's hands rushed to her stomach. "It's my new moisturizer."

"No, I mean a *happy* glow." She gave Sadie a knowing look, then dropped it abruptly with a careless shrug. "Not everyone is brave enough to have a kid in their late thirties. Trust me, Maddie was Jack's idea, not mine."

Jack entered the kitchen, Maddie perched on his shoulders, squealing and latching on to his hair. "She's nonrefundable, Quinnie. It's been nearly three years; you can't back out now. Tell her, Maddie."

"No back, Mum!"

Quinn grimaced. "Ugh, we talked about this. *Mom*, Maddie. I'm Mom. Not Mum. I don't care what Daddy says."

The toddler squealed again. "Mum, mum, mum, mum!"

Jack's eyes danced, and his body followed as he teasingly exited the kitchen doing a sort of rumba shuffle, Maddie's song increasing in volume as they left.

Sadie caught herself laughing. "Wow. Poor Blake had to exist on the fringes of this? No wonder he was depressed."

If she thought to entice Quinn's guilt, she didn't know her well enough just yet. But she was learning.

Quinn lifted an imperious eyebrow. "Poor Blake's place in this family has always been his to determine. Now, if you want to say he moped the last couple of years and wallowed in his mistakes until he met a woman tough enough to snap him out of it, then sure, I'd agree with that." She went back to picking through cherry tomatoes.

Sadie crumbled more feta into a pile on the cutting board. "You think I'm tough?"

"I think you have to be. Blake fell apart after what Kira did to him. Losing Hunter tore him up. It changed him, or brought him back to himself. Whichever way you want to look at it."

"Maybe a bit of both," Sadie offered.

"Maybe." She turned away from the salad, leaned against the counter, and made an open study of Sadie.

She was imperious and intimidating, gorgeous and confident. But she was also drily sarcastic, something that came best in small doses, in Sadie's most humble opinion.

"Blake deserves you, Sadie. I don't mean that in a nasty way. I mean it in the best way imaginable. He's been through hell. And yes, he brought most of it upon himself, but I realize it's been hard for him to see Emily and I move on. He probably would've preferred to stay away, but we wouldn't let him, even though it's the most awkward situation on Earth." She rolled her spectacular green eyes. "Have you heard Jack's southern accent? It's terrible. But we all suffered through it, because family is family. *Blake* is family. He's spent a great deal of time punishing himself for things that weren't his fault. He and I had grown apart long before he met Kira. No matter which way I go back and look at it, Blake was bored to tears with me, and I lived in my own little bubble with Seth and my stories. It worked until it didn't."

Sadie was thrown by Quinn's honesty. Blake had finally reached the same conclusion about their marriage, but it had taken him much longer to accept it.

"Emily certainly wasn't the answer," Quinn went on, idly popping a tomato into her mouth. "He was just trying to do something right, that's all. Which is great in theory."

Sadie was sure Quinn had a point in there somewhere. "Not sure what you're trying to say, exactly."

Quinn pressed on as if she hadn't heard. "We all need someone who makes up the other half of us. I need Jack to make my world spin, because without him, it just...*stops*. It goes flat and gray. I'm a black-and-white drawing, and he's acrylic paint. Blake never, not even when were in high school and believed ourselves fiercely in love, looked at me the way he stares at you the moment you step into the room. It's the way Boston's great big blue peepers find Emily the moment she arrives. I know you can feel it, because I can feel when Jack's eyes are on me. He's the first person I search out, without even realizing what I'm doing. I don't think Blake merely existed until you came along, Sadie. I think he was waiting for you. I'm trying to say I'm glad you finally showed up."

Sadie dumped the feta into the salad bowl and issued a low, impressed whistle. "You do have a way with words."

Quinn cast her a sidelong glance, winked, and grinned. "You'd know that if you read my books."

Sadie's face warmed as she responded with an impish smile and picked up the bowl, now loaded with a fully assembled salad. "I'm a fan," she admitted. "But I figured at least half of your charm ought to be a credit to your editors. At least, on paper."

Quinn blasted Sadie with her full smile for the first time and seemed to take in Sadie's whole face at once, light green eyes studying her in amusement. "You're the most perfect person I can imagine joining the family, Sadie. You've already got the mouth for it."

Later, Seth made his excuses and left to meet up with old friends from high school, while he was in town, and Maddie went to bed. As the sun set and fireflies put on a show in the backyard, the six of them gathered on the deck and sipped drinks. Non-alcoholic for Emily and Boston. Whiskey and beer straight from the bottle for Jack and Quinn, respectively. Iced tea for Sadie and Blake.

She leaned into him. "Has it occurred to you we're the boring couple?" She hadn't meant to say it so loud, but heads popped up from relaxed positions and swiveled toward her.

Blake ignored their audience. "Oh? Who's the fun couple?"

With a nod in their direction, Sadie answered. "Emily and Boston." No competition. Those two lived for the outdoors, surfing, and traveling.

Boston smiled, dimples springing into action on either side of his well-formed mouth and wrapped an arm around Emily's waist as she relaxed into his lap. "Nailed it. We're opening a new homeless shelter in Maui next year. We're calling it The Landing."

His wife smiled at him adoringly, but addressed Sadie. "We met when he operated a similar shelter in Honolulu called The Canopy. It's a cause close to our hearts."

Jack cheered, but Quinn tilted her head and pouted. "No nieces or nephews for me, I take it?"

Boston and Emily shook their heads simultaneously. "It's a little late for kids," Emily said. Despite her uniquely feminine appearance, sensually curvy and physically fit, the boardroom still lingered in her commanding tone. "Besides, I've spent most of my life settled down, between college and my old job. I chafe against routine anymore. And it's not fair to take that from a kid."

They all agreed kids required a certain degree of stability.

"Ah, well," Jack said before nudging Quinn and giving her the most devilishly stunning smile Sadie had ever seen. "We'll have to double-up."

Quinn shook her head and sipped from her bottle with a cool expression. "Not happening, Jack."

"Never say never, love. You should know better by now."

Instead of arguing, she seemed to take the sentiment seriously.

Blake and Sadie exchanged covert smiles and dropped them immediately when Emily hitched her chin toward Sadie. "If we're the fun ones, and you're the boring ones, I guess Quinn and Jack are the pretty ones."

"He's a movie star," Blake pointed out. "What chance did the rest of us have?"

Sadie blew out a plume of air. "Actually, I think you're all freakishly handsome."

Jack raised his glass again. "Hear, hear!" He wrapped an arm around Quinn's shoulders and leaned in to whisper, loudly, in her ear. "I like her, Quinnie. Can we keep her?"

Quinn's gaze lingered on Blake, a small smile playing at the corner of her mouth.

It made Sadie slightly uncomfortable, that secret smile. She especially disliked the way Blake returned it. Then she glanced over to see if Jack had caught their exchange, only to find him grinning indulgently, like a child in a toy store.

A peek at Boston and Emily and their sheepish smirks told Sadie something was up.

She turned to Blake. "I want to play too, so if someone could explain the rules, that'd be *greeeat*...." The word faded from her mouth as Blake made the smooth transition from sitting beside her to kneeling before her.

Like every woman ever in that position, she gasped and covered her mouth, knowing before he pulled the ring box from his pocket what was happening.

"Custom designed just for you." He opened it to reveal a silver ring, with a princess-cut diamond embedded deep in the band—a ring that wouldn't get caught on fishing line or snag on a thread inside her work gloves; a ring she could wear all the time. "You'll never have an excuse to take it off." He teased, but nerves danced along the edge of his voice.

She looked from the ring to Blake and back. No one had ever put so much thought and effort into a gift for her. *How* was this man single for five years?

His grin widened. "Do you need to think about it? Because I don't. We can have a lengthy engagement if you're still not sure. I'll wait. I'm a patient guy."

Faces beamed and mooned. Sadie's heart moved in her chest, like a quarter when it falls perfectly into a coin slot.

Blake licked his lips nervously. His smile faltered. "I-I shouldn't have put you on the spot, Sadie—"

"Oh, God, shut up." She grabbed his face and brought his mouth to hers, taking both of their breaths away. She pulled away with a gasp. "Yes. Hell, yes."

Clapping and cheering followed. Sadie wiped away a tear from the corner of her eye as Blake slid the ring onto her finger and reclaimed his seat beside her, pride practically bursting from him, evident in the smile threatening to crack his face wide open.

Emily applauded fiercely. "Well done, Blake! We've got our fourth and final Cobb!"

"The last Cobb!" Jack joined in with his glass raised high.

Blake subdued their celebration with a small shake of his head. "No, actually, I don't think so. Sadie will probably want to keep her own last name. I think enough women in this family have had mine." He turned to her questioningly.

She stroked his cheek lovingly. "I'll show them how it's done, babe."

Boston laughed out loud, Jack whistled, and Quinn and Emily swapped approving glances.

Blake's smile turned teasing and he kissed her. "Well, okay. If you're prepared to walk into this family with a name like Darling Cobb, I've got your back. But don't say you weren't warned."

There was laughter and jokes, none of which bothered Sadie in the least, because the company was well-meaning. Mostly, Quinn and Emily empathized with her, having had the surname Buzzly their entire lives, while Jack and Boston ribbed Blake.

Jack nodded apologetically. "It really does help to have a cool last name, mate."

Boston raised his glass with an identical expression. "Really does."

Sadie curled into the crook of Blake's arm, drawing his attention, as Jack and Boston delved into the deeper meanings of names, and Quinn jumped in with her thoughts on naming characters.

Sadie traced a heart on his knee and spoke low, so only he could hear. "You're my darling Cobb. I don't see why I shouldn't be yours."

THE END

Keep reading for a special sneak peek of Roxanne Smith's novel

Relapse in Paradise

She likes Hawaii, but she just might love Boston...

Still stinging from her recent divorce, Emily Buzzly heads to majestic Hawaii to soothe her wounds. But once she arrives on Oahu, Emily discovers that a man she assumes is a beach bum is in fact her personal tour guide, hired by her sister. With his long hair and tattoos, Boston Rondibett is everything Emily detests—despite his sun-kissed surfer body. And with her straight-laced, executive persona, Emily is everything Boston rebels against. But both have a lot to learn about making snap judgments...

As it turns out, Boston's real job, the one he truly cares about, is running his soup kitchen and homeless shelter. Embarrassed by her assumptions, rather than lazy beach days, Emily soon finds herself feeding the hungry, and even involved in the search for an AWOL soldier. And to Boston's surprise, she's loving every minute of it—and he's loving seeing her loosen her chignon and be the admirable, beautiful woman she is. As each works through the challenges of the past, these two very different people just might find their hearts are on the very same page...

Chapter 1

Boston rubbed his forehead and let his exasperation show plainly in his tone. "Hani, I don't have time for this, man."

Even doubled over with his head stuck inside the cold oven, the overgrown Hawaiian took up most of the space in the dark galley kitchen. The one narrow window set above the porcelain sink had been scrubbed just last week. Boston had watched Akela bring down the threadbare curtains and take a sponge to the glass pane with his own eyes, but the room seemed to stay gloomy.

Boston blamed Hani's giant body blocking out the sunlight. Or scaring it away.

Hani's head came out of the oven and cocked to one side in annoyance. Despite it, his clear, dark eyes held only concern. Maybe a hint of fear. "Don't push me, *haole*. If we don't get this stove working, we ain't feeding nobody. Akela's bringing plates she made from home, but that won't get us through the day. And if Mama finds out she's helping here, Bos, it won't be good."

Fair point. Hani's sister did a lot around the shelter, without her family's consent or knowledge. Since Hani had left home and landed on the streets, they'd had little to do with him. Less so after he took up running The Canopy with Boston. Except Akela, who refused to disown her only brother.

Boston pulled a wad of bills from the side pocket of his maroon cut-off shorts with tired reluctance. The frayed end of his shorts tickled his shins and got caught in his leg hair, but they were his favorite pair.

Probably because Hani hated them. Boston figured he'd picked them out this morning in a subconscious effort to antagonize his business partner.

He held the fat wad of cash aloft to give Hani a better view. "Relax, big guy. See this? It's my paycheck from the job I picked up last week. Money just came down the wire."

His friend didn't appear impressed. Hani had never much cared for money. It was hard to work up a whole lot of concern for something they never had. "Whatcha gonna do, huh? Hand it out? We're trying to give these poor folks a decent plate of rice, not send them back to the liquor store."

Boston put zero effort into hiding his impatient groan. "Your brain's as thick as your barrel chest sometimes. Hell no, I'm not about to sprinkle cash on a bunch of homeless guys. But I bet I've got enough right here to pick up an old used oven at the appliance yard downtown. Relax, man. We're in paradise, remember?" He gave Hani his best cheesy smile, the one he might use on folks if he ever turned to selling cars to make a buck.

The big man stopped fooling with the lost cause of an oven to put a hand over his large belly and laugh lazily.

Like Boston knew he would. If the famous Chef Hani of The Canopy, Honolulu's poorest and smallest soup kitchen, didn't have a sense of humor, no one did.

He shook his head, a slight smile on his wide mouth. "You're funny, Boston. Real funny. You try that paradise talk on the next straggler who finds his way in here. Wait till I can watch, though, 'kay? It's been too long since I seen you get your ass handed to you. In fact, I think it was Jordan who gave you your last shiner, huh? A girl, even."

Boston's insides seized up in his gut like a bad toe cramp. Not the result of nostalgia, loss, or even heartbreak, but fear. Happened every damn time Jordan's name found its way into a conversation. Or into his head. Or he caught a glimpse of the tattoo in his reflection. He absentmindedly rubbed the spot on his ribcage where the ink etched into his skin, barely visible through the threadbare white T-shirt he wore.

A hui hou, it read. *Until we meet again.*

So much for that.

Hani must've caught his expression. He ran a flat palm over his face as if to wipe away the grin he'd already dropped. "Hey, man. I'm sorry."

Boston waved him off and forced a smile. "Don't be. We've got bigger problems."

Hani was back to fiddling with the knobs of the broken oven. "Damn thing." He sighed. His shoulders drooped. "I like to see the money but hate to see it spent before you even go over the books. Tell me about this new job you got before I call Thompson down here to help me move this thing." He kicked the bottom of it. "Stupid piece of junk."

"What about Kale? Did he finally do the right thing?"

Hani grunted. "Whatever *that* is. Like either of us would know."

They were certain Kale was an AWOL soldier from the army base at the center of Oahu, but neither of them felt any compulsion to turn him in. Boston would be damned before he'd do it.

The Canopy was a soup kitchen/sometimes shelter when weather hit and they brought a few poor souls inside, not a halfway house or rehab facility. They fed people a couple times a day, as many as they had rice for and nothing more. Hot food, no soapbox talk. Guys like Kale and Thompson relied on the place for a safe haven, and Boston relied on them for help maintaining the shelter. Damn hard to make payroll without liquid assets.

Hell, without *any* assets. The building itself wasn't worth the broken industrial oven they were about to toss on the curbside.

Hani's thick, black eyebrows drew together in a concerned wrinkle. "I ain't seen Kale in a while, but something tells me he didn't turn himself in at the base. His face would be all over the news if he had."

"How would we know? You see a television in here?"

Hani rolled his eyes. "I may not get out much, but you do. You would've seen something, heard something. One of the boys would probably know."

The boys. That's what Hani called them even though a few women made their way into The Canopy from time to time. The stragglers, the panhandlers, the bottom-feeders. Sometimes, in his more poetic moods, they were the lost souls or the forgotten.

Boston ran a weary hand through his shoulder-length hair. "Nothing I can do for a street kid on the run from the Army. But I can tell you about the job. About two years ago, when I first started doing the guide thing, this couple came from London on their honeymoon." He scratched his chin. The lady was American, he recalled. "Or was it California? Can't remember. Anyway, great couple. Totally laid back." He snapped his finger. "Jack, that was the husband. Jack and Quinn. If all my clients were as chill as these two, I'd love my job."

Air blew from Hani's lips with a rude noise. They called it a raspberry back on the mainland, but there was probably some Hawaiian word for it Boston didn't know. "Whatever, man. You know you love dragging mainlanders all over the island. Don't lie."

Okay, yeah, so he loved it, but what wasn't to love? Oahu did the work; Boston only had to drive and point. "Well, they called last week. They're surprising some family member, a cousin or something, with a plane ticket and hired me to meet her at the airport and show her around the island."

Hani finally gave up on the oven dials with a disappointed, thin-lipped grimace. "You'll probably have it easy if you liked Jack and Quinn so much, eh?"

Boston sucked in air through his teeth. "Nah, I don't think so. Quinn booked this lady's room at the Hilton. Right on Waikiki. She and Jack, they were down for the full experience, you know? They stayed in a little cottage on North Shore that didn't have air-conditioning or sealed windows. Given that, the lofty hotel reservation gives me the impression their cousin—aunt, sister, whatever—isn't made of the same stuff. You smell what I'm cookin'?"

"Oh, I smell it, brother. Smells like you got a rough job ahead." Hani stopped short of whatever he'd been about to say next to give Boston a lingering head-to-toe appraisal. "She's gonna dig for spare change when she sees you, man. Then, when she finds out who you are, she's gonna call the lady who hired you and ask her what the hell she was thinking. *Then* she's gonna go straight to the Hilton Village and hire one of them real guides. The ones who wear the mint green polo shirts and have official stuff like clipboards and name tags."

Upper crust business rivals. Well, not really rivals. The people who came to Boston were usually the ones intent on avoiding things like client rosters, preplanned lunch menus, and name tags. *Especially* name tags.

Boston ran a critical eye over his shorts, which were doing their job offending Hani. "She'll get used to me. She'll have to. If Quinn's buddy ditches me, I'll owe her back the deposit. Since I'm about to spend it on an appliance we need to operate this place, I'd better have something up my sleeve, huh?"

An anxious grunt escaped Hani's lips. "Damn right, you better. Hey, you heard what happened to Ryder, didn't you?"

Boston nibbled the inside of his cheek and thought hard. Ryder... Ryder, sure.... Or, wait. No, that was Robert. Wasn't it? He scratched his neck. "Too many, man. Not enough time for me to get to know them all." At the rate their homeless patrons came and went, who but Hani could keep track? He had the benefit of both working and living at the shelter. Boston's part was making the money to keep it going. On a good week, he'd get to The Canopy once or twice. During a bad week, he made it daily, but it meant no money coming in. "Remind me."

"Guy could've come straight from some bank downtown. Like he might be the CEO or something. Suit and tie."

"Oh, yeah, I remember him. Expensive haircut, trimmed nails, tailored slacks. As recent as they come." Boston had spotted him twice. The first time had stopped Boston in his tracks. His heart had thudded in his chest, stupidly hoping some benevolent rich dude had discovered their operation and came to donate. Until Boston saw him chowing on one of Hani's rice plates. The second time, Ryder hadn't looked so fresh. His button-up was wrinkled, his slick black hair a little less slick. "What happened to him?"

Hani's flat gaze stilled on Boston. "He got arrested last night." A pause. "In Kalihi. I was thinking if bail is set low enough, maybe we can pull something together. Ryder's a good dude."

Boston checked a sigh. Hani reminded him of a spoiled wife sometimes, asking for a new car at the same time Boston was breaking his back just to pay the mortgage. He shook his head slowly. "Kalihi is bad news, man."

Hani's plaintive stare didn't waver.

Boston ran a hand over his smooth cheek. Shaving. His only concession to societal niceties. He tended to get more business when clean-shaven, like facial hair was some sort of trustworthiness gauge. "I don't know, Hani. Guy like that, maybe he developed an expensive habit—the kind of habit that takes a man to Kalihi in the middle of the night. If that's the case, I'd just as soon not get involved." Kalihi had no shoreline, no draw for tourists. Just a working-class neighborhood with the crime and drug problems encountered in any city. It had to go somewhere.

Hani didn't let go. "You can't assume nothing. We don't even know what he was arrested for. One of the boys let me know about the arrest, but he didn't have any other info."

Boston hated to let Hani down but couldn't promise the money was enough. "Let me see what I can do about the oven. Maybe I can pick up a used one. If there's anything left, we'll talk about what we can do for Ryder."

Hani beamed. "You'll come through, *haole*. That's what you do." He wiped his hands on the apron tied around his expansive waist and turned back to the stove.

Haole. It had taken Boston years to get accustomed to Hani's familiar use of the word, Hawaiians' not-so-nice name for white people. Whether or not it had prejudice connotations depended largely on who was saying it and how. Hani used it as a term of endearment these days, but that hadn't always been the case.

He hesitated to say it, to give Hani hope, but *maybe…* "I might be able to squeeze a little more out of Quinn."

Hani had started sorting through a shelf of pots and pans on the far wall. He didn't look up but raised his voice over the clunks and clangs. "Oh, yeah? How you gonna do that? Be a *real* guide after all? I got a clipboard 'round here somewhere." He hefted a huge stainless steel pot into the sink.

Boston grinned at Hani's doubtful expression. "Hell, no. This lady's vacation is open-ended. No departure date is set. I got a two-week advance. If she stays longer than two weeks, I get to charge for it. The longer she stays, the more I get paid."

"Why can't you just tell them your rates went up? Insurance companies pull that crap all the time. Inflation, man. I'm just saying." Hani's innocent shrug almost made Boston laugh.

"I'm not successful because I gouge my clients. You know that."

Hani gave the stove a frustrated kick and muttered something unintelligible and probably offensive under his breath in Hawaiian. He smoothed down a long strand of hair that had escaped from his braid. "Don't try to sell me your credo, Boston. I think we both know why you're so damn good at this private guide business, and it ain't nothing to do with prices."

Was Hani about to berate him for giving away Oahu's local secrets to tourists? He thought they were past this.

Hani's grin came slowly. "It's them long, golden locks. Akela knows what I'm talking about. You're like a Barbie doll, man. You're so pretty it's confusing sometimes."

Boston refused to be baited. Hani constantly gave him a hard time about his "pretty boy" looks. Maybe he should grow a beard after all, his clients be damned. "Flattery won't convince me to marry your sister." It might be playing with fire to tease Hani about the mean crush Akela had on him, and the pink hibiscus tucked perpetually behind her right ear, a status symbol declaring to anyone in the know that she was both single and available. Unfortunately, Akela didn't merely resemble Hani—they were practically identical. They even had matching braids, big thick black ones they wore straight down their backs.

He hadn't noticed the blue speckled stovetop coffee urn sitting atop the broken stove until Hani reached for it and poured the dark contents into a mug, disgruntled. "Cold coffee, man. How do you like that? I was gonna offer you some brew, but I guess compliments are all I can afford. You'd make a terrible prince, anyway. Don't know why I bother."

Boston's eye roll didn't do the situation justice, but he didn't have time to groan and walk away.

Hani bobbed his head like he knew what was coming. "I know, I know. You don't believe me, but I'm telling you, brother. We're descendants of the royal Hawaiian family. Kemahameha the Great, man. He's my great, great, great, great something. With the conquest of O'hua in 1795, he became the founder of the Kingdom of Hawai'i. Fifteen years and a few concessions later, *bam!* You've got a unified country, my friend." He poked Boston in the chest with a large, stubby finger. "Until your people showed up, anyway. I'd be living at Iolani Palace right now if it weren't for you *haoles*."

On an island where dialects and languages came in many flavors, Boston appreciated the universal. He flipped Hani the bird. "I have to go. Keep an eye out for the delivery guy from the appliance yard. We'll have rice flying out of here by lunchtime."

Hani grimaced after taking a sip of the cold half-brewed coffee. "Hey, you never said what this lady's name is. How you gonna find her at the airport if you don't know her name?"

Boston dug around inside the outer pocket of his frayed cargos and came up with a crumpled yellow note. He unfolded it. "Emily Buzzly-Cobb. That's one hell of a name."

Another grimace from his friend. "I'm starting to feel sorry for you, brother. She even sounds like a stick in the mud."

Boston smirked. "I'll just have to knock her loose."

* * * *

Some places on the Web described Honolulu International Airport as the busiest U.S. airport.

Emily glanced around and doubted it. A seasoned traveler, she'd seen far worse at LAX, O'Hare, and JFK. Perhaps Hawaiians weren't morning flyers. She checked her watch. Six hour flight plus a three hour time difference in her favor meant she'd only lost three hours.

If she didn't calculate for jet lag.

Which she wouldn't. She could sleep when she went back to California. On Hawaii time, it was seven in the morning. The perfect hour to begin her first official day in paradise. First, she needed to get to her room at the Hilton her sister, Quinn, had reserved for her stay.

Her completely open-ended stay.

No return ticket accompanied the surprise flight to Honolulu Quinn and her husband, Jack, had sprung on Emily out of the blue in an effort to help her escape her post-divorce funk. But that was the point—to break free of deadlines. If she wanted to go home after a week, she'd book the flight. If she wanted to stay, she'd stay. Stay and do what, who the heck knew.

Maybe forget Blake Cobb existed for a few weeks. Forget her failure as a wife and her failure to be true to herself. She should've never gotten involved with her sister's ex-husband, especially knowing what she did about him. How could she be so successful in one arena of life, yet such a miserable failure where it mattered?

Usually, Emily had meetings and consultations to keep her mind from such dour reflections. The lack of a schedule and sense of urgency was like having the floor shift beneath her feet with nothing to hang on to. No tether. No one waited for her at the hotel, no one expected her at a function downtown, and no one clamored for her expertise.

Emily caught herself smiling, despite the disheartening thoughts of her ex-husband. No consultations. No meetings. No pencil skirts, panty hose, or sensible black pumps.

She glanced at her pin-striped pencil skirt and slide-on loafers.

Okay, first her hotel room. Then, a gratuitous shopping venture for a vacation wardrobe. She must've gone into autopilot when she dressed for the flight and wore what she always wore. She'd even taken to wearing slacks on the weekend because why buy jeans to wear one day a week? She didn't recall if she even owned a pair anymore.

Emily stopped at the conveniently placed Starbucks kiosk outside the terminal exit and ordered a tall caramel frappe. It was downright decadent compared to the coffee she'd suffered on the plane. With her indulgent coffee in one hand and her luggage handle in the other, Emily navigated her way through swarms of travelers to a cabstand outside.

A native woman greeted Emily with a friendly welcoming smile and a lei of white, heavenly-scented flowers. She inhaled deeply and let the floral aroma take over her senses.

Her shoulders relaxed. This must be the island vibe people talked about. An ocean breeze from the west blew the fine hairs around her face into a playful dance. Even the humidity enticed her. Such rich air. So *tropical.*

She came to a dead halt that nearly sent the scalding contents of her coffee flying. Without blatantly staring, Emily recovered herself and tried to get a better glimpse of the man standing near the cabstand with her name on a sign.

She double-checked the placard.

Yep. Emily Buzzly-Cobb. That was her name. Pretty unmistakable except for the time she'd gone down on a reservation list as Buzzing Cod. Or, more facetiously, the time she'd been addressed as Fuzzy Knob at a school fund-raiser with her nephew.

She regarded the man holding the sign.

Definitely homeless. His unwashed sun-streaked blond hair was a few tangles away from becoming dreadlocks, pulled back into a ponytail at the nape of his neck. His ragged red shorts were hacked off so the hem frayed around his shins, and he wore a tight-fitting faded T-shirt of indeterminable color. It might've been tan or even a light blue at one time. His heavy-duty black hiking sandals with tread like a tractor tire appeared to be the only thing on his person of any value.

His smooth face surprised her. Where did a homeless guy get a good shave?

And why would Quinn hire someone like this to drive her to the Hilton? The last bit of the unsettling image came from the tattoos on the man's arms and legs. Several more on his torso were noticeable through the worn fabric of his shirt.

Emily suppressed a shudder and smoothed her hair into place. Merely examining his made her want to run a comb through hers. Luckily, he hadn't seen her yet and wouldn't recognize her. She made to walk past him.

He pinned her with pale blue eyes the size of half dollars. "There you are."

Her body froze mid-stride. "Excuse me?" The flat question came out sounding like an accusation. She inwardly cringed.

The man didn't seem fazed by her tone or dumbstruck manner. He was probably used to people reacting strangely to him. He stuck out his hand. "Emily, right? I'm Boston. Your ride."

She took his offer of a handshake like she would any CEO's and silently thanked God for the automatic responses her career had ingrained in her. "Boston." This time she was careful to keep her tone neutral. "That's an interesting name. How did you know what I looked like?"

"Quinn sent a photo." He gave her a sort of cockeyed half-smile. Not the genuine article by a long shot, but not quite a smirk, either. A pair of aviator sunglasses kept hair from falling onto his face. He slid them back on his nose, and his cornflower blue eyes vanished behind the reflective lenses.

Cornflower? Really? It was some nonsense Quinn might use in one of her books. Didn't make a lick of sense. Corn didn't grow flowers and if it did, they certainly weren't blue. "Very thoughtful of my sister," Emily mumbled.

At least she wasn't the only one sending out prickly vibes. She blamed Boston's unfriendly bearing, which she gauged by his forced smile, on her choice of attire. It gave away everything about her.

She was one of *them*.

Suits. Working stiffs. Nine-to-fivers.

Otherwise known as someone who worked for a living.

She didn't much care for him, either, which made his dislike easy to stomach. Indeed, the feeling was mutual. Emily only had to survive the ride to the Hilton, and they could dust off their hands and part ways.

Boston offered to carry her bag, and she let him. He could do something to earn his tip besides harbor barely contained displeasure with his fare.

Wordlessly, Emily followed as he guided her though two levels of the parking garage, and her thoughts turned to Quinn. How best to tell Quinn and Jack they sucked at making travel arrangements? They obviously hadn't done their research on cab companies, or they wouldn't have sent a homeless man to pick her up from the airport.

Eventually, Boston pointed them toward a late model white van with a simple logo pasted on the passenger door.

Wonderful. A ride in a nondescript white van with a total stranger.

Emily hadn't realized she'd come to a halt until Boston paused one stride away from the vehicle. He made a lazy about-face with an amused grin lifting one corner of his mouth. "What's the matter? Does my van creep you out?"

Heat flew up from her chest like a rash and spread over her face. Boston had to notice the furious blush on her pale skin, which made it worse. Didn't he know anything about tact? "No, no. Of course not. I was, uh, admiring your company motif."

He gave a doubtful glance at the circle drawn with *The Island Experience* printed in bold maroon script inside. "Whatever you say. You can sit up front if you prefer."

She hitched her chin up a notch and started for the van. "I believe I would, yes. Thank you."

The polite response irked her. She used manners to diffuse social awkwardness, an old defense mechanism. The more dismissive Boston became, the stiffer she'd get. It had worked so well during her marriage she and Blake were on the same sickly sweet polite terms as two soccer moms at a bake sale by the time the lawyers were called in.

She rolled her shoulders in an attempt to loosen the tight muscles. Why'd she care what this bum thought of her, anyway?

"*Mahalo.*" He tossed her bag in the backseat of the van.

She paused in opening the passenger door. "What?"

"It means 'thank you,' among other things."

Boston smoothly navigated the twists and turns of the airport with the practiced ease of a veteran driver. At least he knew his way around, and they wouldn't waste a lot of time getting lost or turned around. Before long, they were sailing down a highway rife with morning commuters in strained silence.

Well, at least on her end. Boston didn't strike her as the type to possess the honed social sense or level of self-awareness necessary to notice something so subtle as an uncomfortable silence.

However, her job had taught her to combat bubbles of discomfort like this one. She walked into businesses and tossed out ideas managers didn't always want to hear with one hand while smoothing their ruffled feathers with the other.

She really ought to be able to handle one lowly beach bum. She keyed in on the only interesting thing about him she'd learned so far. "Are you from Boston, then?"

He kept his gaze on the road. "Would you believe me if I said I was?"

He didn't appear to have come from particularly creative stock and had no discernible regional accent. He could be from anywhere.

"Sure."

He chanced the quickest of glances and flashed his first genuine smile. It stunned her to discover it changed his whole face. He almost didn't look homeless anymore. "Well, don't. I'd be lying. Boston Rondibett from Mesa, Arizona at your service. And I'm never going back to that dry, windy hellhole unless God himself is tugging me by the ankles. Or my mom says please."

"I'm from southern California. Similar climate."

She'd meant to present common ground, but he surprised her. "I know."

Her head snapped in his direction. "How do you know where I'm from?"

He shrugged one shoulder as if the question didn't strike him as relevant. "Quinn told me. How else would I know? I was her and Jack's personal guide when they honeymooned on the island. She asked me to show you around while you're on vacation. Besides, you flew in from LAX on a non-connecting flight. See?" He slipped into an intentionally idiotic accent. "Even a scruffy dude like me can did math."

Normally, Emily would've bounced back with a scathing comment, but her jaw hung loose. "You're my *vacation guide?*"

"Did I stutter? Although, now you mention it, 'vacation guide' makes more sense in terms of a title, but it's kind of a mouthful."

"So, you're not dropping me off at the Hilton and going on your merry way? I'm spending my entire vacation with you?" Emily winced. She might've tried harder to disguise her derision. Still, the guy needed a haircut and a bath. She hadn't forgotten those atrocious shorts, either.

She'd suggest the underside of a sewing machine if they wouldn't be better off in the garbage bin.

Boston didn't say a word. Apparently, he was the kind of man who spoke through action, and his next stunt involved slowing down the van.

She sputtered. They were in the center of a multilane highway with vehicles whizzing past on either side. Emily quit trying to communicate and started praying. If she was going to die, it couldn't hurt to go out with the Lord's Prayer on her lips.

Miraculously, Boston didn't get them killed, mangled to death in a fiery crash of steel on asphalt. He managed to ease over two lanes and come to a stop on the shoulder of the highway.

Emily released her white-knuckle grip on the door handle and seethed. "You're a psychopath."

Boston flicked on the hazards and put the van in park. He swiveled his body toward her and yanked the sunglasses from his face in a quick, agitated movement.

She realized then, regarding him straight on, they felt the same way about each other. Forget disdain. He'd passed judgment and found her lacking.

As she'd done him.

Boston spoke in a measured tone. "I'll put it to you plain, Ms. Buzzly-Cobb, if that is your *real* name. I have a job to do. We don't have to like each other, but it'll make for a better time had by all if we can at least manage to get along. A little mutual respect would go a long way. I'll even give you a reason to try it. I know this island like no one else you're gonna find. Ask your sister if you want my references."

Now, *this* Emily could handle. Directness. "I don't care about your résumé."

"Well, you should. It's impressive."

"Does it include how utterly charming you are? Or mention you've got the hubris of a D-list celebrity?"

He gave her a sad puppy-dog frown. "I'm simple folk. Try to keep the vocabulary at my level."

Something in those great big blue orbs said he knew exactly what she'd said. And some of what she hadn't. "If I don't like you, why should I have to spend the next couple of weeks in your company? Or you in mine, given the feeling is mutual."

"I never said I didn't like you."

"I can read expressions better than you can fake them."

That seemed to catch him unaware. He stared at her unguarded. Finally, the corner of his mouth quirked up. "Me. You." He pointed at each of them in turn and continued with exaggerated caveman speech. "See island. Pretty stuff no one else will show you. Boston good at this." He hooked both thumbs toward himself and gave her a simpleton's grin. "Me already paid. You sit back and get over it."

Good thing she hadn't laughed. Her back straightened. *"Get over it?* No, I don't think I will. Drop me at the Hilton and keep the damn money. I'll pay Quinn back for her trouble."

Boston dropped his goofy act and flopped back against the seat, at the same time gusting out a great sigh. "Man, you don't have any sense of humor at all, do you? Not a shred."

The plainspoken observation was more insulting than anything else he'd said or done in their short acquaintance. "I happen to be hilarious."

He didn't seem convinced by her deadpan delivery. His loss. He wouldn't be around long enough to get to know her unique approach to humor, which tended to run a little dry.

"Fine. If I don't have a sense of humor, it's probably because there's nothing funny about your lack of class or professionalism."

"You basically called me a dumbass. What did you expect?"

Had she? "I don't think you're stupid. Just repugnant."

"Oh, that's *loads* better." He snorted like the whole situation amused him. "I apologize, okay? My mouth does things without permission from my brain sometimes."

He sat up, gripped the wheel, and offered her a small smile. She couldn't tell outright if he meant it as mocking.

"Look at us," he said. "We're a mess and we just met. That means one or both of us have already decided how we feel without giving the other a shot. I have a suggestion, if you're open to hear one."

"Let me guess. You want to start over?" She refused to roll her eyes like a teenager and had to settle for a flat stare.

Boston bit his knuckle as if unsure of his next words. "Anyone ever tell you you're a hard ass?"

A laugh escaped her, unbidden and unexpected. It seemed to surprise them both. "I might've heard it a few times."

"Well, there you go." Relief colored the words like he'd solved a complicated puzzle. "You're a no-excuses kind of girl, and I'm a guy with a pocket full of 'em. No wonder we didn't hit it off."

Great. Now, good-looking surfer dude wants to play Gandhi.

Whoa. Good-looking surfer dude? Had that thought really popped from her cranium? Well, his eyes were pretty remarkable. And his smile redeemed quite a bit of his face. "Why don't you start by telling me just what makes you so special, Mr. Rondibett? Then, maybe we'll discuss second chances."

Boston blew out a stream of breath through pursed lips and slowly shook his head. "You strike me as a tough sell, but I've got faith in the product. First, I gotta know something about you, though. See, there are two types of tourists. You're either a traditionalist or you're an explorer. Trads, they want what everyone wants—the brochure version of Hawaii. Diamond Head. Dole Plantation. Pearl Harbor and Waikiki Beach. Beautiful, special places, for sure, but there's so much more to Oahu. And that's what a real explorer wants to see. The soft underbelly. They want experiences no one else has, pictures no one else takes. *That* is what I can do for you, Emily. So, yeah. I'm mouthy, but I'm worth it."

Natural-born salesman, this one. "You would say that."

His mouth formed a flat line, some of the lightheartedness gone. "Know who else? Your sister. She hired me. I'm guessing not because you'd find me charming, but because I've got something to offer."

Emily had to concede Boston's point. Quinn definitely hadn't chosen him to accompany her based on their likelihood of having anything in common. It left a single alternative. He might actually be something special as far as island guides went. "Okay, Mr. Rondibett. I'll give you a shot purely based on faith in my sister's judgment. Perhaps we can both try to be somewhat less abrasive to one another."

"Does that mean you'll relax a little?"

She cut her eyes to him, a warning not to push her buttons. "If you pretend to have some semblance of professionalism. Now, take me to the Hilton. I have a six hour flight to wash off."

Boston saluted and flicked off the hazards. As he checked his mirrors, engaged his turn signal, and prepared to merge back onto the highway, he flashed Emily a lopsided, dimpled grin that made her question her decision to give this another go. "One thing, miss. We aren't going to the Hilton."

Meet the Author

A Florida native, Roxanne Smith has called everywhere from Houston to Cheyenne home. Currently residing in Asheville, North Carolina, she's an avid reader of every genre, a cat lover, pit bull advocate, and semi-geek. She loves video games, Doctor Who, and her dashing husband. Her two kids are the light of her life. Visit her website at roxannesmith.net, and her blog at smithrox.blogspot.com.